Son of a Sinner

by

Lynn Shurr

A Sinner's Legacy, Book One

Son of a Sinner

Cover Art by *Diana Carlile*

The Wild Rose Press, Inc.
PO Box 708
Adams Basin, NY 14410-0708
Visit us at www.thewildrosepress.com

Publishing History
First Champagne Rose Edition, 2015
Print ISBN 978-1-62830-812-9
Digital ISBN 978-1-62830-813-6

A Sinner's Legacy, Book One
Published in the United States of America

Dean returned, phone in hand, shucked his jeans, and got back into bed. Stacy read the text message typed all in lower case and without punctuation as if the person on the other end didn't know where the shift key was located.

return my call right now important.

"Aunt Nell. I guess I should get this over with."

"Right now?" Dean covered his face with the pillow as if hiding from his all-knowing, all-seeing mother.

"Hi, Aunt Nell. I guess you saw those pictures in the tabloids. No, I won't deny I have feelings for Dean. Yes, I'm on the pill. No, I won't break your son's heart. Yes, I do know marriage between us is legal. I looked it up on the internet when I was fourteen." She listened quietly to the rest of the lecture and half-hoped Dean hadn't heard that bit about how she'd known they could marry since she'd been a kid, information he did not need right now. At last, the conversation ended. "Love you, Aunt Nell. Thanks for everything you've done for me."

The pillow over Dean's face shook. She raised it to find him laughing.

"So you've wanted to marry me since you were fourteen."

"I had a crush, a silly childish crush!" She socked him with the pillow. He wrested it away and hit her back but not very hard. This could be fun, or would have been. Xochi pattered up the stairs calling out, "Anyone home?"

Praise for Lynn Shurr

"Shurr is a wonderful storyteller."

~The Romance Studio

~*~

"Very easy reads, well written, combined with conflict, believable plots and secondary characters that make the story come alive."

~Jane Lange, Romances, Reads and Reviews

~*~

"What I love about these books is that they appeal to any audience, not just those that love sports...Another theme I would say plays heavily into the books is love and acceptance. I love how deep and well written the characters are."

~Juliette Brandt, Paperbacks And Frosting

~*~

"Lynn Shurr stories have that distinctive Louisiana flavor...and make you eager for another taste."

~J. L.Salter, Author

~*~

"Lynn Shurr's sinfully delightful New Orleans Sinners series is sure to please both non-sports fans and sport fans alike. Do yourself a favor and dive into the world of the Sinners."

~Farrah Rochon, USA Today Bestselling author
of the New York Sabers football series

Dedication

For Barbara Gautreaux,
who always makes me feel like a writing rock star.

A SINNER'S LEGACY
The children of Joe and Nell Billodeaux
who fulfilled the prophecy that they would have
twelve offspring, this way, that way, all ways

Dean Joseph Billodeaux—Joe's illegitimate son by a one-night stand with a woman who planned to shake him down for money. He is adopted by Nell, who believes she cannot have children of her own. Current Sinners quarterback. (*Wish for a Sinner*)

Thomas Cassidy Billodeaux—a redheaded son who enters the family through an open adoption with a teenage mother. His birth father is Joe's no-good cousin. He is a kicker for the Sinners. *(Wish for a Sinner)*

Jude Emily Billodeaux—twin of Ann, conceived by in vitro fertilization using eggs purchased from Nell's sister, Emily. (*Wish for a Sinner*)

Ann Marie Billodeaux (Annie)—Jude's quiet twin. (*Wish for a Sinner)*

Lorena Renee Billodeaux (Lori)—First of Nell's little frozen babies to be born, one of triplets. (*Kicks for a Sinner*)

Mack Coy Christopher Billodeaux—Second of the triplets to be born. (*Kicks for a Sinner*)

Trinity Billodeaux - Youngest of the triplets and named for the Father, Son, and Holy Ghost. Smallest of the three and in need of a powerful saintly help to survive. (*Kicks for* a *Sinner*)

Xochi Maria Billodeaux—child of Joe's no-good cousin by a young Mexican woman. She is Tom's half-sister and is adopted into the family after the terrifying deaths of her parents. Her name means "blossom" in Aztec. (*Kicks for a Sinner*)

Teddy Wilkes Billodeaux—a child with spina bifida, abandoned by his mother at Nell's health care center and adopted by the family. He believed himself to be Joe's natural son. (*Paradise for a Sinner*)

Anastasia Marya Polasky (Stacy)—daughter of Nell's sister, Emily, and a bogus Polish prince. She becomes a ward of the Billodeauxs upon her parents' deaths, but by her own wish is never adopted. She arrives on their doorstep the same day as Teddy. (*Paradise for a Sinner*)

Edith Patricia Billodeaux (Edie)—a normally conceived child, twin of Rex. (*Love Letter for a Sinner*)

Rex Worthy Billodeaux (T-Rex)—Edie's twin brother and future Sinner's quarterback, maybe. (*Love Letter for a Sinner*)

Chapter One

Mariah's Place, the French Quarter, New Orleans

Tourist guides touted this venue as the best place to spot members of the Sinners football team sitting at the long, brass-railed bar or occupying one of the bentwood chairs around a table for four just off the small, checkered dance floor. Be careful to approach the players respectfully and not monopolize them, they cautioned, or one of Mariah's two big bouncers would surely see you on your way outside. Despite a rather sketchy past of her own, Mariah did not appreciate low women, hootchie-mamas, or working girls, coming into the club to approach "her boys". She'd discovered her motherly instincts late in life, and they had come on fierce. One other caveat—never, never sit in a more substantial seat marked with a plate reading "Billy's Chair". You will be asked to move no matter how big the crowd. Otherwise, relax and enjoy the smoke-free atmosphere and some damn good jazz and singing.

Dean Billodeaux sprawled at the far end of the bar and chilled out early on a Friday evening before the place became really jammed. He appreciated the new cigarette ban but swore Mariah's years of smokes had permeated all the wood and tainted the air permanently. Right now, his brother Tom worked backstage helping the aged star with her oxygen tanks. She'd huff enough air into her damaged lungs to get through her signature opening version of *Fever* and allow dry ice to substitute for the former natural haze in the room. Good old Mariah—his surrogate grandmother and one tough babe.

Dean sipped his first beer and gazed in the mirror lined with bottles behind the bar. He saw the face belonging to his father, the legendary quarterback Joe Dean Billodeaux, in his youth. Same black hair worn short and that unruly curl that fell across his forehead, a heredity cowlick his mom called it. Other women referred to it as sexy. Thinking he needed to use more hair gel or spray, he pushed it away. Same dark chocolate eyes stared at him, too, along with a strong jaw—always clean-shaven—wide shoulders, and long legs that shot him up to six-foot-four, one whole inch taller than his old man. He'd have his usual two beers and be gone by midnight. He favored Mariah's Place for another reason other than sentiment. If a fan cornered him and just had to say Dean hadn't proven himself yet as the Sinner's latest quarterback and wasn't half the fun as his daddy back in the day, the bouncers would nudge the pest away with one autographed napkin in hand.

Hell, the fans should give him a break. He'd graduated from college, been drafted in the top ten, took over as quarterback that same year when Rex Worthy retired suddenly to take care of his cancer-stricken wife and two young sons. He'd gotten the team to the playoffs, maybe just barely, but still there, twice at an age when his own father still warmed the bench as a backup and spent his spare time womanizing and drinking.

His focus on the mirror gave him an early warning. All heads in the club turned toward the entry where a little sunlight spilled into the darkened room this early in the evening. In that pool of radiance stood two striking blondes. The first, tall, thin, and pale with light eyes and very straight white-blonde hair flowing down her back, took in the sights as she adjusted to the dimness. The second, equally long-legged, her rich yellow curls spilling over her shoulders and a know-it-all look in her wide, baby blue eyes, hunted the midnight corners of the place—his nemesis and cousin-by-marriage, Anastasia Marya Polasky, better known as Stacy. Without turning his head, Dean drew in his legs and hunched over his drink. Maybe she wouldn't see him.

Not like Stacy to appear at Mariah's on a Friday night though she did visit the old broad from time to time. Dean took a quick glance in the mirror to see if she'd spotted him. Not yet. Neither woman appeared dressed for clubbing. Both wore sensible heels and slim gray suits accessorized with plum-colored scarves streaked with gold, though Stacy's flowed freely over breasts even that serious jacket could not suppress. The unfamiliar woman in her company had knotted hers in some complicated arrangement only women knew how to achieve and proudly showed off her own substantial, but probably enhanced, chest. Stacy definitely had the better rack, though he would never, ever tell her that. He stayed completely still, like a squirrel on a tree limb when a cat prowled below. Shutting his eyes might help make him invisible, too.

Nope. He heard the tandem rhythm of their high heels approach his corner.

"Hey, you big lout. Is Tom around?" Stacy asked in a low-timbered voice issuing from pouty lips that could make mostly anything sound sexy in several languages.

He'd never backed down from his cousin unless his parents made him, so he straightened his shoulders, opened his eyes, and looked straight into hers. "He's backstage helping Mariah. You slumming tonight, Princess?"

"I would never call a visit to Mariah's Place slumming," she answered, putting some frostbite into her words. "Really, it's a great place to come for the music and very safe. Of course, it is overrun with football players." Stacy, her blue eyes gone narrow, told her companion.

The other woman stared at him wide-eyed. She waved a long-fingered hand in front of her face and said in a strong German accent, "You are the famous footballer, the-the—how you say it?"

"Quarterback," Dean supplied with a grin, his father's grin. He didn't mean it to be a come-on, but it always turned out that way. He couldn't seem to help himself, and often got this flustered reaction, like it or not.

Stacy sighed as if deeply resigned to having to introduce him. "My sorta-cousin, Dean Billodeaux. Dean, meet Ilsa Beckmann, our newest member at Anchi: Translating and Interpreting Services. She's going to cover German and Russian for us since Xochi and I handle French, Spanish, Italian, and Portuguese."

"My pleasure, Miss Beckmann." He took the translator's hand and caged it top and bottom within his own more to annoy know-it-all Stacy than for any other reason, though Ilsa certainly was very attractive—and completely star-struck.

"Ach, you must call me Ilsa. Why you have not told me this man is your cousin, Stacy?"

"Because I wanted you to meet Tom. He's a wonderful guy."

"He is also a footballer?"

"Kind of," Dean supplied. "He's the kicker for the Sinners, a really outstanding one, and my brother."

"Is he as handsome as you?" Ilsa had moved away from star-struck toward flirtatious.

Dean removed his hands from hers. "Tom is adopted. We don't look alike except around the eyes."

"I see. Stacy hired me from my resumé and a FaceTime interview, and so I am new to the city. She said this Tom might show me around the town. Perhaps, you could do that job? I will make it a joy for you, *nein*?" Ilsa tossed her white-blonde hair, a sure sign of interest.

"Well, I have a home game on Sunday, but I guess we could do an early dinner and maybe a carriage ride around the quarter tomorrow. Where should I pick you up?" He hated to disappoint a lady so eager to please him. Aggravating Stacy simply came as an added bonus. She had a snarl on her very pretty face that Ilsa failed to notice.

"Right now I stay with the girls. You know where Xochi and Anastasia live?"

"Xochi is my adopted sister. I helped haul their furniture up those stairs when they moved in. Is six okay?"

"*Ja*! I am so excited!" Ilsa leaned closer to Stacy's ear and whispered over the bar noise. "*Wo ist die*

5

Toilette?"

Stacy flipped a finger that might as well have been the bird in the general direction. "The ladies room is over there."

Dean watched Ilsa work that slim gray skirt with her narrow hips like a runway fashion model as she crossed the empty dance floor. With her long legs and great looks, she might want to consider applying to the Amberello Modeling Agency here in town instead of slaving for Stacy. He'd suggest it.

When he brought his attention back to Stace, she had her hands on her shapely hips, not a good sign.

"How could you do that!" she exploded, her cheeks turning bright pink in that perfect complexion.

"Do what?" Feign innocence, or she'll attack.

"Come on to Ilsa when you knew I wanted to fix her up with Tom."

"I believe she came on to me. I didn't want to mess up your deal with her by brushing her off. Hey, it's just dinner and a carriage ride. If she likes Tom better, I'll step aside, no problem. You look overheated. Want a cold drink? Jackson, a ginger ale with a twist for the lady," he ordered. He knew very well she wouldn't accept any alcohol when she wore her self-imposed business uniform.

"I don't want a drink. I want to…" She balled her fists. In her fury, she'd failed to notice Tom's approach. He touched her arm, and she jumped a little.

"What's up, Stace? What did Dean do now?" Tom, long and lanky, his fiery red hair combed back and tucked behind his ears because he'd forgotten to get it cut lately, gave her an understanding smile. He had those dark brown Billodeaux eyes, but they came across as warm and friendly, not smoldering hot. A million freckles inherited from his birth mother made him seem harmless and boyish.

"Dean stole away a woman I wanted you to meet. We just get here, and they already have a date for tomorrow."

Tom raised his russet brows. "Really? Dean doesn't usually…ah, go out the night before a game."

"Well, he is tomorrow. Here comes Ilsa. Maybe she'll be so disappointed in Dean she'll want to meet someone else, someone nice like you."

"Hey, Dean is a good guy, too." Then, Tom's sincere brown eyes caught a glimpse of what he'd missed out on by a few minutes. "Wow, gorgeous. You lucky dog, you." He punched Dean lightly on the arm.

Ilsa heard the last remark. "The Lucky Dogs, they are like *wurst, nein?*"

"Sure, hot dogs they sell on the street. I'm Tom Billodeaux by the way." He offered his hand, and Ilsa shook it slightly before seating herself next to Dean.

She helped herself to the newly arrived ginger ale. "Oh, very good. It is so hot to me in here." Ilsa unknotted the purple scarf that had filled the V in her suit jacket like an ascot. The merest hint of a pale pink lacy bra now showed in her cleavage. Stacy wore a light gray blouse under her coat that completely hid her very nice goodies.

"Sit down and watch Mariah's act. I got her all primed to go on. You haven't seen it for a while," Tom suggested. "Bartender, another ginger ale and a draft beer for me."

"Oh, yes, I would like to see this act!" Ilsa added with the enthusiasm she appeared to have for everything and everybody in New Orleans.

"Sure, we'll stay. Mariah is still amazing. She's Tom's step-grandmother." Stacy perched on the barstool next to Tom and stared straight ahead at the first wisps of dry ice fog beginning to seep under the black velvet curtain.

"Very complicated, your family. Is it not?" Ilsa asked Dean.

"Complicated, that says it all. There are twelve of us, of many different parents."

The black curtains parted, the band played the signature song, *Fever*, and the tourists at the tables leaned forward to take in the sight of the fabulous Mariah Coy, a grandmother three times over, and still very hot. She'd let her hair go from red to white after her longtime lover, Billy, passed away beside her in bed, but still the mass of curls covering her head certainly had to be a wig. Wearing a red-sequined gown with a slit up the front nearly to the crotch, she owned that stage and strutted from side to side in shoes with heels thicker than they used to be but still very high. Flesh-colored tights covered any imperfections of those long legs. Her enormous fake bosom jutted proudly out at the crowd. Her entire stance seemed to say, "Move over Cher, Dolly, and Tina, and let me work my magic."

"Good evening. I'm Mariah Coy, and we're going to have some fun tonight," she breathed in her smoke-husky voice. The audience that had thickened close to show time shouted their approval. Mariah launched into her opening song playing to the drum riffs and the men in the front row of tables. She managed one more song before turning the stage over to a young black woman

destined for fame, at least that was what Mariah
claimed. The bald-headed bouncer with the cobra
tattooed on his scalp helped her gently down the steps
and over to the reserved chairs where she would hold
court as long as her damaged lungs allowed. Too many
smokes, too many years. She slung an arm over the
back of Billy's Chair as if the old man who had been
her devoted bodyguard for so many years still sat there.
Some of the more imaginative customers claimed when
the dry ice wafted over that area they could make out
the form of a stooped old man, once a big bruiser but
now whittled in size by age, sitting there. That placed
Mariah's joint squarely on the ghost tour. "Good for
business," the star performer said and left it at that.

When a slow, dreamy number played, the singer
almost cooing the song, Dean asked Ilsa for a dance.
Tom did his duty and made the same offer to Stacy.
"No, thanks, we don't plan to stay long," she uttered—
which didn't prevent Ilsa from jumping up and taking
Dean's hand. He danced like he played football,
amazingly agile, his footwork superb, his timing
excellent.

"Want some loaded potato skins? I'm kind of
hungry, and you look like you could use some food."
Tom bumped Stacy with a friendly elbow.

"What makes you say that?'

"You look sort of pale."

"I'm always pale. I don't think Ilsa is going to
work out. Great time to find out, after we flew her all
the way from Frankfurt." On the dance floor, Dean
gave Stacy a wink as he nimbly swung Ilsa around and
then back into his arms. "Yeah, order the potato skins. I
need to settle my stomach."

The couple stayed there attracting attention until the food arrived. Ilsa dug in with abandon. "So good these potatoes. Always too much rice here with everything. Say, I been thinking. Why not you and Tom come with us tomorrow, a-a…"

"Double date?" Stacy took a swallow of her fizzy drink too fast and coughed. "Tom is my cousin."

"I'm an adopted cousin," he explained for Ilsa's benefit.

"Then all is good, *nein*?"

"*Nein*, I mean no. I have plans," Stacy blurted.

Dean studied her face until she pinked up again. "You're seeing someone?"

"Ah, no. A client who doesn't like to dine alone. Don Juan."

"Really, Don Juan?" He thought he could always tell when she lied; that quick glance away as if she planned a fake play, but he didn't pursue it. "Tom, you have anybody else you could bring along?"

"Absolutely. I might be a lowly kicker, but there are a few women I could call." He pulled out his phone and worked on getting a short notice date.

As clientele came and went, the sunlight no longer lit their way. Outside the door, the French Quarter came alive with Friday night neon and noise.

"We should go before it gets any later." Stacy stood and waited for her new employee to unwrap herself from Dean.

"Yeah, you have to get rested up for Don Juan. Want me to call you a cab?" he offered.

"I could get my own, but it's a short walk."

"Then, we should walk you home. Two women like you might be followed. Come on, Tom." Dean paid their tab and left a generous tip.

"I know how to handle myself in New Orleans. I just hadn't planned on staying here after dark."

"Let's say good-bye to Mariah and get going. Tom, you ready?" His brother nodded, still talking into his phone. "It's on the way back to our place anyhow."

"Sometimes I think you are hard of hearing, Dean Joseph Billodeaux! We don't need an escort." She said it loud enough to alert several autograph seekers who headed their way.

Dean graciously signed whatever they presented, a napkin, a Sinners cap, a hand. Ilsa showed no inclination to walk out into the night with only Stacy for protection, but waited patiently for the line to thin. Tom ended his call and gave them a thumbs-up for scoring a date. As usual, he smoothed things over between his brother and Stacy.

"Dad would be upset if we didn't see you safely home, Stace. You know that."

"Fine!" She stalked over to Mariah and accepted a crushing hug to that broad bosom. The guys both received kisses on their cheeks that left them stained with red lipstick. Ilsa merely got an invitation to visit again, as she wasn't family of any kind, not sorta and not almost, not stepchild or adopted into the big Billodeaux team, unless she married into it of course.

Chapter Two

"You can leave now. See, we're right at the door." Stacy inserted the key in the lock, a brand new lock with a serious deadbolt. She stood under a high-powered security light so bright it made her hair gleam like the gold in a Royal Street jeweler's window and lit the little alcove as if it were high noon. Ilsa appeared ghostly in its glare. Above, a newly installed fire escape stood out in sharp metallic contrast to the shabby rear wall of the three-story building sprouting small ferns between its crumbling bricks. All the safety improvements came with the compliments of Stacy's Uncle Joe Billodeaux. Dean with Tommy by his side did not budge. So like him to be bossy and overbearing.

Stacy opened the door and motioned Ilsa to climb the stairs to the second floor where Anchi Services had its office and the girls their living quarters. A quaint little sign on a cast-iron bracket jutted out from above the door. Purple lettering on a pale gray background proclaimed the business within. Not that many clients came to them. Usually, they met the customer elsewhere, or in the case of fulfilling their contract with the police department, rode in a squad car to their destination day or night.

The short cul-de-sac butting against the wall of a major hotel was perfectly safe. A very pricey boutique hotel, also three stories, claimed the corner on Canal

Street. Their shabby building with a cracked pink stucco façade crammed between the two hotels faced the wide thoroughfare. The first floor housed a Korean electronics store selling cheap goods to tourists and probably burner phones to drug dealers. Their business motto seemed to be "We don't care where your money come from, no question asked." Still, the Kim family who ran the place was very nice and allowed the girls to use an interior staircase whenever the shop remained open. Other perks included a crock of homemade kimchi hot enough to burn out a person's tonsils presented at Christmas. The three businesses got along so well they shared the dumpster pushed against the far back wall.

Dean and Tom still stood there waiting. "Go inside and lock the door," Dean ordered.

Stacy gritted her teeth. She stepped inside and poked her head out. "I'm in. I'm locking. Go away!"

She turned the key hard and hoped they heard the snick of the deadbolt engaging. Stacy progressed up the steep, narrow stairs lit at intervals by replica art deco fixtures she'd picked out herself. Ilsa had left the office door wide open. Evidently the German had no fears when Dean Billodeaux wasn't handy as an escort.

Her new employee had passed by the small but very modern office space and already lounged on a plum-colored sofa inundated with silver throw pillows in the living room overlooking Canal. Drapes striped in silver and aubergine pulled back by tasseled cords framed the view outside one tall window of two trolley cars passing in the night. A second long window let light into their kitchen area though it never reached the small bathroom in the rear that held a sink, commode, and tiny shower and had an access door from the office.

"Do you want anything else to eat?" Stacy offered, though Ilsa had scarfed down more than her fair share of the stuffed potato skins, which caused Dean to order a second platter. As for herself, she'd had as much cheese, bacon, and sour cream loaded on a hunk of potato as any reasonable person could hold, but Dean and Tom had no trouble finishing the appetizers down to the last lump.

"*Nein*, I still have what you call it—jet-lag. Soon I go to bed." Ilsa unbuttoned her jacket, exposing the sheer pink bra edged in lace. "So hot here all the time. We should have more cool dresses *mit* shorter sleeves."

"Most of the places we work have air-conditioning, and I want Anchi to project a business-like image at all times. I suppose we could look into other options in our signature colors. I'll see what Xochi has to say."

"Is *gut*. I go to my bed now." Ilsa stretched her perfect slim and lengthy body, arose and started up the second flight of stairs to the floor housing two spacious bedrooms and a full bath.

Stacy hurried after her. "Do you want to use the shower down here or should I lock up?"

"Later," Ilsa called over a now-naked shoulder with the jacket slung on it.

Stacy stared after her wondering if rumors that Europeans didn't bathe as often as Americans could be true. She'd picked up her new employee at the airport on Wednesday night and didn't recall her washing at all. Well, in this climate she'd better change her habits. On the other hand, if Dean got a whiff of body odor on his date, so much the better. Stacy sniffed the air in the stairwell. It smelled enticingly of high-priced perfume.

Too bad. She followed in its wake after locking off the living area.

The door to her bedroom at the end of a short hall stood closed already. She entered the bath on the other side and made a point of running the water long and loud for a soothing bath filled with lavender-scented salts. Laying her suit out on top of the hamper and disposing of her undergarments inside, she pinned up her hair and soaked for a long time, relaxing and releasing her latest turmoil over Dean Billodeaux. There, she'd washed him away. She dried off and put on a nightgown of thin pink cotton with a little frill on the bottom and a scooped neckline at the top. No need for flannel in New Orleans.

Since Ilsa used her room and hadn't had the courtesy to let her hang up her clothes before shutting the door, Stacy gathered her outfit and took it all into Xochi's room next to hers. Her roommate, business partner, and another adopted cousin, sat up in bed reading a Spanish language book. Her thick black hair waved well past her shoulders. She pushed aside a curl that got in the way of a turn of the page. Xochi placed a bookmark and set aside her reading material. She studied Stacy with large brown eyes that everyone said came from the Billodeaux side of the family since her no-good dead father had been part of the clan, but Stacy suspected she'd gotten those alluring Spanish eyes from her deceased Mexican mother. No pictures survived for comparison.

"Did you find Tom?"

"Yes, and Dean." Stacy rattled a hanger from the closet, hung up her suit, and placed her pumps side by side beneath it.

"Well, they are nearly always together so it figures. You set him up with Ilsa?"

"No, Dean moved right in and plucked her like low-hanging fruit, which I think she is. They have a date tomorrow, and Tom is going along for the ride. She suggested I come, too." Stacy got into the other side of the queen-sized bed that Dean, Tom, and her Uncle Joe had shoved up the two flights of stairs using a bevy of curses for fuel. "As if I would. I don't like Dean."

Xochi cocked her head and stared at her with a wise gaze strange in a young woman in her early twenties no matter how many languages she spoke. Spooky stuff, Stacy thought. When sleeping pills and psychiatrists had failed to quell Xochi's night terrors about witnessing the deaths of her parents, Aunt Nell had given into the last resort and taken her to see the Cajun *traiteur*. An old soul she'd called Xochi, claiming the child would gain control as she grew into her powers. The *traiteur* gave the little girl a simple prayer to repeat and a charm of some kind in a small satin bag to place under her pillow. The nightmares ceased. So far, Stacy hadn't noticed anything too woo-woo about Xochi except her uncanny ability to understand things she should know nothing about, and of course, the auras if they could be considered real. Xo still slept with that little sack under her pillow.

"Dean is a great guy, and you know it."

"How can you say that! He's bossy and overbearing. He ruined my life in high school. I could have been popular." Stacy punched her pillow hard a few times, then sank into it.

"No, Stace, you would never have been popular.

16

You were too pretty, too brainy, and too sure of yourself. All those qualities scare men and cause women to hate you."

"Kent Gonsoulin asked me to the prom when I was fifteen, my first real date, or it would have been if Dean hadn't tattled some story. I had to tell Kent I wasn't allowed to date until next year."

"None of us were allowed to date until we turned sixteen," Xochi reminded her.

"It was the prom! They might have made an exception just once if not for your brother. Kent took over from Dean as quarterback of the Flames after he left for college. I could have dated the quarterback. He reigned as prom king, and his date got to be queen."

"So you still want to be royalty, Princess Anastasia." Xochi's eyes crinkled a little at the edges, a sure sign she meant her words as a joke.

Stacy ignored this indication of good humor. "Don't call me that! Dean does all the time. After my parents died in the car wreck, I was a scared little kid. All I owned was a pile of luggage, a little dog, and a title that turned out to be completely bogus. I hid my fear of being abandoned behind all those things. We've been over this ground before. Don't you start in on me again."

"Just trying to ease the tension. Consider this: Kent Gonsoulin got his date pregnant that night, married her at eighteen under a lot of parental pressure. Now, she keeps the books for his daddy's mobile home business while Kent sells trailers. They have three kids already. Is that the life you wanted?"

"Of course not!"

"Then, Dean didn't ruin your life. He probably

17

saved it."

Stacy wracked her brain for another example of Dean's high-handedness. "What about the summer he took off to go abroad and left Tom to be the only lifeguard at Camp Love Letter? That had nothing to do with me. He dumped all that work on Tom and went his merry way."

"Dean traveled to Haiti to build houses for the poor. Besides, all of us older kids had lifeguard training—even you. You're the one who insisted on rescuing Dean for your test just to show you could haul him out of the pool on your own."

"And I did, too. Don't tell me Dean didn't love being lifeguard at the camp with all the girls swooning over him and bringing him cold drinks and rubbing suntan lotion on his back."

Xochi studied her roommate again. "Dean did love all that. He also made sure none of the little kids got hurt and treated those bald-headed cancer victims like bathing beauties. How many other guys that age would have been so nice to them?"

"I concede that point," Stacy said as if they had entered into a formal debate on the topic: Dean Billodeaux, pro or con? She rubbed her temples. "Look, I need to get some sleep. Turn out the light, would you?" Stacy turned over, showing her back to Xochi and escaping her penetrating gaze.

"I think you are too agitated to sleep." Because it was her bed and her lamp, Xochi made no move to obey. "Tell me why you always pick on Dean."

Stacy sat up again, got out of bed and began pacing the floor. "Because everyone fawns on him. It's disgusting the attention he gets. Someone needs to remind him he doesn't walk on water."

"No, he runs across football fields which in Louisiana is almost as good." Again, Xochi's eyes crinkled. "But you started doing this the day you showed up at Lorena Ranch needing a home."

"He called my little dog a Bitchin' Freeze instead of a Bichon Frise. Titi didn't deserve that. She loves everyone. I was nine years old, all alone in that mass of Billodeauxs, and he had to be mean to my dog." Stacy's lower lip quivered as she remembered the insult to her beloved pet. She bit her flesh to make it stop.

"As I recall, you treated us like country bumpkins. That's what got his back up, Princess Anastasia." This time Xochi showed no sign of teasing. "However, I did laugh the first time you called Dean a big lout. Up to that moment, I think all of us considered him our unchallenged leader. We did what he said, and he looked out for his younger siblings. None of us questioned him, a twelve-year old boy being trained as the next great Sinners' quarterback. You never failed to stand up to him and defend the female point of view. All of us girls appreciated that."

"Standing up to Dean became my role in the family. Now, I don't know how to stop." Stacy ceased pacing as if she'd suddenly admitted a great truth. She returned to the bed and again requested a lights out.

Once more, Xochi ignored her. Her deep brown eyes held Stacy's with a steady stare. "Tell me, how long have you been in love with Dean?"

Stacy slid under the covers and pulled them over her head. In the safety of her hiding place, she mumbled, "Since I turned fourteen."

Chapter Three

Dean and Tom crossed wide Canal Street with their longs legs carrying them over the neutral ground in one turn of the light. Shorter people and the elderly often got caught on the center strip where the streetcars ran, but those who lived in the city became adept at jay-walking. They hadn't far to go after that. A massive building resembling a New York brownstone mansion dominated the opposite corner. It now housed luxury condos, and Dean Billodeaux owned the fourth floor facing Canal. They nodded at the doorman as they swung into the lobby.

"Will you be needing your car tonight, sir?" the man inquired with a broad smile on his brown face.

"No, thanks, Arturo." Dean headed for the elevator and commented to Tom, "Nice having valet parking right across the street, huh?"

"Yeah, but I still don't feel really comfortable living so close to Xochi and Stacy. It's like we're spying on them."

"Dad told us to keep an eye on them. I'm just following orders. It's no joke having two young women to watch out for. I'm just relieved our twin sisters remained at LSU for grad school instead of moving here, too."

Dean punched in the key code, entered the apartment, and reset the alarm. The hell with Stacy and what she thought, he liked this space. The ceilings soared and possessed fine crown molding stained dark that stood out against the off-white of the walls. He had a fireplace filled with gas logs appearing entirely real, even though no one needed a fire to keep warm in New Orleans. A TV as large as he could hang filled the wall above it. A long brown velour sectional sofa filled the area in front of the fake flames. Recliners folded out of either end of it. His coffee table, a large dark block of distressed wood, was rugged enough to put your feet on if you wanted. The kitchen, bigger than he needed, sat off to one side, and four bedrooms lay down the wings on either side, each with its own bath, giving them two private rooms apiece.

Dean had turned his second bedroom into a game room. It was just big enough for a foosball table and a pool table side by side. He'd squeezed in an X-Box system, too. His Heisman Trophy and Tom's Lou Groza Award for placekicking sat on shelves amid other sports memorabilia, piles of CDs and video game packages. Not bad for two bachelors living the life, only they rarely did—on the road too much and often exhausted by practices and workouts.

His interior designer, a motherly older woman chosen by his Mama Nell, said she pictured his style as being very traditional like him: short hair, no tattoos, and the kind of man who still opened doors for a lady and saw them to their front door after a date. She'd pegged that. He'd said he didn't know what his style was, but he wanted a big comfortable sofa and recliners. The decorator shook her head over the one he'd chosen and tried to make it less tacky—though she hadn't used that word—by dressing it up with annoying little multi-colored cushions that usually ended up on the floor when he stretched out and relaxed.

He favored the dining area where a cabinet matching the high gloss mahogany table and chairs in some kind of eighteenth century style held his sound system and electronics rather than china and linens. Best of all, it sat in a bow window overlooking Canal Street and peering down on the building that housed Anchi Services. One of the tall palms lining the street partially blocked the view of the bedroom windows—maybe a good thing, not that the girls ever left their shades open. Instead of turning on the TV or heading for a shower, he stood in that window and stared across the way.

"Xochi's bedroom light is on, but Stacy's room is dark. Guess they really are in for the night."

"That's what I mean about spying. As Xo keeps reminding me, they are both over twenty-one and don't need us to watch out for them any more. You really pissed off Stacy tonight with the overprotective bit."

"I do like getting under her alabaster skin, that's for sure. She's never given me a break. Why should I give her one?" Dean continued to contemplate the distant window. A figure appeared to be pacing back and forth behind the shades. Not like Xochi to be agitated. She owned a sort of deep-seated, indolent calm. Right, Ilsa probably slept in Stacy's room. Had to be Stacy. "I really got to her tonight."

Tom changed the subject, a skill he'd perfected when two people he admired went at each other. "How about that Ilsa? She's something else."

"Not any prettier than Stacy, less I think."

"You want something else to eat?"

"What have we got in the fridge?"

Tom rummaged in a refrigerator so big it made the meager contents seem like they were both on a diet. Not true. He flipped open several takeout boxes. "We can nuke leftover Italian from Vincent's, Moon's Chinese, Joey's red beans and rice with sausage, or thin cut fried catfish with hush puppies from Ralph's."

"The catfish, but heat it in the toaster-oven. I like it crispy."

"Yes, *monsieur*. Whatever you desire." Tom flipped a dishtowel over his arm and bowed.

"Don't you start mocking me now." The pacing across the street ceased. "Say, do you remember when we were trying to figure out a nickname for Princess Anastasia and I suggested Nasty?" Dean grinned with pleasure at the thought.

"I do, vividly. Mom said you wouldn't be allowed to play football in the fall if you kept up that attitude. Close call, bro. That crack could have ruined your career." Tom dumped the catfish and hush puppies on a metal tray and turned on the small oven.

"Awww, Dad would have let me play."

"Don't be too sure. Our parents are real good at the united front or a strong defensive line, as Dad would call it." He chose the leftover lasagna for himself and heated it right in the box after removing the garlic bread to crisp with the hush puppies. "I guess we should have salad with this stuff."

"If you want, but Mom isn't around to make us eat our greens any more."

"But still." Tom rummaged a bag of salad from a refrigerator drawer and dumped the greens into two bowls. "You want beer, milk, or pop with this?"

"I had my beer limit back at the club. Make it milk." Dean did his part by getting out plates and cutlery. His set his place facing the bow window with Tom's chair off to one side in order not to block the view. "Who are you taking on our double date tomorrow?"

"Brigit Murphy. We went to Ste. Jeanne's Parochial with her. She's a year younger than me and just moved to town. Mom ran into her mother and made a point of sending me the number pressed into her hand by Mrs. Murphy. I'm supposed to show her around. This way, I make Mom happy and get it over with."

Dean took the milk jug Tom handed him and poured his own drink. "I don't remember any Brigit."

"She said you didn't know she was alive back then."

"Pretty?"

"Still had zits and braces last time I saw her. She went to college out of state, but I'm sure she's improved. We all have except for you and Stacy—both of you were perfect right from the start, hardly ever a blemish and naturally straight teeth." Tom dumped both meals onto the plates and served the food.

"I wish Stacy had agreed to go with you. Boy, I could have had some fun with that."

"Probably why she didn't sign on."

"You think there really is a Don Juan?" Dean contemplated the thought as he doused ketchup on his fries and broke open a steaming hush puppy to add a dab of butter.

"I can ask Xochi."

"Do that. Maybe we'll show up at the same place for dinner."

"Talking about giving a person a break. You could let Stacy live her life and just butt out if she annoys you so much. Really, she's not a bad person. She helped our brothers set up the Camp Love Letter News and went out and did interviews of the campers for them, took pictures, everything. Now one is a sports reporter, and the other is working on being a computer geek, not that he wasn't already. I think she gave them confidence."

"Stacy never lacked for confidence. Who starts their own translating business right out of college?"

"Who gets to be quarterback for the Sinners as a rookie? You don't lack confidence either. You two are a lot alike. Perfect for each other, in fact." Tom shoveled in some lasagna and waited for the reaction with a devilish look on his freckled face.

"Never say that again! Stacy and me—that would be impossible. We grew up together like brother and sister. We don't even like each other." Dean protested so vigorously ketchup flew off the french fry he waved around to make his point and landed on his three-hundred dollar pure cotton shirt that by some kind of magic did not wrinkle even in the heat and humidity of Louisiana. "See what you made me do. Am I supposed to soak this in cold water?"

"Yeah, I can see you two together, but I don't know about shirts and cold water. Want me to call Mom—or Stacy?" Tom continued to enjoy his food, mopping up the red tomato gravy with the garlic bread.

"No! Our housekeeper will take care of it. Just ask Xochi if there is a Don Juan. You know Stacy has a weakness for Latin types. We need to protect her from herself."

"You mean Dr. Rivera, her Spanish professor at

LSU? That's only one."

"I no sooner graduate and leave for New Orleans than she up and has an affair with a faculty member who took advantage of her. I tried to get Mom and Dad to talk to her, get him kicked out of teaching, but they said to leave her alone to work things out for herself." Dean rose and wet a paper towel, scrubbed at his shirt more vigorously than necessary.

"Yeah, Professor Rivera had a reputation with the young ladies. I took his class for my language requirement. He said the guys would have to work for their grades, but if the girls sat in the front row and wore short skirts, they were sure to get A's"

"No one reported that? No one turned him in for sexual harassment?" He tried to tamp down the instant outrage, but Tom didn't stop.

"In the next breath he said 'only joking', but the pretty girls did get A's. The others, not so much. Hey, he kept it up with Stacy for a year. Most of his affairs only lasted a semester I'd heard, and Xochi said she dumped him, not the other way around."

"That's good news, but then she did junior year abroad. Who knows what kind of guys she got involved with there...Frenchmen, Italians."

"See, that would be none of our business. Not to mention you have plenty of French blood, too, and maybe a little Spanish. Lots of Cajuns do. Maybe you're her type."

"Knock it off before I wash your mouth out with— milk." Dean went for the jug still sitting on a counter.

Tom held up his hands defensively. "No need for that, big brother. I'm going to bed."

"I thought I'd stay up and watch some of the

preseason game tapes. You interested?"

"No more than you claim to be in Stacy. I'm only a lowly kicker. I go out on the field when I'm told, and if I get roughed, the Sinners benefit from the penalty. Dean and Stacy—think about it. I'm going to bed."

Damn, now he would obsess on the thought of himself with Stacy all night long. Dean snatched up a dishtowel and snapped Tom's skinny behind as he passed, but his brother was pretty quick for a kicker and raced down the hall laughing.

Dean cleaned up the dinner dishes because that was the way he'd been taught. You didn't leave a mess for their devoted housekeeper to cope with in the morning and the same applied to their cleaning lady. He kept an eye on the light across the street. The girls must be having a real gabfest tonight. He wondered about their topic of conversation, but eventually settled in front of the TV and got the game tape running. Head in the game, Dean Billodeaux, head in the game.

****

Xochi ripped the covers off Stacy and found her curled in the fetal position. "You cannot hide from emotions like this. You must tell Dean how you feel about him, and if he rejects you, you will heal faster like opening a festering wound and allowing the poison to drain."

"Oh, thanks for the disgusting analogy, and that's what my hidden passion for Dean is—disgusting." She shaded her eyes from the light, or maybe she merely wanted to hide her face again.

"No, I don't think so. You are very much alike in being strong and independent," Xochi scolded her with a wagging finger.

"Dean doesn't want a strong woman. He likes them clingy and helpless."

"You sure about that?" Xochi raised those skeptical black brows.

"I've never seen a picture of him in any of the magazines where he didn't have a beautiful woman hanging on him like one of those sucker fish attached to a shark. Okay, okay, since it is confession time I might as well admit that at first I just didn't want to give up my family name because I still had an illusion I might be royalty."

"We busted up that dream when we tried doing genealogy research. All we ever found out about my parents, Mama Nell already told me. Papi married my Mexican mother at fourteen, and she'd just turned fifteen when I was born in Texas, then back across the border they went. She died at barely twenty when the drug dealer my father worked for killed them both. Now that is disgusting—and sad." Hurt marked her face like a scar.

"I didn't mean to rake all that up. What I meant to say is that I still resisted when I realized how I felt about Dean because I looked up the state law on marrying adopted relatives in Louisiana, and you can if you aren't real cousins. I didn't want him to think of me as a sister either."

Xochi regained her calm as her fingers stroked the small satin bag she'd taken from under her pillow. "That's a long time to fester. We must do something about these feelings."

"I don't see how when he hates me."

"Dean hates no one. He stands up to you when you pick at him is all. What does he do when any of his sisters are in trouble?"

"Rats them out to Aunt Nell and Uncle Joe because he's a jerk, a big handsome jerk?"

"No, he does what it takes to save them in some way. My brother is not a jerk. I know you don't want to hear this, but he burns with a pure white light."

"Because he's sooo saintly." Stacy puckered her lips as she said it.

"No, because he's a protector, the knight on the white horse coming to the rescue."

"And what color am I?"

"Always purple, full of self-esteem. Too independent. We need to set up a few situations where he can rescue you, and you can show you need him, like him, appreciate him, want him. Then, he'll see you differently."

Stacy stuck out her pouty lip. "I don't need his help."

"Okay, fester on as long as you want."

With a resigned sigh, Stacy said, "Where do we start?"

"How about your date with Don Juan tomorrow night? You did call and tell him you'd go after all, didn't you?"

"Yes, I didn't want Dean to catch me lying. But, that sweet old man? He's not a threat. I acted as his interpreter when he went for his medical exam for prostate cancer surgery. He wanted to make sure he understood every word about his treatment, though his English is very good. I've been boning up on my Spanish medical vocabulary lately and..." A small laugh relieved the tension. "I can't believe I said boning up. Anyhow, it's not a date, just a thank you dinner for my service and my discretion. I assured him that wasn't necessary. Anchi Services never reveals information about their clients, but he insisted."

Xochi, who had the ability to lift only one eyebrow when she chose, did so. "I've heard Don Juan Guzmann once had a reputation as a ladies' man. He still likes to be seen with a pretty woman on his arm. That's why he always calls Anchi. We have established a brand for being intelligent, accurate, and beautiful. I am a little bit tired of the plum and gray color scheme though."

"I wanted us to have a sort of uniform look that would make us stand out. The beautiful part is only a coincidence. Now we've got Ilsa. She makes me look like a curly-headed bimbo."

"Oh, hardly! But, back to Don Juan. I can drop a few words to Tom that I am worried about tomorrow evening, that the Don wines and dines young women then seduces them in a luxury hotel. If l leak the location of the restaurant, want to bet Dean shows up there?"

Stacy shook her head. "He'll be preoccupied with Ilsa, but if he does, I'll look into adding more pieces and colors to our uniforms."

"Deal." Xochi tucked her little satin bag under her pillow, reached over, and turned out the light.

Chapter Four

The four of them bumped along the uneven streets of the French Quarter in a mule-drawn surrey just past the worst heat of the day. Yes, it did have fringe on the top, also artificial flowers and loops of Mardi Gras beads, anything to attract attention to this particular vehicle. Dean prudently selected the first in line in front of Jackson Square after they'd crossed the street from Café du Monde where they'd eaten beignets and had iced coffees. No sense in starting an argument among the drivers over who got the Sinners quarterback into their carriage.

Dean found the leg-room cramped and tried to stretch out a little by putting his arm across the back of the seat. He hadn't intended it as a come-on, but Ilsa interpreted his move as one. She nestled against his chest, making him sweat beneath another of those expensive cotton shirts, a pale green one he wore with the collar open and the sleeves rolled up.

Their driver, an old hippie with a long gray braid down his back and a straw hat on his head, popped the mule lightly with his whip urging the animal to pick up its heels a little in the traffic. The mule, also a dappled gray and wearing a similar hat, displayed its rejection of speed by spewing a good-sized heap of manure into the poop bag required on all the carriages. Ilsa held her nose.

"Not a country girl, I take it?" Dean asked while trying to reclaim the arm going numb around her shoulders.

"*Nein*, a city woman, an uptown girl, right?"

Tom's date leaned over the seat from behind. "Not me. I love horses and all kinds of animals. Your dad keeps horses, doesn't he, Dean?" Brigit's complexion had cleared up and her small white teeth were very straight. Not bad looking for a short brunette, but not stunning like Ilsa. Too bad she appeared to be crushing on him and not Tom.

"Yes, but they have to use mules in the city because of the heat. Horses can't take it," Tom informed them. Between the guide's patter he pointed out uniquely New Orleans sights like the Lucky Dog carts and the Roman candy wagon.

"I knew that about the mules," Brigit said.

"Interesting," Ilsa replied in a bored sort of way. Large, dark sunglasses masked her icy blue eyes.

The driver did his thing, pointing out the Cities of the Dead—the cemeteries of tombs raised above the water table—and prattled on about Marie Laveau, the Voodoo queen, of which there might have been several. He revealed that drawing an X on her tomb and completing a simple ritual might gain a person a wish.

"Oh, I want to do that!" Brigit bubbled. She spoke into Ilsa's ear since she couldn't reach across to Dean. The seating arrangements precluded her drooling on his shoulder, too.

"The cemeteries aren't safe unless you go in a group," Dean said. "You can take a walking tour if you want."

"Could we do that?"

"Not tonight. I have a game tomorrow."

"Which means I do, too," Tom chipped in, for all the good it did him.

They clipped past Madame John's Legacy, the oldest house in the city and supposedly the home of a pirate ghost. Dean had no idea how truthful the guide was being. Stacy, a stickler for accuracy, would be correcting the guy right and left by now, and that might have been more fun.

Tom's phone rang. "Sorry, got to take this. My sister is just now returning a call. That so… Really? Doesn't sound good…Yeah, I'll tell Dean."

"No, let me talk to her." Dean used the call as an excuse to withdraw his arm as Tom handed over the phone. "So there really is a Don Juan. The steakhouse right off Jackson Square at seven. Don't worry. We'll keep an eye on them. Thanks for telling us." He returned the phone to the back seat. "Anyone in the mood for a good prime rib?" he asked.

"Oh, I'd rather have seafood," Brigit answered.

"Whatever you want, Joe." Ilsa put a hand on his arm.

"Beef it is, but I'm sure they have lobster on the menu or some other kind of seafood for you, Brigit."

Ilsa had to remove her grip when Dean dug out his phone and searched the number for the restaurant where Don Juan intended to take Stacy. He made reservations for four at seven. The surrey driver completed the loop back to Jackson Square and helped his passengers step down. Even though the fee for a ride was pretty stiff, he tipped the man and scratched the mule behind the ears before taking the ladies into the shade of the park.

"Our dinner reservations are for seven. We have

about an hour's wait, but the restaurant is just over there. We could get a drink somewhere in the meantime if you want."

"I must go back to the apartment and change. I am sweating like a swine," Ilsa said.

"I guess I should put on something else, too, if we are going to do fancy," Brigit agreed.

"Tom, why don't you take Brigit home, and I'll walk Ilsa back to Anchi. We'll meet at the restaurant in an hour."

All agreed, he escorted Ilsa to the apartment and stepped across the street to put on a fresh shirt and a little cologne. Then, he thought he should shave and maybe shower. He wasted exactly enough time in order to return and catch Stacy stepping into a silver Mercedes with heavily tinted windows, the kind that were supposed to be against the law. A uniformed driver held the door for her.

"Hey, Stace. Lookin' good. Is Don Juan in there?"

No lie about her appearance. She wore a skimpy black dress in some kind of material that molded to her breasts and hips. She'd put up her golden curls in an arrangement that allowed little ringlets of it to frame her pale face and seemed as if it would tumble down with the removal of a single marcasite clip in the shape of a butterfly. He hated to admit he liked the notion of removing the barrette and having her hair cascade over his hands.

Her naturally full lips shone with an application of bright red lipstick, the kind men dreamed of kissing and getting all over themselves in other places. She'd given her blue eyes a smoky indigo showcase, but not too much. Always stylish but ever tasteful, that was Stacy.

Her shoes with heels higher and thinner than usual, had ankle straps and open toes, not great if she had to make a getaway. Dean frowned at them.

"I'm meeting him at the restaurant. He sent his car. You look nice, too. What?" She caught his unhappy expression.

"Your shoes. What if you have to run from danger?"

Stacy laughed, a great low-pitched sound. She never giggled. "You think I should wear sneakers with this outfit? Believe me, if I have any trouble I can puncture a man's gonads with these heels, and I've got the legs to do that."

"Yes, you certainly have." Dean kept his eyes down, staring at her toes also lacquered in red. She wore no stockings and probably not much else under that outfit. His eyes traveled slowly back to her lips again, then her eyes, which appeared a little miffed about something.

"Ilsa is running late. You can go upstairs and wait for her if you want. Have a good evening."

"Yeah, you, too."

She ducked into the Mercedes that nosed carefully into traffic. So far, so good. No chance this Don Juan would jump her in the backseat. Dean trudged to the second floor and took a seat on Stacy's purple couch among the silver cushions. At seven-fifteen, his date appeared in a fire engine red dress longer than Stacy's but made provocative by slits in both sides of the skirt to show off her long legs. The bodice bared a good deal of those breasts he wasn't too sure about being real. Seemed like she and Stacy had used the same shade of lipstick only it didn't show as well on Ilsa's thinner lips. Worn loose, her straight, pale hair caped her bare shoulders and back. Her black heels, even more complex and higher than Stacy's, looked like real ankle breakers. He'd better hail a cab to get them to their destination. All decked out, Ilsa topped six feet, but then so did Stacy who less resembled a model and more represented a woman with curves.

He offered the standard compliment. "You look very beautiful, Ilsa."

"Yes, I know," she said, without any false modesty.

He helped her negotiate the stairs and found a cab with ease near the neighboring hotel. At the restaurant, he again lent his arm to get her to the second floor entry of the steakhouse. Tom and Brigit sat waiting at the bar. Brigit sipped a white wine, and Tom drank a Tom Collins simply because he liked the name, as he'd often said. "Our table is ready, but guess who's here?" He gestured toward the dark, candlelit interior of the restaurant.

"Stacy and her Don Juan. I think we should check this guy out." Dean waved off the maitre d' who tried to seat them at a window table overlooking the square. Always good for business to place a Sinner in the window. "Could we sit over there by that couple?"

"But of course, Mister Billodeaux."

It was good to be a Sinner in New Orleans. As they moved to their new location, Dean paused at Stacy's table to say hello oh so casually. "What a coincidence running into you here, Stacy. This must be the famous Don Juan."

The candlelight flattered her date, a man with deep lines in his heavily tanned face, a head of thick silver hair as dense as a fox pelt, and a trim mustache on his upper lip. Beneath his white brows, startling blue eyes glittered. The guy could have been her grandfather, or maybe Xochi's because of her Hispanic blood. Still, he had a smoothness about him Dean distrusted as he rose to shake hands.

"Not as famous as my namesake, I assure you, and a different last name. I am called Juan Guzmann," the Don said in one of those fine Corinthian leather advertising voices. "And you are the much more well-known Dean Billodeaux who plays for the Sinners." He had a firm grip; no old man's palsy.

"Yes, their quarterback. Do you follow American football?"

"Not really, but I have attended the games as a guest many times when here on business."

"Let me introduce Ilsa Beckmann. She works with Stacy as their German translator."

The Don caressed Ilsa's body with the warm glance of a practiced womanizer and cupped her hand as if it were a breast. "A pleasure. If I ever have need of a German interpreter, I shall remember you."

"But your last name is German, is it not?" Ilsa questioned.

"We have German blood some generations back," he answered. "But I have none of the language."

Yeah, right. His Nazi father probably hid out in South America after World War II. The guy spoke great English. Why did he need Stacy around? Only one reason Dean could think of, and nothing else. He introduced the rest of their party. "My brother, Tom Billodeaux, and his date, Brigit Murphy."

"Ah, Tommy the Toe, the very excellent kicker. So

good to meet you."

"Actually, we don't kick with our toes any more. We do it soccer style, but they still call me that." Tom grinned, pleased at the recognition he seldom got.

Brigit chirped, "What do they call you, Dean?"

"The quarterback. Would you mind if we joined you and Stacy?"

Although the Don seemed surprised, especially since very traditional shrimp cocktails chilling in ice already sat before them and they had obviously ordered, he nodded graciously. "Most certainly."

"*Garcon*, could we put two tables together?" Dean said to the waiter who approached with a bottle of champagne in a cooler and sat it next to the Don. Maybe the *garcon* laid it on a little thick, but this man made him want to show some sophistication that he really didn't possess.

"Right away, Mr. Billodeaux." The waiter summoned a small army of busboys who rearranged the furniture to their liking without breaking a single of the multiple glasses on the tables.

"Bring another bottle of champagne. We don't want to hog your liquor, sir."

"Actually, we are drinking a fine Chilean sparkling wine. I represent this winery's interests in the United States among other enterprises. I am sure you will enjoy it."

Dean blocked Ilsa from sitting next to Don Juan by holding out the chair on his far side. He seated himself across from Stacy and watched Tom place Brigit next to her while his brother took the daddy's chair at the far end of the table.

"How about jumbo shrimp cocktails all around

while we study the menu? They really look good."

"Oh, yummy!" Brigit exclaimed. "I'm so hungry."

"Here, take mine. I can wait." Stacy set her appetizer in front of Tom's starving date.

"Thanks! Hey, I know you. Stacy Polasky—you went to Country Day School. When Dean wasn't around, all the guys at Ste. Jeanne's said you were the girl they'd like most to do. You turned down Kent Gonsoulin for the prom. Was he ever burned. He swore to everyone he'd nail you that night." Brigit stuffed a shrimp into her ever-burbling mouth.

Dean's head swung toward Stacy and away from some polite comment the Don made. Neither Ilsa nor Guzmann appeared to follow Brigit's rapid speech or the American idiom, but Stacy's cheeks burned. He started to say something macho like "Good thing they never said that in front of me", but Stacy answered very coolly, "How flattering to be so desired. What brings you to the city, Brigit?"

At least the girl swallowed her shrimp before answering. "I finished culinary school this summer, and I mean what kind of opportunity does Chapelle, Louisiana, offer? Folks there wouldn't know fusion cuisine if you spent an hour explaining it to them and then they'd refuse to eat it. I have to stay with my aunt out by the park until I can find a job here in the Big Easy. Maybe Dean can help me with that."

Stacy shot him an amused glance. The waiter made the rounds with the open bottle of wine, and he took a sip before replying to give himself a minute. "Ah, I don't really have much influence in the restaurants around here. The only people I know are the caterers at the Dome."

"That would be great! It's a start, right? I bet we'd bump into each other all the time."

Stacy buried her smile against the edge of the champagne flute.

Dean said, "I'll check into it. Say, Mr. Guzmann, what kind of business are you into? This wine is great. I'd like to order some for my parents. One of their anniversaries is coming up."

"Import-export, but please, I am Juan to my friends." He handed over two cards from a slick silver case, one for the winery, one for his company. "I keep telling Stacy she must call me Juan, not Don Juan. Your parents are the same who raised Stacy, no? They have two anniversaries?"

"Yes, one for their elopement in Vegas and one in the Church. They celebrate both every year."

"How charming, but then I would expect that from people who raised such exceptional children. Stacy performed an extremely intimate service for me and would not accept jewelry or any gift other than her usual fee. I had to convince her to dine with me tonight before I return to Argentina."

Blessed with the olive complexion of many Cajuns, Dean knew his face rarely reddened, but it did darken when he became angry. He felt that heat gathering now. Don Juan spoke of Stacy as if she were a high-class prostitute. He set down the wine glass so abruptly the contents sloshed on the white linen tablecloth. His very broad shoulders straightened. Across the table, Stacy's blue eyes widened at the expression she saw on his face. The conversation from Brigit's chatter to some comment Tom made to Ilsa ceased.

"I see I have upset you," Don Juan said into the

quiet. "No, no, no, it is not what you think. She acted as my interpreter at the hospital to assure that I understood all about some surgery I required. Afterwards, she came to visit me while I recovered, which was not part of our contract. Her lovely face cheered this old man, but alas…" He lowered his voice so that only Dean and Stacy could hear. "I am now incapable of pleasing a beautiful woman. It goes very hard with me."

Dean relaxed into his chair and picked up his wine again. "Sure, that would be difficult for any man."

"Still, I enjoy having such women as my interpreters. I must look into importing this wine into Germany, but they are protective of their own brands." The Don turned his attention to Ilsa and a discussion of German vintages.

The shrimp cocktails arrived, and the new members of the party completed their orders with Dean and Tom going for that prime rib, medium. Brigit asked Stacy what she had ordered—the filet mignon with a side of mushrooms and a house salad, everything being a la carte—and said she'd have the same. Ilsa ordered likewise and added on the loaded baked potato even though Stacy warned her they were immense. "We share, okay?" Hot, crusty loaves of French bread arrived, and the conversation returned to New Orleans cuisine.

"I mean this is great and all, but any competent chief can grill a good steak," Brigit said. "I like more of a challenge."

"Home cooking is fine by me," Dean answered and asked Ilsa what she thought of New Orleans food.

"So *pikant*." She waved a hand in front of her lips. "But all this I like."

41

The meal progressed pleasantly with the serving of the beef perfectly cooked to order and filets three inches thick wrapped in bacon. It extended to coffee and liqueurs served in small chocolate cups. By the end of the evening, Dean and the Don became so chummy that he offered the Argentinean game tickets the next time he came to town. They parted as friends with one caveat from Dean. "I am counting on you to see Stacy safely home, Juan."

"My pleasure, to be sure. Her eyes, so like my granddaughter's," the sly old man added before a final shake of the hand.

Dean nodded. "Goodnight, Stacy."

"Goodbye, Dean. Have fun with Ilsa," she replied but didn't seem to really mean it.

Out on the square, Brigit was the first to ask, "Where to next?"

"I should get a good night's sleep," Dean said.

"Party pooper," Tom had to say. "We still have time to get in line at Preservation Hall and hear some old time jazz. Let's go."

Dean caught another cab knowing Ilsa would never be able to hoof it in those shoes. They debarked in front of the venerable music hall and moved to the end of a very long and unmoving line that snaked past Pat O'Brien's Restaurant where waiters came outside to hawk Hurricanes and other drinks to the tourists. He got the women Hurricanes in souvenir glasses and listened to them whine when, once inside the building, all the seats were taken and they had to stand in the rear and bear the heat the ceiling fans barely dissipated. Even Dean Billodeaux couldn't get them better treatment. After that, he found another cab and took Ilsa back to

Anchi Services, leaving Tom to cope with Brigit however he wanted. When his date waited for a kiss, he brushed her cheek lightly and held the door for her.

"Be sure to lock up after I leave," he prompted.

"You want to come in?"

"No. Game tomorrow, remember?"

"Always this game." With that final comment, Ilsa picked her way up the stairs.

Chapter Five

Stacy curled on her plum-colored couch and watched the old romantic movie *You've Got Mail*. She identified with the main character, a blonde intellectual who loved books. One day, she'd like to write bilingual children's stories. Wrapped in her pink terry robe and wearing fuzzy slippers, she sipped a cup of tea that should have been herbal at this time of night, but wasn't. The clip of Ilsa's shoes on the staircase made her look at the clock—only eleven, but still enough time for Dean to have taken his date across the street for a quickie. She schooled her face to reflect only nonchalance.

"Have a good time with Dean?" she asked the model-perfect woman. "Would you like some tea? I made a pot."

"You got any schnapps? My feet hurt." Ilsa plunked down on a hassock fringed around its edges in silver and began unstrapping her complicated shoes. "We have to stand to hear the old jazzmen play."

"Oh, you went to Preservation Hall. It's the real deal, but yes, not much seating. I think we might have a bottle of peppermint schnapps left over from last year's Christmas party. I'll get it for you." All the better to loosen Ilsa's tongue.

Stacy found the dusty bottle in a cabinet and poured a measure into a shot glass with a gold fleur-delis on the side. She delivered it and the rest of the liquor to Ilsa who sat rubbing her long toes. "So how was Dean?"

"What you say—the perfect gentleman." Ilsa tossed back the schnapps and smacked her lips. "Better than the Hurricane drink."

Maybe Dean had tried to get her liquored up and failed. Ilsa sure could hold her booze. Stacy turned off the movie and settled on the couch again. "I meant, how was he in bed?"

"Was no bed. We come right back here after all that tooting with the horns, and I get a kiss on my cheek. I dress like this for nothing." She smoothed her red gown down the length of her body.

Stacy took pleasure in noting a slight bump where that huge baked potato must be digesting. Ilsa had given her and Brigit a quarter each of all that starch, and it still filled half her plate. Since the guys had gotten their own, she'd polished off the rest. If Ilsa kept eating like that and absorbing so much booze, she would soon outgrow the fire engine red dress.

"Maybe Dean doesn't expect you to sleep with him until the third date. He can be rather old-fashioned."

Ilsa poured another shot of schnapps, gulped it, and slapped the empty on the glass-topped coffee table with a snap. "No, we had no, what to say—spark. Tom says he is the party pooper. Party pooper, I like that word."

"Maybe next time you could go out with Xo and her friends. They love to dance."

"Not if they are Latins. Always too short, and I do not have the rhythm for their music."

Ilsa raised her swan-like arms far over her head, stretched, and sniffed her armpits. To Stacy's disappointment they were shaven, maybe even waxed. She'd heard sometimes European woman didn't bother. Hairy armpits would have grossed out Dean, but Ilsa's pit hair probably grew in like swansdown.

"And so, tonight I take a shower and go to bed," Stacy's new employee said with finality. She padded off toward the bathroom with her painful shoes in-hand and not a single schnapps-induced wobble.

Stacy started the movie again and waited for Xochi's return. She'd fallen asleep with her head on a star-shaped pillow by the time her roommate came home at 1:30 a.m., turned off the TV, and shook her shoulder. "Off to bed, Stace. I know that sofa fits our décor, but it's not the most comfortable place for a nap."

"True. How was your evening?"

"Fun and same as always. We had a couple of drinks, but mostly danced. More importantly, how was yours?" Xochi said as they entered her bedroom and shut the door.

"As you predicted Dean showed up at the steakhouse with Ilsa, Tom and his date, this mouthy girl named Brigit they both knew from high school. She said all the guys at Ste. Jeanne's wanted to bang me. I guess I was more popular than I thought."

"Not in a good way, but how did Dean answer her?"

"He started to say something, but I just told her I was flattered and turned the conversation to be all about her. That always works."

"What am I going to do with you? You should have let Dean do the talking, a small thing that would have made him feel manly."

Xochi wriggled out of a tangerine-colored dress with thin straps and flounces on the skirt. Stacy wouldn't be caught dead in that bad bridesmaid's dress nightmare, but Xo carried the outfit off just fine. Her cousin removed her hoop earrings and tidily hung them on a holder shaped like a cactus, a birthday gift from Tom. Her undies matched her gown, but instead of dropping them in front of Stacy, she modestly slipped a big sleep shirt over her head, put her lingerie in a laundry bag in the closet, and placed the dress on a padded hanger.

Stacy cringed at the memory of her arrival at Lorena Ranch with a heap of luggage as tall as the Alps and her own butler. Her wardrobe overflowed the generous closet and dresser space in her room, and she'd expected Brinsley, her servant, to take care of it for her. When clothes she left on the floor began disappearing, Aunt Nell's doing, she finally caught on that she'd have to put her things away or lose them. Poor Brinsley had been ordered not to intervene. Now, he belonged to the entire family and was, in fact a vital part of it. Anastasia Polasky should have been branded with an S for Spoiled. It could also have stood for Scared to be alone in the world.

Stacy waved her hand. "Dean had another chance to save me. Don Juan said I'd done him an intimate service and wouldn't accept a gift for it. He made it sound very sexual, and Dean actually showed rage on his face. Scary. I wonder if that's how he looks beneath the helmet on the football field. Anyhow, the Don quickly explained about his medical condition. They ended the evening the best of friends, even dueling over the tab which Dean paid since he'd barged in on us.

That poor, frail old man, for a minute I thought I'd have to rescue *him*."

Xochi snorted. "Poor, frail old man, my ass. A few years ago, Don Juan would have lived up to his namesake's reputation and tried to seduce you. I think he purposely meant to get a rise out of Dean—and maybe a free dinner."

Stacy shook her curls. "No, he took several radiation treatments to make sure all the cancer cells died, and that took a toll on him physically. On the way home, he fell asleep, all worn out from entertaining us with his stories. He's like that most interesting man in the world on the beer commercials. Before I went upstairs he said I needed a virile young man like Dean."

"Fine. Believe what you want. We don't need Don Juan any more. We must find a greater challenge for Dean." Xochi brushed her thick black curls a few strokes. "Let me think a minute."

She left for the bathroom and returned with her teeth brushed, makeup removed and nearly as pretty without it. A snap of her fingers. "I know! There's this fellow in my crowd called Angel Garcia." Xochi very properly pronounced the name, An-hel and rolled the R in Garcia. "He's a great dancer who wants to be an actor. Angel tries out for every movie filmed here and usually gets some kind of bit part. You know, second street punk, that sort of thing. I can ask him to pretend to be less than savory and out to bed you. You are being reeled in until Dean puts an end to it."

"Would we have to pay him to play the part?"

"To guarantee his best performance I think we should."

"Okay, when do we start?"

"No better time than tomorrow. You going to the game?"

"Sure, it's the season opener. The family is coming, all except the twins, I think, but they might show at the last minute."

Xochi considered the ploy as she wrapped one dark curl around a finger. "Say I couldn't come because I had to interpret for some Mexican gangbangers at the police station so you brought your friend, Angel. Wish that weren't so often true. I know we needed that retainer with the city police when we started this business, and the Billodeaux name helped us get it, but I hate being the mouthpiece for scumbags. Those kinds of clients remind me of the people who killed my parents." She shivered and reached under her pillow for the little satin bag.

Stacy hugged Xo's shoulders. "I take those jobs whenever I can because I know how you feel about them, but the cops always ask for you first. You come across as pretty tough. This time you'll just be safely at home watching football. And I guess even scumbags have rights in this country. Are you sure Angel will be available?"

"He'll do it if I don't wake him before noon and tick him off. The game starts at three. He should be ready to go. Did Ilsa mention going out with Dean again, maybe after the game? He might not notice you with Angel if his mind is on her."

Stacy laughed quietly enough not to wake the person in question. "I don't think they will be going out again. Ilsa called Dean a party pooper when she got back."

Even Xochi smirked at little at Dean's expense.

"He certainly can be that." She put two fingers to her lips as if blowing a whistle, and deepened her voice. "No cannonballs off the diving board, no running near the pool, no sandy feet. Wash those off!" she mocked doing a fairly good imitation of Dean as a lifeguard at Camp Love Letter.

Stacy laughed louder. "Dean, the party pooper. I love it—but I hope Angel works better than Don Juan did."

"Next time, let Dean talk."

"I'll try to remember."

Chapter Six

Dean Billodeaux awoke Sunday morning with nothing on his mind but carbo-loading a tall stack of pancakes. He was rarin' to go like a racehorse being led to the gates with the bugles signaling post time and the band playing *My Old Kentucky Home*, only in his case he'd be running through the tunnel and entering the field through the blowup devil's mouth with dry ice steaming around his ankles. For two seasons, he'd gotten the Sinners to the playoffs. This year he intended to take them all the way to the Super Bowl. He could feel it. Yes! He punched the air as he entered the kitchen where Tom slumped over a bowl of cereal.

"Cereal, bro? We need to stoke up on hotcakes. Let's go out and find some."

"I won't be running the length of the field. You're certainly in a good mood. You and Ilsa get it on last night?"

"No way. She's too much like the Amberello Agency models I always get stuck with, but brighter. Anyhow, Stacy's lights were on when I dropped Ilsa off, so I know Don Juan kept his promise and brought her right home after dinner. No more worries there. He's impotent, told me that himself."

"Poor Dean, having to date models all the time. How do you know it wasn't Xochi at home?" Tom finished the little O's swimming in the bowl and drank the remaining milk. He rinsed his dish and put it in the washer.

"Xo always stays out late on Saturdays with her girlfriends. They go dancing and come home in a cab for safety unless one of them hooks up, and you know Xochi doesn't do that. How did the rest of the night go with Brigit?"

"I had the cab take us directly to her aunt's place. The aunt wanted to meet me. We had pecan pie and coffee, talked way too long."

"What about?"

"Mostly you and how you are going to get Brigit a great job at the Dome. Will you?"

Dean put one of the little pods in the fancy coffeemaker and turned it on to brew one strong cup to get him started for the day. "Hell, no, not on this side of the causeway. Lots of new trendy places starting up on the other side of the lake. Maybe if I promised to put in some personal appearances and eat their food, they'd give her a try. As long as she isn't in New Orleans and certainly not in the Dome, I'll be happy."

"Her aunt talks almost as much as she does." Tom screwed fingers into both ears. "Good thing I don't need to hear the plays. I think I've gone deaf from listening to them."

"You heard what she said about Stacy and Kent Gonsoulin and the other guys?"

"Stace handled it well, but did you notice Brigit only gave you credit for defending her reputation. I went to Ste. Jeanne's, too, had your back when you threatened to bash his face in that weekend you came home from college."

"My wingman. If you want Ilsa, she's all yours. I

can't stand women who hang on me and agree with everything I say."

"Generous, but like I said, I can get my own women."

Dean had no memory of life without Tom. Only ten months apart in age and both adopted by Mama Nell who thought she'd be childless before she started popping out test tube babies, they formed a tight unit within the larger family. Wherever Dean went, there went Tom, into trouble and out of it, rarely apart. He led, and Tom usually followed. All except that one time when Tommy ran off to Mexico with his birth father and ended up bringing home his half-sister, Xochi, and a puppy he called Macho. Dean had wanted to go find his brother, but seven-year-olds weren't allowed on the rescue mission. He'd saved all his Easter candy to share when Tom came home. Another thing he didn't like about Ilsa was the way she ignored his brother.

"Yeah, I know you can get your own girls. It's just that some women don't know a great guy when they see one—like Princess Anastasia Marya Polasky."

****

Still pumped at game time and able to convey that to the team Dean Billodeaux ran onto the field. He gave a slight wave to the cheering crowd and a wider one for his family before beginning his stretches. Mom and Dad, always there for home games, sat in their usual box low near the fifty-yard line. Daddy Joe hated the sky-boxes where his "suggestions" to the coaches and officials could not be heard. His five siblings who hadn't left the nest yet lined up with them; Teddy in his wheelchair claimed the end slot. Stacy sat there next to Xochi in the second row behind them. No, not Xo, but some other Hispanic-looking person, a guy with greasy black curls hanging down his neck. He had a thin, handsome face, slim build, soulful dark eyes, and a possessive hand on Stacy's knee. Don Juan had proved to be no threat, but this guy, definitely. He'd come from out of nowhere like a lineman trying for a sack.

Head in the game. Head in the game. Dean stretched. He warmed up his arm. He noticed Stacy hadn't shoved that hand away. She laughed at something the fellow said. As he jogged by the box and reached up to slap the flesh with the kids, he noted the couple jabbering in rapid Spanish. Having picked up enough of the language in high school and from their housekeeper, he could get by in the language, but not at that speed. Tom spoke it more fluently having used it with Xochi from the moment she arrived to live with the family. He swung over to where Tom kicked balls into a net getting that leg ready for the start of the game.

"Say, do you know who that is sitting with Stacy?"

"No idea. I'll call Xo after the game if you really want to know. Seems like she didn't make it today."

"I don't like the looks of him, so do that for me. Thanks."

Tom picked up another football, rotated it in his hands. "You know you could ask her yourself."

"No, that wouldn't be good. Might appear like I'm butting into Princess Anastasia's life."

"Aren't you?"

Dean didn't have to answer because the officials called for the coin toss. He did his thing, electing to receive and get this show on the road. The return team did a better than decent job getting the ball to the forty, setting up Dean nicely for his favorite kind of play, the long spiral forward pass just like his daddy used to do. He called the play. The ball snapped into his hands. Relaxed and trusting his offensive line, he sought the three wide receivers that fanned out across the field, one left, one center, one right. He turned his head too far right and caught a quick glimpse of the hand on Stacy's knee moving under her skirt. That tiny jolt of distraction caused him to miss all three opportunities, each man now tightly covered.

Dean danced in the pocket for a few seconds, noted his protection crumbling. Unlike his predecessor, Rex Worthy, he rarely ran the ball and his opponents knew that. He'd missed his chance to throw the pigskin downfield and saw no other way to gain yardage than to tuck and run as far as he could, maybe a few yards before being taken down like a stag in the hunt. He faked a pass, hid the ball, and raced through the nearest gap. Beyond that, his offense had opened another. Most of the defenders had been drawn toward the far end of the stadium to cover his receivers. Before him lay an open field. Dean put on some speed, stiff-armed a cornerback coming in from an angle and ran like hell. As he approached the goal, Jakarta Jones, an older wide receiver left over from the Worthy years, threw a block that gave him access to the goal line. He crossed over and spiked the ball. What do you know? He'd run in his first touchdown in the NFL. Usually, he just made them possible for others.

Dean caught the football as it bounced up and instead of turning it over to the official, he trotted down the sideline and lofted it directly into Stacy's lap. Like the rest of the family, she was clapping wildly but didn't stand up. Little T-Rex, the youngest Billodeaux, tried to grab it as it passed over his head, but as always Dean's throw went where he intended it to go. Stacy had made him run the ball all the way, and she deserved to hold it for him. He took a moment to enjoy her startled blue eyes, her full pink lips forming a little O of surprise. Then, her companion, who now had his arm around her shoulder, said something in her ear. Smiling, she gave the ball to him. Gloating, the sleaze held it high.

Dean, stunned, simply stood there staring into the stands while Tom left the bench and kicked the PAT with his usual ease. Didn't she know he could be fined for doing this—though probably not as most players were awarded the ball from their first touchdown. He'd pay for the pigskin if he had to, no problem, but she'd given away his trophy as if it were nothing, to some guy he didn't know and had never checked out for suitability. Finally, his father's bellow, one that had issued lots of audibles in its day, penetrated his helmet. "Great job, son, but what happened to that pass?"

Dean shrugged, returned to the bench and accepted a cup of Gatorade after removing his helmet. Tom sat beside him. "Good work," Dean told his brother automatically.

"You weren't watching, just standing there staring into the family box like your cleats were nailed to the artificial turf."

"Sorry, you're the most reliable member of the team. Stacy gave my ball to that-that…"

"Don't say it. No Hispanic slurs allowed in our family."

"Right. Does she hate me so much?"

Tom didn't answer that one. Their rival's return team formed up on the field, and he went to perform the kickoff, launching the ball to land exactly one foot before the goal line on the bounce. "Tommeee, Tommy the Toe," the Sinners fans cheered. He gave them a modest wave as he returned to the sidelines.

The hotshot rookie quarterback leading their opponents did a decent job of working the ball down the field, but in the end ran out of downs. All that time, Dean repeated silently to himself, "Head in the game. I do not care if Stacy has sex with that dude in the bleachers, and they put it up on the big screen. Concentrate, concentrate. Remember what Dad always said. No matter what bothered him, he always tried to play his best game. Good advice if he could take it. For the next three quarters, he pointedly did not glance Stacy's way. In the end, the Sinners prevailed 24-7 with his touchdown, another by Jones, a third by Prince Dobbs and a field goal kicked over the uprights by Tom.

He showered and went to join the family for dinner at Ralph's. He'd ask Stacy to return the ball, that's what. Only she didn't join them. Xochi appeared and apologized for missing Dean's big moment. She sat beside him. "Hey, tell Stace I want that ball back. Who was the guy she brought to the game?" he asked, breaking his own slight resolve to stay out of Princess Anastasia's life. Tom grinned at him across the long table they'd reserved at the premier seafood restaurant.

"Oh, Angel Garcia. He and Stacy are dining elsewhere. He's a good dancer and horns in sometimes with our group. He came over to our place along with a few of the girls last night and hung around. Stacy still had on that black dress she looks so fantastic wearing. Angel hit on her hard, practically invited himself to the game when he found out I had to work. Hey, let's not waste an extra ticket. You know how it goes. Stacy really found him fascinating, but I don't know. He might be a gang member and mixed up with drugs. He's got that vibe about him." Innocently, Xochi put a warm hushpuppy on her bread plate before her younger brothers could gobble them all up.

"Want me to have a word with him?"

"Usually Stacy can take care of herself, but maybe you should. I know they have a date to go dancing next Saturday. I'll find out where. In the meantime, I can ask some of the cops we translate for to run a background check on him." She shot her most adored brother—and it wasn't Dean—a warm smile across the table. "Great game, Tom. They couldn't do it without you."

From the far end of the table, Joe Billodeaux said loudly, "Yes, a great game, but what about that first play? Explain what happened there."

"A moment of inattention, Dad. I won't let it happen again, but I think I made up for it."

"You sure did. So, what does everyone want tonight?"

The family members ordered stuffed redfish, fried oysters, alligator pasta, seafood platters, shrimp remoulade, crab salad, and in little T-Rex's case a whole platter of frog legs because he thought eating them would make him jump higher. After coffee and bread pudding, Dean and Tom departed for the after-game celebration at Mariah's Place, the perfect ending to a perfect but slightly disturbing day.

Chapter Seven

An easy Monday morning opened up before Dean Billodeaux offering September sunshine, fairly low humidity, and promising a team meeting that should go pretty well though he didn't expect his hesitation on that first play to remain unmentioned. Despite a late night, he rose early, put on his sweats and the brand of running shoes he currently endorsed. He added sunglasses, a Sinners cap, and plugged in his ear buds, a light disguise but one that would keep fans from stopping him as he went for a short run to loosen up a little. He put Stacy firmly out of his mind. She rarely went out on weeknights, and Xochi said they'd be helping Ilsa find an apartment today, a nice safe activity. In an excellent mood, he jogged along Canal Street, but only got as far as the nearest coffee shop to his condo.

Stacy, dressed for work, sat right in the front of the place like a piece of attractive window dressing. Across a tall table with a very small top, Angel shared a plate of flaky croissants with her. At this early hour, that could mean only one thing—he'd stayed over at her place last night. Nearly taking out a dog walker, Dean made an abrupt turn into the shop. No better time to have that talk with Mr. Garcia, but he had to make it seem natural. Without looking their way, he strode up to the cashier, removed his ear buds, and took a quick glance at the pastry counter, choosing the first item that caught his eye.

"One of those big oatmeal scones and a tall café au lait." He offered a credit card he'd tucked into the kangaroo pouch of the sweats for any emergency that might come up. This seemed like one to him. He accepted the huge scone in a bag and gingerly picked up the scalding coffee that burned a little even through an extra wrapper. Turning as if to leave, he smiled and said, "Hi, Princess. I didn't see you over there with your friend."

Though their chairs sat up on a small platform, his height still darkened their table as he loomed over them. Dean held out his hand and delivered a crushing shake to her companion's rather long-fingered and delicate hand. "Dean Billodeaux. Stacy and I grew up together." He thought that was the best way to put it. Protection rights asserted. He stared directly into Angel's languid black eyes, an alpha male challenge.

"Dean, this Angel Garcia. He's an actor." Stacy introduced him as An-hel.

Actor—that meant unemployed sleazebag. Although Dean knew she used the correct pronunciation, he went for the American version because it sounded pretty and weak. "Angel, we think a lot of Stacy. You'd better treat her right."

"Or what you gonna do?" Angel slouched in his seat and fingered the pocket of his worn jeans as if it might contain a switchblade. Ironically, he wore a red Sinners T-Shirt, the nasty one with the evil devil on the front, not the cutesy kind kids bought for souvenirs at the games.

Actually, Dean hadn't thought that far in advance.

Usually his size and fame kept things from going any farther. He fell back on Xochi's idea. "Check your police record. See if you are breaking any paroles."

"The cops ain't never caught me doin' nothing," Angel answered with a heavy Latino accent and a sneer on his thin lips to show he had no fear of Dean.

"Good for you. Stay clean. By the way, I'd like that game ball back."

"Don't got it on me, man." He held out his thin brown arms as if Dean might want to pat him down. "You could autograph it for me sometime. Then it be worth some big bucks. I could use a little extra cash."

"Please don't sell it, Angel. It means a lot to our family, Dean's first touchdown ball," Stacy interceded.

"For you, my *bonita* Anastasia, I keep it." Angel broke off the white carnation in the bud vase on the table and placed it with a caress behind her ear.

Dean clenched his fists. A splurt of hot coffee erupted from the lip of his cup and dribbled to the floor. The scone broke in half.

As if to keep the conversation pleasant, Stacy quickly said, "I saw you bought a scone. I thought you didn't like them. When I first asked Brinsley to get some for me, you wouldn't even try them."

"Well, now I love them." Dean opened the bag and bit off a huge triangular corner. He chewed and tried to swallow the dry lump. It lodged in his throat. He coughed and took a swig of coffee. It burned his mouth, and he grimaced.

"Here, mine is cooler."

Stacy held her cup to his lips. He tasted a hint of sugar she'd left behind.

"Yeah, man. We don't want you to choke, no.

What would the Sinners do then?" Despite the nice words, Angel leaned back as if he could really care less.

"They'd get another quarterback. Say, you have a pretty thick accent for an actor, Angel. Doesn't that keep you from getting roles?"

"Hey, I was gang member #2 in the detective flick they just wrapped here because I got some experience in that area, you know. I like to stay in character. Stacy loves it."

"You do that. I need to get my run in before team meeting. Take care of yourself, Princess."

Before he could do anything that would get him on the front page of the tabloids, Dean left the shop and continued down the block. A grizzled old black man slumped in the doorway of a store with dirty windows and a heat-curled For Rent sign in the window. He handed him the scone and the coffee. "Watch the heat, and if you don't want that scone, feed it to the pigeons."

"God bless you, sir. Got any spare change?"

"None on me, sorry." He jogged away weaving through a thickening crowd of people on their way to work and tourists hoping to beat the heat of the day. Running faster and farther than he'd intended, the pounding of his feet matched the throbbing in his head. Be an example for your team. Be a leader. Stay out of bar brawls and away from bad women. As if his dad ever had—at least in his early years as a quarterback. Wasn't Dean himself the product of a drunken one-night stand with a woman Joe barely knew?

Mama Nell always told the truth as far as her children could understand at whatever age a question came up. Dean knew Daddy Joe had fathered him and wanted to know why she'd adopted him. Where was his real mother? After all, Tom knew *his* mom. She visited often. Because his had died giving birth to him after a tragic accident, his mom said when he brought this up at age five. Mama Nell followed this news with how much she loved him and thanked his mother for bringing him into the world.

She took him to visit the niche holding Margaret Stutes' ashes in the huge cemetery on the edge of New Orleans, held him up to place a bouquet of silk flowers in the holder beside the plaque with her name and dates engraved on it and paid for by Joe Dean Billodeaux. Content with that, he'd questioned no more until his early teens when additional details of the sordid story came out—the ugly legal battle for custody staged by Margaret's lawyer and the obvious ploy to shake down the famous quarterback for money. Mama Nell said she had no more to tell. She'd met Margaret only briefly a few times, one of those times being at Stevie Dowd's reception after her wedding to Connor Riley.

Before he left for college, he pried the rest of the sorry tale out of Stevie Riley, a no-nonsense woman who admitted Joe slept with Margaret as a favor to her in order to get a job as team photographer with the Sinners and be closer to Connor. "Joe had to get really drunk to do it," she said. "Margaret wasn't his type." Meaning not very attractive, he guessed. When he looked in a mirror, he saw only Joe Dean and none of his mother. Maybe a good thing.

So, his dad could get away with all kinds of bad behavior and still come out a legend and a great husband and father. His family, his coach, his team expected Dean to be a leader and role model fresh out of the box. As he turned a corner to head back to his condo, he wondered what they would have thought if he'd thrown Angel Garcia through the plate glass window of the coffee shop this morning exactly like he'd wanted to do.

Arriving home, he found Tom had already left for the meeting. He showered in haste and skipped the shave. Dean Billodeaux never came late to team meetings. Other guys still hung over from last night's celebration would, but not Dean. He had to set an example.

****

Stacy pondered Dean's last words to her. "Take care of yourself." Did that mean he had no intention of trying to save her from the lecherous Angel? She was on her own? She finished her coffee, setting her lips exactly where Dean's had been. "You can have the last chocolate croissant," she told Angel. He didn't hesitate to polish it off.

With his mouth still full of crumbs, he said with no trace of a Spanish accent, "Thanks for the breakfast and dinner last night, Stacy. I think we got the script all worked out. I'll do a great job for you."

"One thing, no more hand up the skirt. I want Dean to notice me, not ruin his career."

"Whatever you want, boss. Man, that dude is even bigger and better looking up close. I know he wanted to bust my chops, I was that convincing. Glad he has no anger management issues, then all this glory would be ruined." Angel framed his angular face with his long fingers for a moment before getting up and heading off to another audition. "See you Saturday."

Stacy watched his skinny ass sway down the street. He was so not her type, but she'd go dancing with him and hope Dean showed up to prevent her from making a big mistake. In the meantime, she could sleep with that football she kept under her bed—once she got Ilsa the hell out of her room. She swore they'd find a place today for the new employee and eliminate her as a further temptation for Dean, party pooper or not.

Chapter Eight

Not a bad week, all things considered. Sure, it started out with that close encounter involving Angel Garcia and moved on to a light reprimand about hesitating on the first play and giving the football to the family. After that, hard practices because the always-important Falcons game lurked ahead on Sunday afternoon. That kept him tired enough to sleep well without any thoughts of Stacy.

Dean adjusted his striped silk tie in the mirror and asked Tom, who lounged nearby stabbing his finger at the screen of his cell phone, "You got the address? You know where Angel is taking Stacy tonight?"

"Paco's. It's a few blocks into the Treme. Xochi says they already left, and Stacy dressed really hot for the date. The good news, Angel doesn't have a record."

"He said he'd never been caught. He's taking her back of town. That's a-a..."

Ever the diplomat, Tom filled in the blank. "Was racially-mixed neighborhood the word you wanted?"

"Yes. I know nice people live there and some great musicians, but it can be dangerous. We need to get going before anything can happen to her."

Tom looked him up and down. "You don't want to shave first? That makes twice this week you've skipped."

"What are you—my fashion consultant or gay like

Uncle Brian?"

"Brian would probably do a better job on this, but tonight all you have is me, your very straight brother. I'd lose the jacket and tie and try to blend in a little better. How about that tropical shirt Adam Malala gave you? Take off the Rolex, too. No use tempting anyone."

Dean ditched the watch on his dresser top and reluctantly found the short-sleeved shirt bearing a print of parrots and big leaves on a pale yellow background in the back of the closet. He shucked his blue sports coat, tie and dress shirt. Bare-chested, he held up the Samoan attire. "Loud parrots will help me blend in—right?"

"It depresses me that you make that shirt look so good. Put it on, but don't tuck it in. I think the black pants are okay and the loafers since they don't have tassels. I need to change, too. Only be a minute."

Tom reappeared shortly wearing a short-sleeved Kelly green shirt that made him appear to be kin to a leprechaun. Dean wore the damned parrots and summoned the truck they'd shared when both became old enough to drive from valet parking. Since it was all about fitting in, he left behind the massive red SUV and the black Mustang GT convertible he'd craved since a movie star showed up at the ranch driving a red one when he'd been around seventeen. Signing bonuses were good for many things including getting the car you always wanted without the approval of parents who didn't believe in spoiling their children.

Dean decided to drive and let Tom navigate with the GPS on his phone. They went south on Canal, rounded the casino, and crawled along in the traffic by the riverfront. Passing the French Market, they swung onto Esplanade with its restored nineteenth century Creole mansions and pleasantly green neutral ground. As they approached its border with the Treme, however, the houses grew smaller and shabbier. Closed shops with broken windows occupied the corners farther from the French Quarter.

"Turn right at the next street," Tom said. "Go three blocks in, then another right turn. Paco's is in the middle of the block."

Dean completed these maneuvers overshooting Paco's with its name in orange neon and a tilted margarita glass displayed on the sign. He wedged the truck into the first parking place they found, and they retraced their path back to the club. Like many nightspots, the two large front windows in its brick façade were blacked out making it impossible to see inside, but people standing on the curb could feel the beat of the fast-paced Latin music being played behind its walls.

Dean and Tom entered the shabby front door and stood just inside allowing their eyes to adjust to the dimness. Along one side, a bar with huge drums of icy margaritas, strawberry daiquiris, and pina coladas swirling in the wall offered these drinks in thick, oversized glasses along with a selection of Mexican beers. Dozens of piñatas hung from the low ceiling— traditional orbs, burros, pigs, cactus, even a ninja turtle, some with their sides bashed in, a true fire marshal's nightmare of papier-mâché. A few of them grazed Dean's head as he wove around the crowded tables and homed in on the music coming from a courtyard.

The band huddled under a shed-like structure toward the rear, protection for their marimbas and maracas if a sudden storm blew up in the moody New Orleans weather. The dance floor glowed with brilliant tiles of orange, green, and turquoise set between two wings, one with a takeout window dispensing tacos and nachos, and the other housing the restrooms. Colored light bulbs crisscrossed the open space and twined their way down two palm trees on either side of the band's shelter.

In the midst of it all, Stacy, standing a head taller than most of the dancers, swung her hips to the rhythm of a samba. She wore hot pink, low-cut and ruffled around her cleavage dewy from her exertions. Her skirt, above her knees, wasn't tight at all and moved gracefully with her motion. She held up her loose blonde hair with one hand as if to cool her long, white neck, and silvery bangle bracelets jangled down her pale arm.

Around her slithered Angel Garcia all dressed in tight, slinky black showing off his fancy footwork, the snake-like movements of his pelvis, some chest hair, and a few gold chains. When he noticed Dean, hard to miss in a shorter crowd, he slid behind Stacy, put his long fingers around her waist, ground against her backside, and whispered in her ear. Her blue eyes half-closed as if enchanted—or drugged—opened. She smiled dreamily Dean's way. Good thing he'd gotten here in time before Angel dragged her off to some ratty motel and had his way with her. Angel kissed her nape.

Dean started onto the dance floor, but the music ceased and the couple headed back to a small table occupied by an abandoned frozen margarita turning from slush to liquid in the warm, humid night and a single empty beer bottle. Changing course, he grabbed an extra chair from another table and joined them without asking permission.

"Some place," he said to Angel.

"One of my favorite spots for dancing with pretty women, and tonight I got a beautiful one." He leered at Stacy's breasts, not her face.

Stacy sat, crossed those long, long legs, and eyed his parrot shirt. "You get lost on your way to a luau or a fia-fia, Dean?"

In many ways he was glad of her sharp answer. She hadn't driven too far down the road to destruction yet if she could still criticize his attire. "Maybe. Thought I'd join the fiesta for a while first. Xochi says the music is the best here."

A chubby waitress with a very short black skirt and low-cut, ruffled white blouse sauntered over. "More drinks?"

"*Tres cervezas con limas,*" Dean said, hoping his slight grip on Spanish would prevent Stacy and Angel from holding a private conversation in that language.

"Which kind of beer?"

"Whatever he's drinking. Stace, you want another margarita?"

"I haven't finished this one." She reached for her glass.

Dean's hand shot out and got there first. He dumped the contents on the tiles. "You shouldn't drink something left unattended. Get her a fresh one," he ordered. "Hey, Tom, over here."

In a population many shades of brown and black, his brother stood out like a tall, white candle with a blazing hot tip. Dean with his black hair, dark eyes, and olive skin blended in better despite the loud shirt. Tom hauled a spare chair with him. He drew the eyes of several women who stared as if they hadn't seen anyone so pale and redheaded before in their lives, at least not in Paco's, maybe at an Irish pub.

"I ordered a beer for you. We should have something to eat with all this alcohol. You mind standing in line for loaded nachos?"

"No *problema*." Tom started for the takeout window, but the band struck up another throbbing tune, and he got caught in a tidal wave of dancers surging from their tables. In a second, a striking Latina girl took his hand and led him into the mass of swaying torsos. He bounced around like a bright red bobber on a fishing line with his impromptu partner.

"I guess we can wait for the nachos. Stacy, you want to dance?" Dean held out his hand.

"Don't make a fool of yourself like Tom. Angel knows the steps for salsa and you don't."

"That remains to be seen." He yanked her out of the chair with a sharp tug on her wrist that set those silver bracelets chiming.

At the edge of the floor, he twirled her three times around, then pressed her tight to his chest. With quick cross-steps, he got them to the center where, with more room, he spun her away the length of his arm and snapped her back again hard against his hips. For several long moments, they danced as if glued together at the pelvis, then another spin out, return, and a deep dip that had her blonde curls dusting the tiles. As she came up, she wrapped one long leg around his waist and he bent her in the other direction. Restoring Stacy to her feet, he took her hand and they did a few quick steps side by side. Dean passed in back of her and swayed against her with his hands on her waist much as Angel had done, but not grinding against her behind. She reached back and stroked his rough, unshaven cheeks. A twirl and she returned to his arms. He buried his face in the side of her neck and her slender, white fingers raked through his hair. The light scent of a floral perfume rose to his nostrils from her heated skin. He felt the quickness of her pulse against his lips and the surge of desire in his loins. The music stopped. They stood there, dazed with each other for a moment. Around them, the dance floor had cleared. People applauded. Camera phones appeared and flashed as brightly as lightning. A little thunderstruck himself, Dean led her through the crush of people toward the table.

When Stacy caught her breath, she asked, "Where did you learn to dance like that?"

"In Haiti. We didn't only build houses for the poor. Nights we went out. The people we helped wanted us to have a good time, and dancing is free if you can get a little band together in one of the squares. They pass the hat for the musicians. You should come with me some time."

"I-I'd like that. I think I'm a little dizzy. Maybe there *was* something in that drink."

"Where did you get your moves?"

"From Professor Rivera. We went dancing sometimes."

"Yeah, that guy. Let's get you to the table, Princess." With an arm around her waist, holding her close, he escorted her back to their seats. Dean waited for Stacy to call him a big lout for manhandling her. Nothing came out of those pretty hot pink lips but a slight sigh as she slid almost boneless into her seat and drank from the fresh margarita.

With his narrow black brows snapped together over those liquid dark eyes, Angel stood, grasped Stacy's wrist, and pulled her upright. "Now you come dance like that with me, bitch. You're my woman, not his, Princess An-as-ta-sia. Show me how you love me. Give me sugar."

He moved in for a kiss, but she stepped back. "I feel wobbly. I need the ladies' room." Stacy fled for the rustic door marked *chicas* above a painting of a pretty *senorita* wearing a mantilla.

Dean's large hand replaced hers on Angel's wrist. He ground the delicate bones together until they almost touched. Pain flashed on the Latino's face. "Don't hurt me," he pled in perfect whining English.

"When it comes to Stacy, never use the bitch word again. And only I get to call her Princess Anastasia. You got that? She's not your woman either."

"Okay, okay, she belong to you." The Spanish accent popped back into Angel's mouth like a tiny bit of chili pepper on the tongue. "I can't get no part with a cast on my wrist. You let me go, *por favor.*"

Still, Dean couldn't seem to release his grasp. He wanted to feel bones snapping beneath his fingers. Someone short and brown tugged on the sleeve of his hideous parrot shirt. "Hey, hey, you Dean Billodeaux, no?"

"I'll give you an autograph after I finish making my point with this douche bag." Dean kept his eyes on Angel's as they filled with water and released a few tears.

"Please, you don't hurt my cousin. He's gay, man.

He won't do nothing to your girl. He just like to dance and play at being tough, you know?"

At the mention of the word "gay", Dean opened his grip and let his hand fall. Being stocky and bearing a small mustache, the fellow in no way resembled Angel. But then, Dean didn't look like Stacy. There were all kinds of cousins.

"This true?"

"*Es verdad.* Stacy, she's helping me prepare for a role, that's all. Honestly, I'd rather date you, big boy." Angel rubbed his swelling wrist and produced his most winning white-toothed smile.

"You lying…" Dean gathered the lapels of Angel's slick black shirt in one hand and drew back his fist. The cousin grappled with his arm. Some men, a few with bottles in their hands, drew closer, the beginnings of a bar fight.

Tom appeared burdened with two trays of loaded nachos. "I beat the line when everyone stood aside to watch you and Stace make a spectacle of yourselves. Why don't we all sit and get something in our stomachs to go with the beer? Everybody down. Drinks for the house." Tom handed their buxom waitress a credit card. The gathering crowd followed her bodacious behind to the bar.

Dean dropped his fist but held on to the shirt. "Angel claims he's gay. I'm not so sure. You saw how he pawed Stacy, and you missed what he called her."

"I'm an actor. I can play straight or gay," Angel swore.

"That's exactly what I'm thinking. I want my cousin treated with respect and taken safely home, you hear. After tonight, you never see her again."

"My word on that."

"Nacho?" Tom offered, chowing down on one himself. "Pretty good, spicy, extra jalapenos."

"I couldn't eat." Angel fanned his face with a decidedly limp wrist.

"Well, I believe you're gay, buddy. We have lots of gay friends, Uncle Brian, Aunt Jackie."

"We have a few gay friends," Dean corrected. "Let's not *lie* about it."

Tom offered Angel's cousin a nacho. The man shook his head. He whispered something to Dean. Dean unbent and took a swig of his beer. "All right. I believe you aren't lying about your sexual orientation. You treat Stacy like a lady, and we're square."

The topic of their conversation rejoined them at the table. She seemed better, more collected, pale, but then she usually was.

"We can take you home if you feel sick, Stacy, and save Angel the trouble. Damn, we brought the pickup. Tom, you'll have to ride in the bed."

"That's illegal."

"Break a rule for your cousin."

"No, no, I'm fine. Dehydrated, I think." She held up a bottle of water she'd stopped for on her way back. "Got it free. Someone is buying drinks for everyone."

"That would be me," Tom admitted. "Worth every penny for this evening's entertainment." A small brown hand reached over his shoulder and snatched a nacho from the tray. "Xochi! You here with your friends?"

"As I said, a good place for dancing. We were inside taking advantage of the free drinks. The place is packed, no seats anywhere this time of the night." She took a sip from a pina colada and shook her black hair behind her shoulders.

"Those drinks are courtesy of me," Tom admitted. "Tell your friends what a generous brother you have. I think I could get into salsa dancing."

Dean stood. "You looked spastic out there. Take my chair, Xo. I need to get to a luau."

"That explains the shirt, but why not stay and enjoy the night with us and Angel."

"I think he might be leaving, too, since you can take Stacy home now."

Angel jumped from his chair. "Yes, I'm leaving. *Buenos noches*, everyone." He squirmed his way through the maze of crowded tables. His cousin followed closely.

Tom negotiated the bar tab so they could be on their way, but he glanced back regretfully at the table now festooned with Xochi's girlfriends all dressed up and ready to dance. "Do we really have to leave? The night is young."

"Yes, we do. We have a big game tomorrow. I have a lot to get out of my head."

They walked into the night under the sign of the tilted margarita and reclaimed the pickup half a block down. "You drive." Dean tossed the keys to Tom, took the shotgun seat, and stared into the night as if anticipating trouble on every street corner.

Tom kept his eyes on the road, but initiated an unwanted conversation. "How long have you had a thing for Stacy?"

"What thing? I don't have a thing for the princess."

"The two of you generated enough electricity on that dance floor to pay Paco's light bill for a month."

"It's just a style of dancing. One you will never

master." He hoped a mild insult would shut up the one person in the world who knew him best.

"There was more to it than wanting to protect Stacy from the wrong kind of guy. I got a strong whiff of something back there, and it wasn't the nachos. I think I scented jealousy up till the minute you believed Angel really was gay. What did his cousin say?"

"Not a cousin, a lover."

"That explains why you backed off, but then you couldn't wait to get out of there. I tell you, I convince you to wear that gross shirt as a joke, and you still come off as Mr. Macho, *muy guapo*. I think every woman in the place wanted you."

"Not Stacy. She hates me, always has."

Stopped at a red light, Tom shot him a glance. "You couldn't see her face when you were twerking her bottom or when you had your head buried in her neck like a vampire starting to feed. Oh, Dean!" He ran his own fingers over his freckled cheeks and up into his mop of red hair making it stand on end.

"Angel twerked her. Not me. I only rubbed lightly, and even that almost did it for me."

"When did this passion for Stacy start? Level with me."

The light changed. Tom had to pay attention to traffic and that helped, not having his eyes staring at him. Dean wouldn't have to see the shock.

"When I came home from my freshman year of college. I'm eighteen, she's fifteen. I go away to training camp the summer before, play football for LSU, don't get home very much. I take my semester and spring breaks in Cancun and on the Cajun Riviera in Florida. I return late that spring, and she's not a kid with a flat chest, the legs of a colt, a baby doll face, and a smart mouth any more. She's got all these curves on display when Dad opens the pool, and she's wearing this bikini, not even a tiny one, but it might as well have been."

"The twins were wearing them, too," Tom said objectively.

"The twins look like Mom. Stacy doesn't. There's another thing. She never fawned on me, never expected me to be the best all the time. I liked sparring with her. Not physically. I never touched her except maybe to dunk her to the bottom of the pool—until tonight. Jesus, why do you think I volunteered to go to Haiti that summer? Sure, I wanted to help with Rex Worthy's mission, but not for the purest of reasons. Lusting after a kid who is almost your sister is sick."

"You handled it. If I didn't notice, no one did. You know once a person is past twenty-one, three years is no big deal when it comes to age." He stopped in front of their brownstone condo and gave the night valet the keys and a tip. The conversation continued as they crossed the lobby, but Dean passed the elevators and took the stairs.

"I need some hard exercise." He started running. "Don't encourage me when it comes to Stacy. I know what I feel isn't right."

"You should talk to Mom about this."

"Mom must never know. You were still in high school with that jerk-wad, Kent Gonsoulin, the biggest braggart in the locker room. I couldn't let him bag Stacy and tell everyone. Then she says I ruined her life, those big blue eyes filled with tears, lots of slamming doors. She didn't talk to me in all the time before I left for Haiti, not a single insult."

Tom shrugged as they rounded the second floor landing. "Girls, especially teen-aged girls, are like that, and our house was filled with them. So much emo. I'm sure she's over it by now."

"Not Stacy," Dean said very definitely. "Then, the second I graduate from college and can't watch out for her, she takes up with Rivera."

"Better that than any of the guys on the Tigers' team, I guess."

"Oh, I warned them off the second she set foot on campus."

"But you had no influence on a professor. Hmmm."

They started the final climb to the fourth floor. "Big help Mom was then. Young women must make their own decisions regarding their sexuality when they are over eighteen, she says."

"Pretty much what she said when you stopped coming home for most vacations. That really tore her up, but she told Dad you needed to establish your own identity away from the family."

"Yeah, I'm still Joe Billodeaux 2.0, plays great but isn't much fun. I guess that's how Stacy feels considering the guys she's been seeing lately. Mom is the best. I'm sorry I hurt her, but I couldn't be around the princess."

"Talk to her."

"No way."

They arrived at the small foyer fronting their condo. "You're not in such bad shape for a kicker." Dean punched in their access code.

"I'll still need a shower."

"Me, too—a cold one and good night's sleep, that's all I need."

Inside, Tom veered toward to his own suite. "Night."

Dean went to his room and peeled off the parrot shirt stuck to his chest with sweat. He gave it a good sniff to see if it needed to go into the wash and inhaled Stacy's perfume. He'd held her so close, so very close, the way he'd always wanted. Dean hung it on the corner of his studded maroon leather headboard and made for the bathroom repeating, "Cold shower, cold shower, cold shower."

That didn't help. Nor did a glass of milk or reading the playbook. He slept very poorly that night.

Chapter Nine

Stacy picked the jalapenos off her nacho and nibbled on the edge. Xochi ate hers at full strength. A man approached their table and asked Stacy to dance. "No, *gracias*." He chose another of the ladies at their table.

"I don't understand why both Dean and Angel left," she pondered.

"You missed all the action. Look, I have it right here." Xo produced her phone from a small, dangling purse. "I had to take it between two guys' armpits so ignore the dark border."

She watched as Dean mauled Angel's wrist and hauled back to hit his victim. "I wonder why he stopped, not that I'd want Angel to get hurt."

"Must have found out Angel is gay." Xochi sipped her icy drink and also turned down a chance to dance.

"Gay—you didn't tell me that."

"He's an actor. I figured he could play the part of a Latin lover."

"No wonder it didn't work."

"Oh, it worked, for a while anyway. Rachelle, did you get their dance? Send it to my phone." Xochi waited a moment, then turned the screen over to Stacy. "I was too short to catch it. Ai-yi-yi, the two of you nearly burned the place down."

Stacy watched, mesmerized. "I could have stayed

in his arms like that all night. He comes here in that silly shirt, those big biceps filling the short sleeves and the parrots plastered against his pecs by the heat of the night. When he crushed me against his chest, it was like hitting a brick wall with a beating heart inside. I think I felt some action below the tails, too."

"Please, you're making me hot, and I haven't been on the dance floor yet," Rachelle complained. One of the taller and less attractive girls in Xochi's group of friends, she streaked her dark hair with henna red and overdid the makeup to compensate for that.

"Now that he knows Angel is no danger, he'll back off again," Stacy claimed.

"We have to find someone better for Dean to take on. Who does he dislike the most in the whole world?" Xo asked.

"Me."

Xochi replayed the dance. "No, I don't think so, not by a long shot."

"Dean would say he doesn't hate anyone."

"On the Sinners team, who do we all despise?"

"That's easy. Prince Dobbs. It's a wonder he can run so fast carrying around that huge ego and that immense weave." Stacy waved away another dance partner. He took Rachelle instead.

"I'm surprised he can get his helmet on. You know Dean never could stand him."

"But, he sucks it up for the good of the team. I've heard him tell Uncle Joe that Prince is their fastest and best wide receiver regardless of how he feels about him."

"The Sinners only took him in the draft when he slid way down in the numbers because of bad behavior on and off the field. I think his poor father begged management to give him a try." There wasn't a person in the Billodeaux family who couldn't discuss football knowledgably, including Xochi. "Hang on Prince's every word at Mariah's one night and see what happens. Anytime now it's got to dawn on Dean that he loves you."

"Love?"

Xochi ran the dance again on her phone. "That's what I see right here. I'm surprised you don't."

"He was trying to outdo Angel, that's all."

"Love is blind in so many ways," Xo said, worldly wise as always. "I came to dance. How about you?"

"I think I'll call a cab and go home. I really don't want to dance with anyone but Dean."

"Suit yourself." Xochi accepted the next man who approached and waved goodbye.

Stacy waited just inside the doorway for her ride. She dialed Angel to make sure he was okay.

"You know I could have lost some teeth, and I don't have dental insurance. End of my career just like that. Julio is icing my wrist as we speak," he fussed.

"I'll put some extra on your check." Why hadn't she seen him as gay? A better actor than she supposed maybe. "Take care, Angel. Bye."

Her stomach churned and not from the nachos. The thought of having to flirt with Prince Dobbs sickened her. But if that's what it took to bring Dean to her side, she'd do it.

****

Dean apologized at the press conference following Sunday's game for his lackluster performance. "But, we have a great team. We owe our victory to the defense, a touchdown scored by Prince Dobbs and those four field goals completed by Tommy the Toe. Next week when we take on Minnesota, I plan to bring my best game."

He would do better because the Sinners played away, far away from Stacy who'd sat in the stands cheering and clapping for him while he threw a pick six allowing the other team to score. The touchdown throw to that showboat, Prince Dobbs, evened things out. When Dean couldn't seem to get another play close to the goal line, Tom—kicker, brother, friend—saved the day with field goals, 19-14, a little too close for comfort.

Much as he didn't feel like it, he needed to go over to Mariah's and buy a few rounds for his team. He dragged his feet getting there. By the time he arrived, Prince had already surrounded himself with a crowd of lovelies who hung on his every word as he recounted how he'd scored.

"That ball come in so low, so poorly thrown, it's a miracle I got under it and found my feet to take it in for the goal," he boasted so loudly the music from the bandstand couldn't drown him out. He shook the weaves tied into a bundle at his nape like a lion tossing his mane before a roar.

Dean remembered when Prince had done the gangsta bit in his teens and smiled when he recalled how Daddy Joe made the boy belt his sagging pants at the barbecue. He'd tried to do his part by defending Riley Bullock's looks when Prince hurt her feelings, but he'd made a teenage boy mess of it, only embarrassing the poor girl more. That prick made fun of Adam Malala's cute, fuzzy-haired children, too, but not directly in front of the big Samoan. His skinny wife had cut the obnoxious boy down to size pretty handily without any help. No one who really knew him admired Prince Dobbs regardless of the great hands and fast feet.

The one thing Dean did appreciate about Prince right now was the distraction. He moved quietly across the club and took his usual seat next to Tom at the bar. "You were the real hero today, not that loudmouth asshole," he said only for Tom's ears to hear, surprised his brother didn't seem happier over the victory. After all, he wasn't the one who'd screwed up.

"I do my job just like you. We have a bigger problem."

"We do? Just a sec. Bartender, I'm buying a round for the team."

When his teammates all had a drink in hand, he raised his bottle for a toast. "To the best damned players in the NFL." That drew plenty of applause. He turned to Tom. "You were saying?"

"Notice who is sitting right next to Prince and admiring his tats."

"I try not to give Prince any extra attention…Stacy, it's Stacy!" Dean got to his feet. "She knows what he is. Hell, the only thing we agreed on for years was how much we really disliked Prince."

Stacy had her hand on the wide receiver's bare bicep, and Prince made it jump beneath her fingertips. She giggled. A giggle, not Stacy, maybe his twin sisters, but never her. Dean knew that particular tattoo from the locker room. It appeared to be a bushy-topped palm tree bearing two large coconuts, but when flexed, it became something obscene. Prince had rolled up the sleeve of his bright red Sinners' jersey to display the full effect. The man possessed an ego so immense he wore his own specially chosen number, 88, in the club.

Dean crossed the floor with Tom on his heels saying, "Easy, go easy." He arrived in time to hear Stacy coo, "It's so big and hard."

"You should see the real thing, baby," Prince said. "How about we go out when I get back from Minnesota? I always liked you best of all the Billodeauxs. You didn't put up with any crap from Dean and neither did I. You grew up gorgeous, too, real hot, not like that frizzy-headed bitch, Riley Bullock."

"Riley plays Women's Professional Basketball now, and she's engaged to an NBA player," Stacy told him, making a feeble case for her friend.

"So, they'll have grotesquely tall, ugly children. Me, I want mine as golden and good-lookin' as I am." Prince twined one of Stacy's curls around his finger and drew her face closer to the obscene tattoo, no longer a palm tree but a penis. "Want to kiss it?

Dean's hand stopped the action before her lips met flesh. "How about a dance, Stacy?"

"Not now, Dean. I'm busy."

"And we bound to get busier," Prince added with a sneer.

"We really need to talk, Princess. Now!" Dean drew back her chair to encourage her to rise.

"The princess don't want to go wit' you. You got some kind of problem because your cousin is with a black man, Billodeaux?"

Black man, my ass, Dean thought. Prince had his stunning mother's honey-colored skin and sharp features. Not a bit of that old warhorse tight end Asa Dobbs turned up in his son, not the team mentality, not the devotion to the game, and certainly not his dark complexion and blunt, wide face. Truthfully, Dean admitted to having had a slight crush on Sharlette Dobbs who always wore animal prints and high heels even to barbecues back in his early teens, but he found nothing to love in her only boy child. Prince marred that fine hide of his with a mass of threatening tats— barbed wire, skulls, and snakes that helped disguise the pornographic palm tree—and had not a single cross or sign of devotion to his mother among them as many of the guys did. He'd added a few blond strands in that light brown weave of his to top it all off.

"Not with a black man, only you, Prince. I know how you treat women."

"Lyin' bitches, most of them. That coed at Alabama fell all over me, then cried rape. The charge was bogus which is why the Sinners bought my exceptional talent." Still, one or two of Prince's female admirers on the edge of the circle backed quietly away. Prince jerked Stacy's chair closer. Dean yanked it away again.

Finally, Stacy stood up. "Dean, you are interfering with my life again. First Angel, now Prince. What gives you the right?"

Dean's facial muscles locked into place. How could he answer that? Because I want you. Because I'm the better man. Instead, he said the first thing that came to mind that didn't expose his raw emotions. "Maybe because I'm a better judge of character. You realize Angel is gay."

"Maybe that's why she craves a real man now." Prince rose from his chair to get directly into Dean's face. "Stay out my business, Billodeaux."

They compared in height. Dean might have a little

more muscular weight, but if it came to a brawl, the match would be fairly even. Prince pushed Dean in the chest. Dean straight-armed him back. "Keep away from Stacy."

A chair fell over behind Prince. The band went silent. Into the void, Mariah's smoke-roughened voice wheezed, "Brock, Bobby, break that up."

The bouncer with the cobra tattoo on his scalp and the improbably boyish name of Bobby muscled between the two men. "We don't want no trouble in Mariah's Place. Youse guys know the rules. Break it up. Go home."

"Not until Stacy leaves," Dean demanded.

"Not until she leaves with me," Prince countered.

Neither broke eye contact with the other like two dogs fighting over a bitch in heat. "How about Stacy goes with me?" Tom said. "I'm the only true gentleman in the bunch." He offered his arm, and she took it eagerly. They moved toward the door. Prince shouted after her, "I'll be in touch, babe" and made the phone me sign with his fingers. Dean simply stood there watching them go. A minute later, he walked out of the club as Prince Dobbs settled back into his circle of admirers. He looked right and left and didn't see a sign of where Stacy and Tom had gone.

****

Tom let out a breath. "Right now I'm counting my blessings." A cab had drawn up to the curb to disgorge a load of tourists at Mariah's Place and allowed them a fast escape.

"Jeez, Stace, what were you doing back there? You know Prince once stomped on a college kid in a bar fight and kicked him in the head more than once. Asa paid the medical bills, and the family dropped charges. Ace always bails his son out. You want something like that to happen to Dean?"

With her arms wrapped around herself, Stacy huddled shivering in a corner of the cab, not that the vehicle had great air-conditioning. She felt a chill inside over what she'd done. "I think Dean can take care of himself, and so can I." Her voice lacked conviction even to herself.

"Lately, it's been one thing after another with you. Granted the first two men were incapable or not interested, but Prince, he'd force himself on a woman." Tom's forehead wrinkled as if he pondered something very deep. He sucked in some air before speaking. "Maybe I shouldn't be telling you this, but Dean has some feelings for you. They're all locked down and mixed up, but you need to give him a break while he sorts it out. I hope you don't believe this is all wrong because he does."

"No, I don't think there is anything wrong with his having feelings for me." She held her own confession tight.

"Good, now there's a start. You should tell him."

"I can't. You do it."

"Oh, no. I'm not getting into the middle of this."

"You already are, you and Xochi."

"Xo?"

The cab turned into the cul-de-sac by the Anchi Services sign. Stacy got out and waved to Tom to stay seated. "I'll be fine. Go."

As the cab backed up and turned toward Canal Street, Stacy steadied herself with one arm raised on the lowest rung of the fire escape and vomited beneath the planters of purple sweet potato vines and dusty miller she'd placed there for color. Letting Prince touch her made her physically ill. She doubted if she could continue this game, not with him, even to get Dean to open up to her.

Chapter Ten

Dean walked home from Mariah's Place to let off some steam. He rarely got angry, not like this. Hot heads had no place on the football field. He passed one of the many convenience stores still open this late that sold beer, liquor, sunglasses and souvenirs to the tourists. Pausing, he turned back and entered the place with aisles so crowded with cheap junk only one person could pass at a time. He found the rack he'd noticed out of the corner of his eye. It held cheap scarves in many colors like the ones people liked to wave above their heads when second lining behind the brass bands that often marched through the Quarter.

Dean fingered one of brilliant red made of some synthetic material, not silk of course. He paid a few dollars cash for it and accepted his purchase lumped into a small plastic bag by a sleepy-eyed Indian cashier. Veering toward Stacy's place, he arrived at the cul-de-sac shortly. Some drunk had puked beneath her pretty planters on the fire escape. The princess could never allow anything to be simply ugly and utilitarian but always had to dress it up. Gently, he tried her door. Good, locked tight. He debated whether to ring the buzzer. Second and third floor lights were still on, but he decided to wait until morning to present his idea. Right now, Stacy was probably still irate because he'd interfered with her life again. She'd be more receptive once she cooled overnight as he had done in walking it off.

Instead, he continued back to his place. Tom sat in the living room watching ESPN and indulging in a late night snack of recently delivered pepperoni and mushroom pizza that made their condo smell like an Italian restaurant. He glanced up as Dean entered. "Glad you're home. After I dropped Stacy off, I debated whether I should swing by Mariah's again and see if you needed any help with Prince."

"Yep, I can see how concerned you were, but it didn't kill your appetite any." Dean eyed Tom's lean build. "Where do you put it all?" He took a seat on the plush brown sofa, tossed the scarf aside, and helped himself after picking the mushrooms off a slice.

"Stacy seemed pretty shaken. I thought I'd stay close in case she needed someone to come over."

"You did the right thing, bro. I can handle Prince all by my lonesome. I followed you out, but you'd vanished like a volunteer in a magician's trick." Dean folded his slice New York style and went to the fridge for a glass of milk. How many times had Mama Nell told them not to drink from the carton?

"I see you calmed down enough to go shopping," Tom said with a nod to the bag. "A cab was at the curb when we came out. So what are you going to do about this Stacy-Prince thing? You know maybe if you told her how you feel, she'd dump him."

"More likely she'd jump right into his arms to get away from me. I did come up with an idea in case she needs my help. I'll tell her about it the morning. You go ahead to team meeting without me. That's enough pizza for me. Clean this up before you go to bed. Miss

Krayola is coming tomorrow."

"We must be the only men in the world who worry about making work for their cleaning lady."

"That's how we were raised." Dean took the bag containing the scarf into his bedroom and debated if he should wrap it as a gift. No, that would be overkill. Keep it casual. Don't make the princess feel she is being smothered. The scent of Stacy emanating from the parrot shirt filled his nostrils as he got into bed, but he slept well all things considered.

****

Covered with only a towel from the waist down, Dean leaned close to the steamy bathroom mirror to complete his shave. He heard the bedroom door bump open. Usually, he'd cleared the place before Miss Krayola arrived. A hefty late middle-aged black woman hired by Mama Nell, she came a couple of times a week to dust, vacuum, scrub the bathrooms, and do laundry. He always added a Miss to her name out of deference for her age. As for the rest of her title, her own mama had just liked the sound of the name on a box of crayons but changed the C to a K to make it classier she'd told him.

Dressed in a maid's white uniform and wearing thick-soled nurses' shoes but ornamenting her head with a multicolored do-rag, Miss Krayola poked her head into his bathroom. "You still here, Mr. Dean? Well yes, you are, you certainly are."

She looked him up and down in a highly interested way that Dean found shocking in a woman pushing sixty. "No tattoos, thank Gawd for that. Jus' gettin' your laundry together. I suspects this shirt goes in the wash." She waved the parrot shirt and sniffed the air.

"Ah, no. Leave it where it was, please."

"Sho' will," she said in a knowing way. "Not like you to leave anything on the bedpost though. Y'all are the tidiest young men I ever did see."

"My mama wouldn't have it any other way." Dean wiped the remaining shaving cream off his face. "Would you mind giving me a little privacy? I'm running late."

"Be a minute. Jus' let me get the dirty towels, all but the one you gots on." Grinning broadly, Krayola emptied the hamper, added the towels to the laundry basket she balanced on one hip, and left the room.

Dean grabbed some boxer briefs from his dresser and shoved his long legs into a pair of worn jeans. He threw on a black knit Sinners shirt with their logo on the pocket and put his feet into his running shoes. Seizing the bag with the scarf, he went into the kitchen to brew a cup of coffee and rummage in the refrigerator for something quick to eat, settling on two slices of cold pizza. Watching the front window as he picked off the mushrooms and wondering why Tom always ordered it that way, he soon sighted Stacy crossing Canal Street for the coffee shop where she stopped most mornings on her way to the World Trade Center.

"Now that ain't no breakfast for a man. Let me scramble you some eggs and cook you up some grits," Miss Krayola said as she emerged from the alcove that held the washer and dryer at the end of the kitchen. "You surely gonna need your strength today. I got this feelin' I sometimes gets."

"Uh, no thanks. I'm in a hurry." Leaving a half-eaten slice behind, he grabbed the sack with the scarf, ran down the four flights, and called to the doorman to get his Mustang out of valet parking as he passed.

Rounding the corner, he nearly knocked Stacy and her cup of coffee to the ground. No Angel with her today. "Sorry, Stace. I needed to catch you. Here." He held out the crumpled bag.

"A gift for me?" She drew the scarf partly out of the sack. "I think cheap red scarves are more Ilsa's style."

"Haven't seen her since she moved out of your place so I wouldn't know. Look, I have an idea. I know you don't want me butting into your life, but I need to make sure you're okay. See, you can put this scarf in your window if you need my help for anything. I can see your place from mine, and I'll come right over in case a date is giving you a hard time and you can't get to a phone. Or if we are at the same place and you want to get away from someone, just wave it around a little and I'll get you get home safely."

Her smooth white brow furrowed. "Have you been spying on me?"

"No! Hell, no. I mean your shades are always down. All I can see are lights going on and off. Please, would you do this for me, Princess?" When had calling her Princess changed from being an insult to a verbal caress he had no idea, and now he found himself begging her for a favor. He really was messed up. Dean waited for her to throw the small gift in his face.

"Actually, that's very sweet." She shoved the scarf into a large gray leather handbag worn crosswise over her chest on its long straps and rooted in its bottom. "Here, this is the spare key Ilsa was using. If you have to rescue me, you'll need to get in. Thanks, you big lout. I need to get going."

"Me, too. Have a good day, Stacy." Dean watched her move away marveling at how sexy she could make a business suit appear. The nicely rounded bottom and long legs did it. Once he pried his mind off her body, it occurred to him that she'd said "you big lout" almost as an endearment. Smiling, he started back for the condo, and then the great start to the morning cracked open like a breaching levee.

The news and tobacco store next to the coffee shop displayed the latest tabloids in its window along with boxes of cigars. There he stood with Stacy in those last seconds of the dance at Paco's when both of them still seemed to be under some sort of sexual spell. She stroked his rough cheeks, and he swayed against her backside with his eyes closed and his mouth partly open as if he'd orgasm at any moment, pretty close to the nasty truth. Later, he'd been thankful for the long hem of the parrot shirt.

He recalled lots of people taking pictures and thought nothing of it then. Fans photographed him all the time with or without permission. He'd been on the cover of *Sports Illustrated* twice, appeared in magazines like *People* and *Us* often with the starlets and models who wanted some publicity, but basically he'd led a blameless, boring life since coming to New Orleans. Everyone said so. Now the headline of this rag asked the question *Kissing Cousins?*

His body had blocked the view of the shop as he stood there talking to Stacy. What would she say when she found out? For that matter, what would his parents think?

Head in the game. Team meeting. Couldn't be late. But he was by a good ten minutes.

Chapter Eleven

Joe Dean Billodeaux, gone iron gray in his retirement but still in very good shape, sipped coffee with his little wife at the kitchen table. Shopping for the eleven people remaining on the ranch took lots of time, over two hours if you counted the drive into the small town of Chapelle. Corazon would figure out what her employers been up to once the five children remaining at home left for school and she drove away with her long list of provisions, but he didn't care. In fact, he prided himself that Nell still retained some of the afterglow from this morning's romp in their king-sized bed. Since they no longer had to worry about pregnancies, he considered their sex life better than ever. The sound of their housekeeper's vehicle returning indicated playtime had ended for the morning.

Hefting two loaded grocery bags with her usual guilty pleasure trove of tabloids stuffed in the side, Corazon Polk hustled into the kitchen at Lorena Ranch. The passing years had made her wider and painted thick streaks of gray in her black hair, but she could still bustle around the big house. She smacked the sacks onto the counter and turned to face her boss and his wife.

"Need help bringing in the groceries?" Joe asked, trying to figure out the source of her agitation.

"Soon, not now. We got a big problem." She

unfurled one of her magazines and placed it before them on the table.

Her boss raised one eyebrow and a slight smile settled on his lips. "I always wondered when Dean would cut loose a little." Then, he stared more closely at the photo and the headline. "Jesus, Mary and Joseph, that's Stacy!"

"Let me see." In her race to grasp the paper, Nell upset her husband's coffee cup, and Corazon stepped in with a dishtowel to wipe up the mess.

Joe rose and went to pour another cup, not that he needed more caffeine to wake him after seeing that picture, but he wanted something to do with his hands. "I admit I didn't see that coming. I mean, Dean never got in any real trouble, just kid's stuff with Tom. He didn't smoke, drink very much, or do drugs. No begging for tattoos or fast cars either. He only had sex with his steady girlfriends and always used a condom. I taught him that. No matter what they say, use a condom."

"Hush, Joe." Nell scanned the article. "At least they got their relationship right, orphaned cousin by marriage, raised by his parents—the well-known Joe and Nell Billodeaux. Magazines are always writing about our family. They must have had that on file. She is an interpreter and translator, speaks three foreign languages, runs her own business, and obviously enjoys salsa dancing. Could be worse. It notes they danced only once and didn't leave the club together, but hotcha, what a dance. Their words, not mine. More pictures inside. Oh, my." She returned the open paper to her husband.

"I knew Stacy had long legs, but I've never seen

her wrap one around a man before. By the expressions on their faces, they might as well be in bed. Say, maybe we should take up salsa dancing."

"I'm too short and way too old."

"Not too old to try. I could lift you up for a leg wrap. You still don't weigh much more than on our wedding day." Nell ignored his rather nice compliment she was that upset, and he thought he'd crafted it so well.

"Let me see." Corazon studied the photos. "You know in the salsa dancing the look on the face is important like on *Dancing with the Stars*. I watch that show regular." Corazon studied the photos. "I think they scored a ten."

"I did not raise Dean to be a womanizer." Nell tore the tabloid away from their housekeeper.

"Hey, he had two girlfriends in high school and two in college, nothing serious since then. They only seem to last two years, and when they don't get a class ring or one of those promise rings or a real engagement ring, they bail. I wouldn't call that womanizing," Joe said.

"You wouldn't, Mister I Slept with a Hundred Women before settling down. Your mother spoiled you because you were her only boy and then expected the nuns at Ste. Jeanne Parochial to straighten you out."

Oh, the double whammy of their marital life, how many women he'd had and how his interfering mother didn't raise him right. To give Nell credit, she rarely mentioned either. She must be really, really upset. Joe dug deep to find the right words. "The nuns couldn't save me, only you could."

Nell pried her gaze from the picture and looked up

at her still handsome husband with tears gathering in her big, brown eyes. "Oh, Joe. Thank you for saying that. When the reporters followed us around that was one thing. We were all grown up. But what else are they going to say about my sweet baby boy?" The tears spilled over.

Joe cupped her face in his hands and smoothed back her short brown hair with nary a gray one in it. He used her pet name. "Tink, our son is the same age as I was when we met, and Stacy isn't much younger than you were. They *are* grown up."

"What if this attraction started here right under our noses and went on for years?" she asked.

"Hmmm, I don't think so. All they did was argue. He'd call her princess in a sneering sort of way. She'd come back with that big lout business. Other than trying to drown each other in the pool, I didn't see much physical contact back then. By the time Stacy developed enough to be of any interest, Dean had his regular girlfriends and went off to college."

Nell took a deep breath and let her psychology degree come to the fore. "Sometimes fighting substitutes for foreplay."

"Don't I know it?" Joe's hands moved down her body to her waist, just skimming her breasts as he passed. He could never get enough of his little pixie of a wife. She fingered that unruly curl turned gray that fell across his forehead and gave it a small tug.

"You want I should leave again?" Corazon said. "But out in the car, the ice cream is melting and the milk goes bad."

"Right, the groceries. I'll call Dean tonight and see what I can find out."

"I'll do the same with Stacy. Corazon, lead us to the frozen foods."

****

Dean sat at his dining room table and watched Stacy's windows as he ate Thai takeout from the boxes. Tom had gone to Mariah's in case she showed up tonight, but Stacy rarely went out during the week. Prince would be there for sure probably mouthing off about what happened in the locker room this afternoon. After arriving late for team meeting and paying his fine without protest, he'd stayed on for some weight work and light training. They'd be back on the practice field tomorrow. Unfortunately, Prince Dobbs followed the same schedule.

With a trainer spotting, he'd been working on the bench press when Prince sauntered over and drew a phone from his sweat pants. Dean had no desire to know where he'd carried it.

"Listen here, Billodeaux. I'm calling Stacy for a date tonight. No sense letting a bitch who is hot for you cool off for a whole week."

Unruffled, Dean continued to do his lifts with the trainer counting. "Don't bother. Stacy rarely goes out during the week. She doesn't keep her phone on when she's working with a client either. I do know her a little better than you."

He could tell by the sour expression on Prince's pretty face that his call went to voice mail. "Hey, babe, this is the Prince. How about we hook up together tonight around eight?" He disconnected.

"She won't go out with you."

"Says who?"

"I do. She has better taste than that." With a final

grunt, Dean put the weight in the bracket and slid out from under it. He wiped the sweat from his face with a towel that Prince Dobbs ripped from his hands.

"Look at me when you say that, sucka."

"Sure. I said Stacy will never date you."

Prince searched the gym for allies before saying in a voice that could be heard in the far corners. "You just don't want me screwing her lily-whiteness."

Eyes turned their way, but none of the players moved to back up Prince. Tom jumped off the treadmill.

Dean stared Prince in the eyes before speaking. "It's not the color of your skin. It's the content of your character."

"You quoting Martin Luther King, Jr. to me, white boy?"

"Paraphrasing." Dean enjoyed watching Prince struggle with the word. For a guy who spent three years at the University of Alabama, he certainly had a limited vocabulary and poor grammar. "You should listen to what the great man said. It is character that counts and yours is low. She could go out with Jakarta or any other man on the team, and I wouldn't care." He lied. He wanted Stacy for himself but couldn't let that get out. Still, he'd made his point. "Doesn't matter if you're black or white."

"You leave Michael Jackson out of this. Jakarta is married and got three kids. What she want with that old man? This between you and me."

Dobbs threw the first punch. Dean expected it, ducked aside, no damage done. He hooked a foot behind Prince's ankle and shoved him to the floor on an exercise mat. The man got to appreciate the soft landing for a moment before Dean sat on his midsection and glanced a blow off one perfect cheek. The fight ended right there with trainers breaking it up by prying Dean off before Tom or any other players could get involved.

Jakarta Jones helped his counterpart up. "He's a hothead, Dean. I'm trying to teach him how to keep his cool, but he won't listen. Come on. Let's get some ice on that cheek."

A trainer bent over Dean's hand checking for damage. "I'm fine. Leave me alone."

"We should ice it just in case."

Dean submitted to the treatment and went home shortly afterwards. Now he sat here feeling like a donkey's ass for letting Prince get to him, though when he really thought about it, the incident had been the other way around. Mostly he worried that the man would turn up at Stacy's tonight and take their argument out on her. The Pad Thai lost its sweet taste.

His phone rang. Dean checked the incoming number and saw the call he'd been dreading all day. "Hi, Dad."

"I noticed you've been off your game some. Maybe your sophomore slump came a year late, huh?"

Wonderful, his father wanted to talk football. Home free. "I'll do better against Minnesota. I've been watching their film. Their defense is weak this year. Good news for me."

"Yes, that is good news. Now about the other news, the kind that gets you on the front page of those grubby tabloids. What's going on with you and Stacy?"

"Nothing really. We were at the same club. She said I couldn't do salsa dancing. You know how we always pick at each other. I showed her I had the moves."

"Looked like more than moves to me and your mother."

"It's a style of dancing, that's all."

"Your mom is worried sick that you and Stacy might have—ah—been intimate while you both lived here."

"I swear to God, no. She was way too young."

"Let me tell you the hardest thing about raising girls is seeing them grow up. One day they're boobless and skinny-legged, and the next thing you know they turn into young women with knockout figures. You just want to shoot any guy who sniffs around them. But Stacy isn't too young now."

While his father waxed sentimental, Dean swore he'd seen a red Lamborghini at the stoplight. He moved to a better angle to discern if the sports car had rounded Stacy's corner. How many people in New Orleans had one of those extremely high-ticket items besides Prince Dobbs? His dad droned on: treating women with respect, thinking before he acted on his urges, using condoms always. Yadda yadda.

"Wait, what did you say?"

"I said your mother and I discussed this situation. She says marrying an adopted cousin isn't illegal in Louisiana. I tell you me that come as a shock." Joe added some Cajun levity to relieve the tension. He turned serious again. "If you really care for Stacy, you have our blessing to go ahead, but please proceed with caution. If this deal crashes and burns, it would do terrible things to our family. Your mom has been trying to call Stacy but can't get through to her. She hates that texting business. Says this matter is too important, and it is."

Blessing, he had their blessing to be with Stacy. That's about all he heard as his dad rambled on about texting. Neither of his parents thought of his feelings as wrong, immoral, or illegal. Now if only he could convince himself. His dad reached the signoff point of the awkward conversation. "We love you, son. Take care."

"Love you, too." In the Billodeaux family no one got away without saying the words even if they were mumbled during the teen years or whispered into a phone before a game. Mama Nell always said it was important, as you never knew what the next day might bring.

The call improved his appetite. Dean put the phone away and dunked a spring roll in the peanut sauce, never taking his eyes off Stacy's windows. He'd worked his way to the fortune cookies, not a particularly Thai custom, but they always put a handful in the bag. He cracked the brittle shell and popped a piece of it in his mouth while reading his fortune. "Life can change in a flash."

Not too profound or oriental sounding, he thought. Yet in the instant he'd removed his glance from the windows across the street, the red scarf had appeared hanging from the top of the blinds in Stacy's bedroom. Life did change with a flash of red.

Chapter Twelve

Stacy's phone rang again. She shut it off. One more call from Prince Dobbs and she'd kick herself for starting this whole mess. He'd begun by inviting himself over tonight. "No, I'll be too tired from work," she replied in a text.

"Dean got to U, baby? U let him run ur life?"

"No, just tired."

The messages got uglier as the day progressed. Busy, she didn't bother to reply but cautiously saved each one. They'd reached threat level by the time she got home and changed out her pumps for ballet flats, her suit for an oversized black Sinners tee that came to her knees and bore only the team logo of the little red devil. A note from Xochi sat on the kitchen table. "Have to go interpret for some more jailbirds. Couldn't reach you by phone. Don't know how long it will take. Love you, Cuz." She could imagine Xo wrinkling her nose at the assignment, then smiling ruefully as she penned the message.

The phone beeped again. Another in-coming call. She hated to turn it off in case she was needed at the hospital or elsewhere, but figuring it would be Prince, she declined to open it until she got something in her stomach. A client would try Xochi next. But why couldn't it be Dean calling? She laid her phone on the table and taking a low-cal meal from the freezer, she nuked it into near edibility. And the doorbell rang. She debated answering, but it might be Xo who often forgot her keys or Tom visiting—or Dean checking up on her. She hoped for the last.

Stacy went down the flight of stairs and peered through the peephole but whoever it was stood to one side. Cautiously, she opened the door a crack, and Prince Dobbs had his big foot in the opening that fast. Yeah, everyone said he was quick. She maintained what pressure she could on that foot. Maybe fear of having it injured would stave him off.

"Hey, baby. The Prince come to take you out on the town."

"Like I said, long day, too tired." She started to say maybe another time but stopped herself. This should end right now. She'd known Prince since childhood. He came from a nice family who'd spoiled him rotten, but she didn't consider him any real danger. Not to her, but maybe to Dean if she didn't straighten things out. "Come in. We need to talk."

He dogged her steps walking way too close going up the stairs. "You sure ain't dressed to go out, but on the other hand you do look ready for bed."

That made her glad she'd kept her underwear on when changing into something comfortable. Stacy led him into the kitchen and away from the more comfortable sofa. "I was getting ready to eat when you buzzed. Can I get you something?"

"None of this crap." He dumped her meal into the sink and lounged against the counter. "But I do see something else I'd like to take a bite out of. Let's send out for something better before we get down to it. Or you can put on a slinky dress, and we'll go over to the

Prince's Palace. You never seen my place. It's baaad, babe."

"Prince, we've known each other for years and years. Our families are friends, right? You know how Dean and I bicker. Last night at Mariah's I was only trying to get to him by flirting with you. He's so contained. I wanted him to blow up for once." Not the entire truth but close enough and a good enough explanation for Prince.

"He blew up all right. He give me this." Prince pointed to a bruised cheek she assumed he'd gotten in practice.

"Oh, I'm so sorry that happened. Would you like an ice pack?" A little sympathy might cool him down.

"I've had all the ice I want today. Now, I'm ready for something hot. Go put on something pretty. We going out."

"I think I just explained that I have no intention of dating you."

"You saying you a tease, Stacy Polasky? No one makes a fool out of the Prince. The Prince knows how to make a tease pay up."

He reached to grab her arm, but Stacy leapt out of his reach. Maybe doing Pilates did pay off along with courses in basic psychology that Aunt Nell said would be invaluable to her. "You know, I do owe you at least one date. Let me get all dressed up nice for you. Maybe we could have a drink at Mariah's and dance a little. I'll go upstairs and get ready."

Dean and Tom might be at the club to protect her and if not them, then any of the older team members who'd known her for years, only most of them were family men probably at home tonight. Failing that, she could depend on Mariah and her bouncers. She literally bounded up those steps to her bedroom. Another option, lock herself in and call the cops, but she heard the heavy thud of Prince's footsteps right behind her, and damn, her phone lay on the kitchen table. He'd be entirely capable of kicking in her door. She grasped the red scarf on the night table and threw it over the top of the shade. No telling if Dean had stayed home tonight, but she'd let no chance go by to escape. Meanwhile, she was on her own.

"No, babe, we ain't going to Mariah's."

Before she could turn, Prince shoved his arms under hers and clutched her breasts hard enough to bruise. His crotch pressed against her behind. She froze. Then, the words of her self-defense instructor came barking back to her. A Brit, the female teacher said, "Women have big bums for only three reasons—to attract a mate and give birth easily and to use in order to distant one's self from an attacker who comes from behind. Thrust out those bums, ladies. Push him away. If you still can't escape, stomp hard on his instep. Thrust! Stomp!"

Glad for the first time she didn't have Ilsa's narrow hips, Stacy bent and shoved. Prince's fast hands slipped from her breasts, but he hardly retreated. Not a small woman, she put all her force into the stomp and dearly wished she hadn't changed to soft-soled shoes. Still, that must have hurt because Prince doubled over. Outside the window, brakes squealed and horns blared as if applauding her effort. She tried to move around him, but as an athlete used to playing through pain he recovered quickly, grasped her arm and gave her a backhand blow across the cheek.

"Stupid bitch, you'll pay double now! I'll do you front and back."

He threw her on the bed so very easily. She bunched her knees to kick him away. Most of her life she'd been around football players, and all had treated her well. She'd forgotten how strong and fierce the professionals could be on the field. Prince simply jumped on top of her like three tackles coming down hard and forced a muscular thigh between her legs. She had only a second to rake her nails across his face before he shackled her wrists in an unbreakable grip above her head. He used his other hand to work his fly open. Next, he'd have to remove her panties. She might have a chance at another kick, but he kept all of his weight on top of her and probed into the side of those simple cotton bikinis with something other than his hand.

"Relax and enjoy the Prince," her assailant advised in a silky and satisfied voice.

She would not! Stacy bucked as hard as she could and made no progress at unseating him, but at least she put off penetration. She closed her eyes unable to bear the sight of Prince with the bloody scratches on his face leering at her helpless and unable to stop him in any way. The pressure on her body lightened slightly.

Stacy opened her eyes. There stood Dean with a hand in Prince's collar and another on his belt. He heaved, and the weight crushing her into the mattress lifted entirely. His arm, mighty from all those forward passes, wrapped about her assailant's neck in a chokehold that would have been illegal on the playing field. The wide receiver's long, tumescent penis deflated and sagged to one side as his arms tried to rip

Dean away, but he found no purchase on Stacy's hardwood floors. Dragging Prince backwards, Dean hauled him to the head of the stairs and kicked him a good one in the backside. His opponent did a header down the steps. Stacy arrived in time to see a handful of his weave catch on a nail she'd been meaning to hammer down. A few of the strands tore free along with a little bit of scalp.

The momentum of the fall sent Prince tumbling down the second flight, but he managed to twist his body to take it feet first before ramming into the door. Pulling himself up by the banister, he shouted at Dean who had put an arm around Stacy. "If she cries rape, I'll ruin you and your pasty-faced cousin, Billodeaux. She wanted me. You hear?"

"I hear you're delusional, Prince. Get out before we call the cops."

Leaning heavily on the doorknob, Prince answered. "You won't do that because it will hurt the team. Go fuck yourself, Dean." He hobbled into the night.

Dean turned to Stacy, and she buried herself against his chest, not crying, simply shaking. Just where she'd always wanted to be, but not like this. "I thought I could handle him. I was so stupid. Dean, tonight you really were my hero, cheesy and trite as that sounds."

Dean pressed his lips against the top of her head and ignored her hero comment. She waited for him to gloat a little, but no. "You, stupid—never. If I had your grades in school, I could have played for Harvard. Not that they ever have a very good football team. Sometimes we all need an assist, Stacy. Glad I could be here for you." He laid another kiss gently on her forehead.

"You want me to do what's good for the team like he said and keep this quiet, right?"

"Princess, you do what's good for you."

She thought of ugly stories in the tabloids adding tarnish to Dean's pristine image, months of lawyers, and a possible trial. How many people had witnessed her fawning all over Prince Dobbs at Mariah's Place? He'd say she invited him in, and she had. No rape occurred but only because Dean prevented it.

"I don't know what to do right now. I want to take a shower. Would you stay while I do?

"I'll stand guard."

"Would you do one other thing for me? Take those braids outside and put them in the dumpster. They're coiled on my steps like a bunch of snakes."

"I will."

****

Once the water began running in the shower, Dean collected the strands and headed for the dumpster. He encountered a pair of tourists in the mouth of the cul-de-sac, one of them talking frantically into a cell phone.

"Yes, that's where we're staying on our vacation. This big man with a bloody face came from out of nowhere and exposed himself to us. He took off in a fancy red sports car. No, we didn't get the make or license number he went so fast. A description, I don't know. What would you say, Minnie? Mixed-race, light-skinned, huge brute over six feet tall, close to two-hundred pounds I'd guess. He had—what do you call it?—a weave with blond streaks in it. I mean he could be dangerous."

Evidently, Prince forgot to zip up before leaving. Dean kept moving toward the dumpster but thought better of it. He picked up a fast food bag lying on the ground, coiled the braids inside of it, and went back to speak to the couple who had finished giving their report.

"I'm sorry you had a bad experience in New Orleans. I don't think the police will do much about it though. They have a lot on their hands and no one got hurt."

"I can tell you this doesn't happen back home," the man said as he put away the phone and retrieved from the sidewalk a half-spilled container of fried seafood and dirty rice he surely didn't need to take back to their room considering his weight and age.

"It most certainly does. Once at the public library—well, let's just say I've seen one before," the wife answered. "We're Minnie and Carter Hicks of Sioux Falls, South Dakota."

"Dean Billodeaux." He shook the slightly greasy hand of the man and waited for the recognition to set in.

"The quarterback for the Sinners? Well, I'll be. Would you sign this box?"

"Be happy to. Did either of you get a picture of this guy?" Dean asked as he scrawled his signature with a pen Minnie took from her handbag.

"No, too startled," the man said.

"I did." His wife held up her little pink phone. "It's not very clear, he moved so fast."

"Would you share it with me? If I see the guy around again, I'll report him."

The Hicks were delighted to share. What a story they'd carry back to Sioux Falls.

Chapter Thirteen

Dean left the small sack of braids at the very bottom of the stairs and returned to do whatever he could for Stacy. He settled into a little quilted chair upholstered in lavender brocade sitting in the corner of her bedroom, stretched out his long legs and waited. He gained some time to think. She came from the bathroom in the hallway with her golden hair pinned up and wearing a simple long, white sleeveless nightgown, not low-cut or particularly sexy but with little tucks fitting it to her body and bits of lace on the bottom and around the neckline. She'd removed her makeup, and a bruise purpled one cheek of her delicate white skin. Still, she looked as beautiful as a fairy tale princess.

Stacy walked barefooted to her bed and straightened the silver duvet until the imprints of Prince's knees disappeared. "I want to erase every trace of him from this room and from my mind."

"I'd like to help you do that, Stacy." Dean rose and wrapped his arms around her. He kissed that bruise so carefully and moved to her plush lips, tasted them as he'd always wanted, licking across their surface but not attempting any entry. How soft they were. He smoothed her shoulders and rubbed her back lightly. One strap of the nightgown dropped and revealed the ugly blotches of Prince's fingertips impressed into her breasts. He kissed each one wishing he could make them disappear altogether. Drawing the gown down a little farther, he suckled one pink nipple far more gently than a babe did its mother.

A thought dawned on him, the words about respecting a woman's wishes. He raised his face to gaze into her eyes and noticed some signs of tears gathering there. "Do you want me to continue, Princess? I know it's been an awful night for you."

She bit her full lips, and that tugged at his heart. "If I didn't want you to do this, I'd have kneed you in the groin by now, you big lout."

"That's my Stacy." Very glad of her response because he grew heavy between his thighs, Dean kicked off his sockless loafers, scooped her up and carried her to the bed, laying her softly on the covers. He released her hair from the clip and indulged in one of his favorite fantasies regarding this woman, running his fingers through the blonde strands as they cascaded around her, spreading out those silky waves like a halo on the pillow and burying his face deep in the curls. "Smells so good," he murmured.

"Lavender shampoo." She tugged on the plain black T-shirt and made him raise his head to take it off.

In turn, he lowered her nightgown to her waist and rubbed his chest against those ample breasts, soft, soft, soft the only words he could use to describe them, except for her peaked nipples. As for himself, he'd turned hard, hard, hard below the waist. Stacy worked on his belt and zipper now, but he took her hand away. "Not yet."

Instead, he removed the nightgown the rest of the way and soothed every inch of her naked body with his hands. His fingers came to rest in her cleft, and he stroked lightly, working that tiny nub at the top with his big thumb. She moaned and arched for him. "That's my princess. Come for me." Stacy had never obeyed him before, but she did now with moans and a tightening of her body that made him regret he hadn't delved inside yet. He let the waves of her orgasm wane, still letting her decide if this went any farther.

To his great relief, she worked at his buckle again. He helped with the zipper and cast off the jeans he'd donned without briefs for a night at home with no plans to go anywhere. No place else he'd rather be now than here.

She cupped him and stroked his length, but that wouldn't do for long. A man only had so much restraint. He glided inside her on the sea of moisture he'd created between her legs. Pumping slowly until he couldn't hold back any more, he finally spent himself, but kept moving until Stacy took her pleasure again. When she lay still and panting, he removed his weight from her body, rolled to one side, and opened his arm for a cuddle. One good thing about having a reformed womanizer for a father is you did pick up some tips on how to please a woman.

****

Stacy lay listening to Dean's heart thud in his chest, its steady rhythm lulling her. He'd covered them both to keep her from feeling chilly. No chance of that with the body heat he generated. Now, he dozed, but she didn't care as long as she could stay here in his arms, toasty and protected.

The one thing she hadn't expected from him was tenderness, and that nearly brought her to tears. She noted how careful he'd been to do nothing invasive until the end and then on her terms. He'd treated her like the princess so delicate she might feel a pea beneath the mattress and for now, that was lovely and perfect considering her earlier experience with Prince. Stacy pushed that thought away.

She'd learned about sex from Dr. Hugo Rivera who could certainly do a grand tour around woman's body stopping off at all the best places. People might claim he'd taken advantage of her, but she knew better. Not wanting to learn with a fumbling college boy, she'd responded to the professor's advances and soaked up all the knowledge she could as she always did. To think that the salsa dancing he'd taught her brought her into her first full body contact with Dean.

Junior year abroad, she'd tried a Frenchman and an Italian and expanded what she knew of men, but none touched her in the way Dean had tonight. He'd gone straight to her heart. But then, it had always been Dean since that fourteenth year of her life. Since coming to New Orleans and seeing him so often, she'd turned down numerous opportunities for sex. No one else appealed to her. Why bother?

The next time they were together though, she'd do more than lie there luxuriating in his touch on her flesh. The next time she would give back. Stacy reached up to stroke Dean's stubbled cheek long past its five o'clock shadow deadline. He'd been so careful not to give her a trace of beard burn, but the thought appealed to her now. Still, how gently he'd kissed her bruises. She leaned over and kissed his lips, so beautifully sculpted. He had Uncle Joe's good looks, no doubt about it, but didn't use them to attract a new woman every day of the week, thank heaven. Dean's thick black eyelashes flickered open over those Billodeaux brown eyes.

"Stacy?" He sat bolt upright spilling her onto the pillow. "Jesus God, I forgot the condom! I never forget the condom. I had one in my jeans. Always be prepared. And I wasn't. But it felt so good that I lost myself in you. What if…

Stacy pressed him down into her bed again. "I'm on the pill. As Aunt Nell says, a woman must take responsibility for her own body. I'd guess the Sinners make sure you are in perfect health, no matter how many women you've been with since they took you in the draft."

"Not that many, not since you came to New Orleans and I couldn't get you out of my head."

"Really?" No other words that might make her happier—except one.

Dean sat up again but brought her close against his side. "Dad called tonight. My parents know about us. He told me to be careful with you—and I still forgot the condom."

"Forget about that." She moved her hand down his body under the covers.

On the second floor, her phone rang. Not likely to be Prince. He'd be licking his wounds somewhere and thinking up excuses for his injuries. "I really should answer that. I've been dodging calls all evening."

"Let me get it for you." Dean rose from the bed and stepped into his jeans.

Stacy eyed his lean, muscular backside. "You don't need to dress up for me."

Dean gave her one of those to-die-for smiles over his shoulder. "No, but if Xochi walks in I'd just as soon have something on."

Her cousin and roommate! She'd totally forgotten the master plotter who'd brought them together. Stacy rummaged in the bed to find her nightie in case she needed to put it on. Dean returned, phone in hand, shucked his jeans, and got back into bed. Stacy read the text message typed all in lower case and without punctuation as if the person on the other end didn't know where the shift key was located.

return my call right now important.

"Aunt Nell. I guess I should get this over with."

"Right now?" Dean covered his face with the pillow as if hiding from his all-knowing, all-seeing mother.

"Hi, Aunt Nell. I guess you saw those pictures in the tabloids. No, I won't deny I have feelings for Dean. Yes, I'm on the pill. No, I won't break your son's heart. Yes, I do know marriage between us is legal. I looked it up on the internet when I was fourteen." She listened quietly to the rest of the lecture and half-hoped Dean hadn't heard that bit about how she'd known they could marry since she'd been a kid, information he did not need right now. At last, the conversation ended. "Love you, Aunt Nell. Thanks for everything you've done for me."

The pillow over Dean's face shook. She raised it to find him laughing.

"So you've wanted to marry me since you were fourteen."

"I had a crush, a silly childish crush!" She socked him with the pillow. He wrested it away and hit her back but not very hard. This could be fun or would have been. Xochi pattered up the stairs calling out, "Anyone home?"

Dean dove for his small pile of clothes. Stacy shrugged into her nightgown damning its length that twisted around her legs. By the time Xo reached the bedroom, she'd propped herself on two pillows and pulled the blankets up to her chin.

Dean sat in the little chair again fully dressed and looking immensely uncomfortable, but he spoke first. "I'm glad you're home, Xo. Prince Dobbs tried to rape Stacy tonight. I came over as quickly as I could. Damn near got hit by a cab crossing Canal against the lights, but I think she needs a woman to talk to, so I'll be going now. I'll lock the door on the way out." He moved off faster than a receiver with two tackles on his tail.

Stacy got out of bed to watch him cross the street while Xo questioned her about the attack. "Yes, it was terrible, but you know Xochi, your plan worked. He is my hero."

Chapter Fourteen

Dean got to training on time, but he should have arrived earlier. With one foot in an orthopedic boot and the other ankle wrapped tight, Prince had hobbled in on a pair of crutches an hour before, possibly the only time he'd been the first to arrive for a workout. He'd told quite a tale about being with "his woman" when Dean barged in and knocked him down a flight of stairs in a jealous rage. Didn't everyone know how their quarterback acted at Mariah's and in the gym yesterday? There should be fines, big ones, penalties and punishments. The team doctors took over where the emergency room left off. Diagnosis: a broken bone in one foot and a high ankle sprain in the other leg, numerous bruises, a small scalp wound, some deep facial scratches, and a slight concussion. They placed the wide receiver on the injured reserve list despite his protests that he'd be good as new in a few weeks.

Coach told Dean the general manager and his crew waited to hear his side of the story, not the best way to start a day. Marty Buck sent him off with a pat on the back. The GM, Mitchell Michener, was a distinguished man with a permanent crease in his forehead and an ulcer in his belly that had him tossing down antacids like malted milk balls. He asked Dean to be seated upon his arrival at the office.

Sitting quietly to one side, Dr. Edmund Funk, team

shrink for going on thirty years, held a pen poised above a paper notebook, very old school. The man Dean's dad called Dr. Mind Fuck, usually following that up with "Sex addiction my sweet Cajun ass", had gone completely bald only increasing his egghead identity. The public relations director, Acton Jackson, better known as Action, filled another chair. With one leg crossed over the other, Action's foot jumped nervously as if he would have preferred to be pacing the room. No sign of the legal team yet.

After listening to a recording of the accusations and marveling at how Prince's grammar and respectful attitude had improved, Dean admitted, "Partly true. He attacked my cousin, Stacy Polasky—and she's not his woman. Stace broke his foot and raked his face defending herself, but I did throw him down the stairs. Probably got the sprain and concussion then."

"You rip his hair out?" Action thumped a folded newspaper against his thigh.

Dean placed the bag containing the braids on the desk.

"You brought breakfast to this meeting?"

Dean suppressed a grin. Last evening, Tom mistook the evidence for a sack of hamburgers when he came home hungry as always. The sight of the weave with its particle of skin attached grossed him out big time. "Some of Prince's braids, though they do smell a little like french fries now. They caught on a nail on his way down. I didn't pull them out. He's welcome to have them back. I'll bet the blond streaks cost extra."

Not a single person smiled. Mitch Michener wagged a finger at him. "We gave away three years worth of early draft picks to get you on our team,

Billodeaux. Hell, we had to take a kicker the next year we fell so low."

"Tom worked out great for you, right?"

"Yes, but this isn't about Tommy the Toe. We expected you to set a shining example of what a quarterback should be, and up until recently you did. Prince Dobbs wouldn't be on our roster if we'd had any better choices this past year. We counted on you to work with him."

"I've tried. When he drops a pass, it's my fault, he says. When Stacy didn't want to go out with him, he hit her, left bruises on her body, and tried to rape her. With Prince, it's always some else's fault. I have pictures of him leaving her place still unzipped. A tourist snapped it. Here's more of Stacy's injuries." Glad Xochi had foresight to take those pictures after he'd left, Dean passed his phone around the group. Dr. Funk said, "Hmmm," and the PR man made a small whimper deep in his throat.

"How much do you think she'll want?" Action asked. "We have to keep this quiet."

"No money and certainly not notoriety. I talked to her late last night. I needed to be sure she was okay. Stacy wants Prince Dobbs gone from New Orleans and for any other team that takes him to be made aware of his problems. She says he needs mental help. If you can't do that for her, she'll report this to the police and take out a restraining order on him. You know that will make the press."

Mitch appeared pleased with the deal but still dug several antacids tablets out of the jar on his desk. "Anyone else?" he offered. The PR man took one. Dr. Funk shook his head.

"I'd expect someone raised by Joe Dean Billodeaux to be a team player. Sounds like Stacy is. Most women would milk this for every cent."

Dean kept his hands gripped tightly to the armrests of his chair to prevent himself from committing his own assault on the GM. To his right, Dr, Funk stated mildly, "I will see the recordings of both these meetings are transcribed and append copies of those pictures to the Dobbs file. I have observed none of his father's proclivities for sexual dalliance in Dean and would take his word in most situations. Prince, however, is a raging egomaniac of the worst kind. While he is unable to train, I'll schedule some mandatory sessions with him to discuss anger management and sexual harassment, but unlike Joe Billodeaux, most men don't change because they have no desire to try. Dump Dobbs as soon as you can."

"He won't be traveling with the team any more. We'll put out a statement that he injured himself in an off the field accident and will be out at least six weeks," the PR man stated.

Mitch crunched his tablets before saying, "Once he's healthy again, we'll try to work out a trade, maybe for Little Joe Bullock up in Cleveland."

Dean no longer felt he had to suppress a grin. "That would be great! There's no better lineman, and Little Joe hates Cleveland winters and Ohio food." He'd grown up with Little Joe, son of the great cornerback, Revelation Bullock. The Rev and his offspring shared the same massive build and appetite.

Action Jackson thumped that paper in his hand one more time before he unfolded it. "I'd save the happy for later Billodeaux. You seen this?"

Dean opened another of the scandal sheets that filled the news racks. This one featured a very clear photo of Prince and Dean facing off in Mariah's. Stacy appeared as a slightly blurred blonde harder to identify and for that Dean felt grateful. She was named within the article. The headline read *Dean and Dobbs Collide over Cute Cousin.*

"No, I hadn't seen this. I apologize for my unprofessional behavior in a public place."

"Never heard that one from his daddy," Dr. Funk remarked.

"But I'd toss Prince down a staircase again if I had to. What I stopped was a rape about to happen. This only amounted to a little push and shove. I left as soon as Mariah sent her bouncers to break it up."

Unable to restrain himself any longer, Action Jackson began to pace. "We'll need the girl to give a statement and sign an agreement not to press charges or hold the Sinners' organization liable. The press and the public will put two and two together when they see this and figure out how Prince came by his injuries, but we don't need to confirm anything. Meanwhile, stay away from the young woman. Prince has his orders, too."

"She's my cousin, part of our family. We see each other all the time."

"Not now you don't. Cool it with her and stay clear of Dobbs."

"Is that all, sir?"

The GM leaned back in his chair, one hand on his flat aching belly. "We're fining both you and Dobbs the same amount for this debacle." He named a sum that would have made a player less well paid than the quarterback wince.

Dean merely nodded. "May I go now?"

"Get out on the practice field. Let's see how you manage against Minnesota on Sunday without Dobbs as a receiver," Mitch said with a flick of his hand.

"Oh, I'll manage just fine, sir, just fine." Dean held in his burning desire to hit something all the way to the field. There he got the anger out of his system with sweat and hard work, but who were they to tell him he couldn't see his own cousin whenever he wanted?

****

He'd called after she got home for the day. Stacy had kept her phone on for a change hoping to hear Dean's voice telling her everything went fine and maybe something more personal. Instead, she'd been asked by a man named Acton Jackson to come to Sinners headquarters and fill in some paperwork regarding the incident with Prince Dobbs. Busy with a client for the day, she'd set an appointment for the following morning and debated trying to get in touch with Dean, but he'd be at practice. Bad form to call him at work and worse form to hound a guy by phone after a night of sex. Though the clock said seven p.m., evidently Dean Billodeaux was the one man in the world who did call the next day. She didn't like what he had to say.

"I'm so sorry about this mess, Stacy. Sorry you'll have to go in and sign papers clearing the Sinners organization. Just tell them what really happened between you and Prince, no more and no less. The lawyers will be there."

"Did you say we made love afterwards?"

"Had sex? No, that's none of their business, but maybe I took advantage of you in a weak moment."

"Believe me, I am not weak, Dean."

"I didn't mean it in that way. Anyhow, the GM and the PR guy don't want us to see each other for a while, especially not out in public. Does anyone else know that we did it last night?"

She guessed she'd been fortunate he hadn't said "hooked up" or "bumped uglies", but what they'd done amounted to far more than having sex in her opinion. They'd broken through a barrier separating them for years, and he only showed concern about who knew it.

"Xochi figured it out," she replied tersely. "If she knows, so does Tom, they're that close." Actually, Xo had asked for all the details, and she'd supplied them while getting weepy again over his tenderness. "Did Tom say anything to you?"

"Not so far. I think he knew something was up. Said I seemed pretty relaxed and happy for a man about to be chewed out by the brass. I'll ask him not to say anything to anybody, especially the rest of the family. Would you ask the same of Xochi? Dad told me to proceed with caution. You know I didn't. We should cool it for a while."

Stacy imagined Dean tugging on that same curl on his forehead he'd inherited from his father as he sometimes did when stressed. She wished she could rip it out by the roots right now like that piece of Prince's weave.

"If that's the way you want it, you big lout," she said, putting some sting into her words.

"Don't get up on your high throne, Princess. This isn't the way I want it. It's for your own good. I never want to see your name or face in the tabloids again. After this blows over we can…"

"I think I know what's best for me!"

"Like flirting with Prince Dobbs?"

"Sure, throw that at me, too."

"Just a reminder to be careful while I'm on the road and not around to protect you."

"Oh, go protect yourself—and use a condom next time." She disconnected. They were right back where they'd started from. Stacy punched one of her silver cushions in frustration.

Chapter Fifteen

Dean guessed he'd shown management how little he needed Prince Dobbs on the field. Two long passes to Jakarta Jones—one into the end zone, a hand off to the running back—and a short pass to his tight end, all resulted in touchdowns, leading to a final score of 28-21, Sinners. If the defense had been able to hold better, the end result wouldn't have been nearly as close. Trade asshole Dobbs for Little Joe Bullock, and they'd be doing a whole lot better.

Good team meeting this morning with nothing said about the absence of Prince in their midst. They'd be preparing for another away game with Dallas this week. Right now, this second, Dean believed he couldn't be defeated. He seemed to have been born with his father's boundless optimism in all matters as well as his looks—except when it came to Stacy Polasky.

Dean stared at her window again wondering if she'd stayed home tonight. No lights on this early.

"Come on," Tom urged. "We deserve to celebrate at Mariah's tonight."

"I don't know. I should avoid run-ins with Prince and stay away from Stacy in case she shows up there."

Tom snapped his fingers. "I forgot to tell you when I was listening to your play-by-play of dragging Prince off Stacy and heaving him down the stairs—choke hold, drag, boot to the rear! Wish I could have been there. Anyhow, he's been banned from Mariah's Place. After we left, he continued to mouth off. Called you the m-f word."

"Tom, Mom isn't here, and we're all grown up." Still staring out the window, he thought he noticed a light go on in Stacy's living room. Hard to say with the sun at its current angle.

"Okay, he claimed you were a worthless motherfucker who wouldn't be able to put a score on the board without his help. Lots of the team still in the club that night, and they told me about it. The temperature in the place rose when he said that. Mariah herself went over and told him get out and not come back. It takes a lot to get her out of her chair these days. Might be part of the reason he wanted to harass Stacy the next night. You know Mariah regards all the Billodeaux kids as grandchildren even if the connection is pretty loose, and she doesn't put up with crap from anyone where we're concerned."

"Yeah, Mariah is something else. In that case, I'll go have a few drinks with the guys. Stacy should be fine. I doubt if Prince could make it up her stairs in his condition."

"That's the attitude. Drive or walk?"

"Walk, I guess."

Glad of that last decision, one beer and two hard shots later, he and Tom traversed the edge of the French Quarter with a mild buzz on. Thinking about being buzzed seemed to have activated the phone vibrating in his hip pocket. He fumbled it out.

"It's Stacy. What should I do?"

Tom gave him the no-brainer look. "Answer it."

"Hi, Stace. We're walking back from Mariah's

right now. What can I do for you? Be right there, only minutes away."

"What?" Tom asked.

"Something terrible happened. She's crying." Dean picked up their pace, stretching out those long legs, eating up the crumbling sidewalks of the Quarter.

"Prince?"

"No. Something else. She's a little incoherent."

"Where's Xochi?"

"Out to dinner with friends. She's all alone." They arrived in the little cul-de-sac. Dean took out the key Stacy had given him. He always had it on him now just in case.

"You want me to stay, too?"

"No, I can handle this."

Tom raised his dark red eyebrows. "If you think so. I'll be right across the street if you need me." He continued on his way as Dean opened the door and shouted up the stairs, "It's me."

****

Stacy knew she was taking a chance, a big one, but in all truth she couldn't stop blubbering, and she did want Dean's arms around her right now providing comfort. She supposed she could have asked Ilsa to come over, but for a German she had strangely little love for dogs, all except the Lucky Dogs sold from a cart near her new apartment. May she gain twenty pounds!

Simply hearing Dean's voice made her feel a little better. Stacy managed to blow her nose in a tissue and wipe her eyes before he rushed up the stairs so swiftly he must have taken two steps at a time. Exactly as she'd imagined, he said, "Tell me what's wrong," and opened his arms. She ran to him and pressed herself against all that warm muscle.

Looking up, blinking back more tears, she told him. "Titi is dead."

"Your dog died—that Titi?"

"There is no other Titi. Oh Dean, Lorena went to bring her inside this evening and found her dead."

Dean let out a sigh that he should never have expelled. "That's all? Stace, Titi was a very old dog. Her time had come to go to the big dog park in the sky."

Stacy drew back sharply leaving a wet patch and some eye makeup behind on his light blue shirt. "You never liked her!"

"I didn't care for the way she bossed big old Macho, always nipping at his heels and chasing him around the ranch."

"They were best friends. He chased her, too. Then, they'd go lie down under that oak tree, rest, and slurp up water. I think they would have been more than friends if Aunt Nell hadn't had her spayed." She waited for the comparison to sink in.

"That was the right thing to do. A big ranch dog like Macho would have torn that little bit of fluff apart if they'd mated."

Why did he have to be so reasonable? "You wouldn't let her sit in your lap or lick your face. Titi wanted to love you."

"Jeez, Stacy, no guy in his teens wants to be seen with a fuzzy little dog in his lap, but I did admire her spirit. Titi had more bark in her than dogs four times her size. I remember when she nipped at that big movie star who barged onto the ranch looking for Rex Worthy.

She did know who to trust."

Dean hung his head and paused as if getting ready to make a big confession. Stacy held her breath. "The reason Titi always wanted to lick my face is that I used to give her treats on the sly. She liked those terrible dry scones. I guess they tasted like dog biscuits to her."

Shoving aside her disappointment, Stacy said, "I thought you'd finally developed a taste for scones. You bought one the other day."

"Nope. I had you and Angel on my mind and just pointed to the first pastry in the case."

That cheered her a wee bit. "I think I need a cup of tea. Can I get you anything?" She shivered a little remembering how Prince answered that question and where it led.

"Coffee. I could use some coffee if it isn't too much trouble."

"No trouble at all." She made a mug of herbal tea in the microwave and started the dark roast dripping into a regular office style carafe. Again she had a flash of Prince lurking in her kitchen instead of Dean already comfortable at the table.

"Let's go into the other room while the coffee perks. I guess I need to talk a little."

They settled on the plum-colored couch but not as close together as she would have liked. "I should have taken Titi with me to college. I just abandoned her at the ranch, and she'd always been my best friend."

"She would have been miserable in a small student apartment all day with you gone. You turned her care over to Lorena who did a great job. You know that."

"I guess, but I think Titi grieved for Macho, that big lug, after he died of old age. That's where they found her tonight, lying on top of his grave under the oak tree. They buried her next to him—and I wasn't there to say goodbye." Stacy couldn't help herself. The tears gathered again and dripped into the mug of herbal tea as she tried unsuccessfully to hold them back. Dean slid closer and put an arm around her.

"The big lout and the big lug, that's what you always called me and Macho."

"Affectionately."

"Pretty hard to tell back then."

"Dean, kiss me." That came out more as an order than a suggestion, but she had no need to worry about the response. His lips pressed down hard on hers, and this time he demanded entrance for his tongue. She smelled good bourbon on his breath and that might have explained his lack of hesitation, but she didn't care. Intending to stay home, she hadn't dressed for seduction, but her fitted pink tee and really ordinarily bra peeled off just as easily beneath Dean's fingers.

He, however, wore a dress shirt with the collar open and the sleeves rolled up, his usual casual style. Opening all those buttons down the front infuriated her, especially when he arched his body to suck her bare breasts, not so gently this time. She tore one button from its threads in her haste, and when she finally exposed that smooth expanse of muscle with a trifle of black hair between the pecs arrowing toward the end zone, Stacy shoved Dean back and went to work on his nipples with her tongue. She grappled with that belt buckle again, but his khakis slid down his hips far more easily than jeans. She thumbed his boxer briefs off with them, and the loafers cooperated by falling to the floor. There, she had Dean Billodeaux naked and raring to go.

Except, he pushed her back into the purple upholstery and upended her hips to shake her out of pair of tight skinny jeans and fairly skimpy undies. She'd been padding around the apartment in cute pink sequined flip-flops and those flew through the air presenting no problem at all. Dean mounted over her with one leg bent on the sofa, the other on the floor, and the notorious third leg ready to go to its destination. Stacy hated to say the words. "Upstairs is better. What if Xo…"

She didn't have to finish the sentence. Dean threw her bare buck-naked body over his shoulders in a fireman's carry very similar to the one she'd used to haul him from the pool for her lifeguard test. With an ease that left her breathless, he hauled her up the stairs to her bedroom. Kicking the door closed as they entered, Dean paused only slightly to rip the duvet still bearing a light stain from their last encounter off the bed and dump it on the floor. He laid her on the pale gray sheets with a slight bounce from the mattress springs and wasn't far behind in assuming the sexual position again.

Dean stopped. "I forgot the condom again. It's in my khakis downstairs. Be right…"

Stacy gripped his shoulders. "I told you I'm on the pill. You can trust me. I won't be having your babies any time soon."

"Thank you," he said and plunged in to the hilt.

She couldn't have been much slicker if they'd spent a half hour on foreplay. Strong, fast strokes brought her near climax, but she dimly remembered she wanted to show some skills this time around. Stacy raised one hip and pushed against his broad shoulder to indicate she wanted the top position. A slight smile on those great lips, he gave in without a struggle for supremacy.

"Whatever you want, Princess. It's all good." He reached for her breasts, fondling them firmly, as she rode him.

Too late to do some fondling of her own between his legs, Stacy felt the tightness building, the spasms starting and continuing as she tried to hang on a little longer. He should give in and go first this time. But, he didn't. When she flattened gasping against his chest, he rolled her over much like Macho did to Titi with one big paw when they'd played together and continued to pump until she came again. Then, he took his turn. As he lay with his head pressed between her breasts, he murmured. "Man, holding back is harder without a condom."

"Get off me, you big lout. I tried to make you come first, my treat, since you were so considerate last time."

"Don't pout, Princess. You didn't enjoy it?"

"Oh, shut up! I enjoyed it—twice—before you did."

"Thought so." He bore that same slight smile again. Wrapping blonde ringlets around his fingers on either side of her face, he kissed that pout away, then tucked her against his chest. They lay there quietly, letting their heart rates lessen and the sweat dry on their bodies.

"I've been thinking," Dean said.

"About?"

"I really can't get away easily during the season, but we have a bye week coming up in October. I remember how it helped when Mama Nell took me to place flowers at my mother's niche. I guess she'd call it closure. When I can swing a day off, we should drive back to the ranch and put flowers on Titi's grave, maybe even get a little marker for her and Macho."

Stacy experienced a small pang in her heart. For the past half hour, she'd forgotten the reason that brought Dean to her house and into her bed. "I'd like that very much."

"Good. It's a date then. We still shouldn't be seen in public together, but this is more important and personal. Mitch will have to understand."

"Yoo-hoo, Stacy. I'm home," Xochi called, using the fake Ricky Ricardo accent she liked to put on when joking. "I brought leftovers, good ones."

"Go away!" Stacy shouted as loud as she could, but clearly Xo had entered the kitchen to stow the food. Her next stop would be the living room to turn on the TV where strewn clothing, both male and female, cluttered the way. Silence, absolute silence, then Xochi's light footsteps on the upper stairs.

"I am placing the clothes of the absolutely anonymous man in there with you outside the door. Yours, too. You know how I hate a messy living room. Now, I am backing slowly away. I have a sudden yen to visit my brother Tom across the street. I might be gone as long as an hour. Who knows? Plenty of jambalaya in the fridge to feed two. I'm going, going—gone." Xochi's feet hit the stairs and continued all the way to the bottom. She made a point of slamming the door.

"I never realized Xo had such a great sense of humor," Dean said.

"Oh, what you don't know about Xochi would amaze you."

"Jambalaya sounds good, and I never did get that coffee."

"Well, if you'd rather eat first…"

"Maybe just a snack. We have a whole hour and maybe more if I call Tom and ask him to keep her at our place."

"That works for me." Stacy left the bed and moved naked to her closet. This time she found a pink lace nightie worthy of the occasion and drew it slowly over her head. "Let's eat."

Chapter Sixteen

Dean went into the locker room to use his phone during a break in practice. Tom craned over his shoulder trying to see what he was doing. "You've been on your phone every spare second we get. Trying to call Stacy?"

"No, something else. Last night we talked about our old dogs. At least, I think we were talking about dogs. I'm not too clear on that, but I'm trying to track down another Bichon Frise for her. The AKC has a site that will find a puppy for me within a hundred miles of New Orleans. I bet I won't have to go that far. Maybe I can pick up the dog on Saturday morning before we take off for Dallas. Stace was so broken up over losing Titi I want to do this for her."

Tom offered his mischievous leprechaun's grin. "Oooh, Mr. Sensitivity. You had to stay and comfort her, huh?"

"You could call it that. Do you think Xo really didn't know who Stacy had in her bedroom?" Dean's fingers continued to flick against the screen.

"If she couldn't figure it out, she'd have checked your wallet to be sure. The mysterious Xochi knows all and sees all." Tom moved his hands as if clearing the fog inside a crystal ball to get a better look at someone's future. "She could make it as a fortuneteller if being an interpreter didn't pay more."

"Do you really think she checked my pockets? My condoms were still in there. She'll know we had unprotected sex."

"How was that? I always follow Dad's Rule Number One: Never forget the condom."

"Great, really great. Having a woman you can trust like this is fantastic. Your day will come. Thanks for keeping Xochi occupied for a few hours."

"No problem. We played foosball. Xo is remarkably good at it, very quick. Too bad she isn't taller, bigger, and a guy. She could replace Prince on the team. We ended up tied. When I got tired of being jealous that you were in bed with a beautiful woman and I wasn't, I walked her home."

"Good timing, too. We passed on the way."

"Oh, Xo had a phone call before we left. I suspect Stacy gave her the all clear to return."

"Not psychic after all. What a disappointment. Got one! A private breeder on the North Shore, Covington, has one pup left from a litter. I'm telling him I want the dog." Dean's fingers flew on the virtual keyboard.

Coach Marty Buck stalked from his inner sanctum where at his age he might have been taking a power nap, not that anyone would dare suggest it. More crotchety than ever, he shouted, "Put those damned gadgets away and get your asses out on the field. Big game Sunday. Move it, move it, move it!" When Buck barked, the players obeyed.

****

Burdened with a pet carrier and a large PetSmart bag containing kibble, bowls, training pads, a leash, collar, and a doggie bed he thought might match the décor because Stacy would care about that, Dean rang the bell in the cul-de-sac midmorning, Saturday, using his shoulder. He'd called first wanting to make certain she'd be in.

"Sure, come over. I'm not doing anything better than studying my Spanish medical terms. Xochi is out interpreting for a Portuguese sailor who jumped ship here and got picked up by immigration. I have coffee and chocolate croissants. No scones, sorry," she teased.

Dean noticed her blue eye at the peephole. "Stand directly in front of the door," she shouted. Good, she'd learned caution after Prince. He held up the carrier. She opened the deadbolt. Man, she looked fine wearing just a plain white shirt and a pair of slim black slacks with those sparkly pink flip-flops on her feet.

"I wondered why you didn't use your key."

"Hands full and I didn't want to set this stuff down in the alley. No telling who peed or puked there lately. I brought you a present." He offered her the carrier where a small black nose poked through the grill.

She didn't reach for it but started up the stairs. In the kitchen where her laptop sat open and a half-eaten croissant lay on a silver-rimmed plate, he sat the crate on the floor. "It's a puppy, a Bichon Frise, but not a Bitchin' Freeze."

"I can tell that. Dean, this is so kind and thoughtful, but I'm not ready for a Titi replacement yet."

Could it be he'd made her sadder? Dean knelt down and opened the cage. A small snowball of a dog jumped out. He scooped it up before it could make a break into the living room and held the pup under its forelegs with its belly stretching down. It squirmed to get free, as hard to handle as a wet football. "It's not a Titi replacement because it's a boy. See?"

Stacy looked at the tiny pink and white penis sticking out of the white fur. She smiled. Good deal. "Definitely male."

Dean moved closer, and the pup licked her face with little pink-tongued kisses. Now who could resist that? Unfortunately, the newly liberated and excited dog started to pee.

"Aim away from the laptop!" Stacy cried. Her crisp white blouse already bore a yellow stain.

Dean set the puppy on the floor. It took off running, circled the couch three times and started to raise a leg by the end table. "No! Bad dog!" He stopped the desecration in time. "There's training pads in the bag. Everything you need really, according to the PetSmart clerk." Dean drew out the doggie bed. "Look, gray with a purple lining. You won't even notice it a corner of the room."

The puppy began to explore again, returning and sniffing Stacy's naked toes. He followed that up with a lick of approval. She giggled. Stacy Polasky giggled. Now that came as a complete surprise. In the past, she'd mostly snarled at him.

"If you don't want him, I understand. I'll take him back when I return from Dallas, but the breeder is across the lake. Can't do it today. I have a plane to catch in a couple of hours."

Gazing down on the dog's curly head, Stacy said, "Maybe you should keep him."

Visions of returning to a condo smelling of urine-soaked pee pads and finding his Italian leather loafers punctured by small teeth marks danced through his head. Not to mention the ragging he'd take from the team for buying a fluffy lapdog. Some of them owned pit bulls. He'd never hear the end of it.

"Um, I'm gone too much. I'd just have to ask you or Xochi to take care of him while I'm away. If you could keep him over the weekend, I'll take him back Monday. I promise. He was the last of the litter, so he'll be all alone for a while." Dean appealed to her with his own version of puppy dog eyes.

Begging to be picked up, the puppy whimpered and put his paws on Stacy's knees. "You're hoping I'll fall in love with him while you're away."

"Maybe."

"Too late." She held the pup against her damp blouse. "I'm already in love."

Dean stilled and said not a word. Did she mean with him or the dog? No room for error here.

"His name will be Mati in memory of Macho and Titi."

Oh good, the dog, but still he felt a tinge of disappointment. She'd wanted to marry him at the age of fourteen, but what about now? "You always had a way with words. I don't."

"French immersion program in school, practicing my Spanish with Corazon. Italian wasn't all that hard to pick up." She shrugged her shoulders modestly and put Mati down.

Yeah, Dean wondered what words she'd practiced with Dr. Ugo Rivera, but he said, "I'm glad you're going to keep him. I figure he'll bark if a stranger comes around, and if he takes after Titi, maybe he'd bite an ankle to protect you when I'm on the road."

"I'm sure he would." Stacy set out the bowls and filled them with puppy chow and water. She placed a training pad in the laundry area and the dog bed near the sofa. "All set up."

"There's a blue collar and leash in the bag, too. Promise me you will never humiliate this dog by putting a rhinestone collar on him or having his nails painted."

Stacy stepped forward and tugged on his collar. "I promise."

Dean didn't care if she smelled of puppy pee instead of perfume. He stripped her of the damp shirt and opened her front-clasped bra to spill her full breasts into his hands. He didn't bother with her trim black slacks before carrying her up to the bedroom, this time held close to his chest with her head on his shoulder. Normally, he wouldn't engage in sex the day before a game, saving his energy for his job, but what the hell, nothing was normal about what he felt for Stacy.

"How long do you think it takes to interpret for a Portuguese ship jumper?"

"No telling," Stacy answered. "Don't you have a plane to catch?"

"I've got enough time." He shut the bedroom door with one loafered foot.

By the time they finished, Mati had puddled next to the training pad, torn up one silver throw pillow and dragged Stacy's bra into his dog bed for leisurely gnawing. Neither of them cared.

****

The Billodeauxs came for a weekend in the city and crammed their youngest five children into their apartment, once the slick bachelor pad of their formerly womanizing father. Lorena, now seventeen, always claimed the pale blue Madame Pompadour bedroom with is crystal chandelier over the bed, but she didn't mind sharing the space with tiny seven-year-old Edie. The three boys fit themselves into the old nursery, once Joe's Chinese Bordello room, but not any more. No one suggested the youngest two sleep with Mom and Dad in the remodeled bedroom where both had been born.

They'd taken the boat up river to the Audubon Zoo on Saturday where the teenagers feigned boredom but still laughed at the seal act. Now, the kids gathered in front of the big flat screen to watch their brothers play football in Dallas. Just before kickoff, the doorbell rang and Xochi and Stacy entered.

Stacy held up the puppy. "Newest family member. This is Mati. Dean bought him for me."

Joe and Nell exchanged glances. Lorena's eyes grew a little misty. Edie squealed and held out her arms. "He's like Titi only smaller and younger."

"Why don't you hold him? He loves to sit in your lap." Xo took the dog from Stacy and passed him to the littlest Billodeaux as she bumped the biggest of her siblings off the long and now very battered leather couch to a place on the floor. Daddy Joe, a beer in hand, reigned supreme in his recliner.

"I'll help Mama Nell with the snacks." Stacy followed her aunt into the kitchen where the popcorn pinged inside the maker and a vegetable tray with a yogurt dip already sat on the counter. As a concession to the men, a chili-cheese concoction to go with the corn chips heated in the microwave. With the chatter of the children, the yip of the puppy, and smells of popcorn and chili filling the air, they could be at the ranch, a place where she'd never quite fit in, maybe her own fault because she didn't want to.

Hard to believe sometimes that the triplets had

been born from her own mother's eggs and that she shared blood through her aunt with the youngest, Edie and T-Rex. Though both large and small in size, all of the five were Billodeauxs through and through with their dark hair, Cajun eyes, and olive complexions. Xochi fit in well with her light brown skin and long, black curls. Aunt Nell hugged Stacy around the waist. At five-ten compared to Nell's barely over five feet tall, a shoulder squeeze would have been impossible without bending over.

"So good to see some of my grown up girls. Dean bought you a puppy to replace Titi. I've raised a considerate young man."

"Yes, he is that." Both in and out of bed. Stacy turned quickly to staunch a blush. Her pale skin always betrayed her. She grabbed the veggie tray. "I'll carry this out for you."

Strange how tiny Aunt Nell could block an exit when she wanted. "How are you and Dean getting along?"

"Great. We don't argue very much any more."

"You are proceeding slowly with this relationship, right?" Oh, how those warm, brown eyes could search a person's soul.

"Absolutely." If only jumping into bed and having sex without condoms were considered moving slowly. The burn reached Stacy's cheeks. "I'd better get this tray on the table. The guys won't eat anything green once the chili dip arrives."

Nell allowed her to go without further probing, but when she followed carrying a huge bowl of popcorn, her aunt raised her eyebrows at her uncle. He nodded and took a sip of beer. They either believed her or positively knew she was lying, Stacy couldn't tell which. Dean appeared on the big screen in hi-def so clear she wanted to reach out and touch his cheek. He did the call for the coin toss and lost. Dallas elected to receive. All the chatter in the room ceased as Tom kicked off placing the ball neatly at the ten-yard line and allowing for a bounce to the eight. Despite having to execute a long return, Dallas eventually scored a touchdown as they poked holes in the Sinner's defense.

Dean returned to the field and on his second throw got a man into the end zone. He set a pattern for the game with no interceptions and only one sack that Stacy felt viscerally as he went down hard. For years, she'd been careful not to exhibit too much emotion when Dean took a hit. Now, the thought of him being injured made her blanch and squash the cherry tomato she'd poised over the yogurt dip. She held her breath until he got up again and walked it off. More meaningful glances passed between her aunt and uncle.

"It's part of the game," Uncle Joe remarked mildly.

The veteran announcers, Al Harney and Hank Wilkes, waxed eloquent with analogies. "Billodeaux is on fire this afternoon, shooting one pass after another like flaming arrows down the field."

"It's *The Hunger Games* out there, and Dallas isn't going to survive," Hank remarked in an attempt to be current.

"The only people with short careers in football are the players. Those geezers have been around since my rookie year and before that. Just look at Coach Buck still pacing the sidelines like the Sinners were down three touchdowns instead of three ahead. I tell you me, one day the old man is going burst a blood vessel right there on the field. One of the good things about retirement is not hearing his gravelly voice on Monday mornings telling me all I did wrong. I guess he won't have much say to Dean after this game." Pride crept into Joe Billodeaux's voice.

Final score 42-17, Sinners.

Chapter Seventeen

Hotter than hot the sports pages said about Dean Billodeaux, and they weren't talking about his sexual allure though he had that also. The Sinners quarterback polished off two more teams, one at a home game and one away racking up high scores as if he simply couldn't stop himself. The paparazzi, however, lurked in the coffee shop and at a café near Stacy's apartment that offered outdoor tables. One posed as homeless person and took up a spot by the dumpster, a good disguise until the camera popped out and Stacy requested the police to move him out of the private cul-de-sac.

Dean took care about his visits, using his hoodie or a ball cap along with sunglasses when he crossed Canal Street and slouched low among the tourists and city dwellers to reach Stacy's place. When the false indigent jumped up with the camera as Dean inserted his key in the lock, he waved the man away. "Visiting my sister. Give me a break." Evidently a picture of him standing before a door lacked punch and never appeared in the scandal sheets.

Sometimes, Stacy came to him in unlikely disguises far different from her usual stylish, professional identity. He especially liked the coveralls, painter's cap, and grungy sneakers, all very easy to take off especially when she wore nothing beneath the clothing. The hooker in the patent leather mini-skirt, fishnet stockings, and red wig fooled even Arturo the doorman who'd seen some amazing sights in his day. Once so icy and aloof, Stacy's ingenuity amazed Dean. He hoped the fun would continue if—when they took their relationship to the next level. As for Tom and Xochi, they seemed to have developed very full social schedules giving the couple the space they needed.

Today, Stacy met him in the parking garage where the Mustang waited to take them to the ranch. She'd dressed like an old time movie star with her hair bundled in a silk scarf and her pouty lips painted red. Large and expensive sunglasses covered her blue eyes. Her full-skirted dress sported black polka dots all over its white surface. She dangled a small funeral wreath around one wrist like a bracelet and held Mati's leash with that hand while towing a stylish black leather overnight bag with the other. As she moved briskly along, people took her picture hoping to learn later that they'd spotted an eccentric celebrity. She eased into the convertible with its top down on a perfect October day, and they roared off to Chapelle on the Friday of Dean's bye week. Slowing only for the small town speed traps and otherwise speeding, they made excellent time with the wind blowing Stacy's scarf back and Mati sitting happily in her lap.

Always thrilled to have one of her *ninos* return home, Corazon buzzed them in through the gates of Lorena Ranch. The younger children hadn't gotten home from school yet or they would have been swarmed as soon as they drove up before the mansion, the epitome of Southern dreams with its white columns, verandahs and setting of live oaks, hardly a ranch house by any definition. Stacy put off going inside and instead went directly to the small mounds beneath a large oak near the front of the house. Two little headstones reading Titi and Macho marked the graves of the beloved pets. She placed her wreath between them and touched Dean's arm.

"Did you arrange for the markers?"

"I called and asked Dad to see to it. He grew up on a farm and isn't as sentimental about animals as the rest of us."

Stacy raised her eyebrows. "No? I thought when Lazy Boy died he might put up a bronze statue in front of the barn."

"He really identified with that old stud horse, but in the end buried him with a backhoe under his favorite tree in the pasture—horse heaven."

"Seems strange not to have those two dogs barking and running out to greet us." When Mati sniffed Macho's marker and raised a wobbly puppy leg to pee, Stacy jerked him back with a strict, "No."

"Yeah, it's a little too quiet," Dean said.

But not for long. Corazon's voice sounded from the impressive front doorway with its beveled sidelights. "What, you not coming in? I bake peanut butter cookies for you, still warm. Better get some before the others come home."

They left the little graves and followed Corazon's wide rump through the length of the house to the kitchen where much of the Billodeaux family life took place. The scent of brown sugar and roasted peanuts filled the room. Automatically, Dean lifted a gallon jug of milk from the fridge and poured a glass. Stacy helped herself from the always-ready pot of coffee.

"Sit, sit. You are early and everyone is gone. Your mama is still at the clinic seeing patients, and Mr. Joe and my husband gone to get a load of hay for the horses." Corazon filled her own red mug with coffee and carried a plate of cookies to the table.

Dean bit into one of Corazon's specialties and closed his eyes. "Oh, so much better than scones."

"They have oatmeal and extra peanuts in them to make your mama happy. Always must be so healthy, the snacks. But, tonight, I do not cook. We all go to see your brother and my Junior play football. Your father says hotdogs, hamburgers, and nachos for everyone. We don't got to be healthy eating all the time." Corazon helped herself to a second cookie.

"Yeah, Dad still can't get over Mack wanting to be a wide receiver instead of a quarterback and have Connor Riley give him pointers, but Uncle Connor is pretty pleased since his oldest boy wants to play golf."

"Stevie is glad her son doesn't have any interest in football. No head injuries to worry about in golf unless you get hit by a ball," Stacy added while primly dipping a single cookie into her coffee and eating it in tiny bites. Mati got up on his hind legs to beg, a trick he hadn't been taught. She rewarded him with a doggie treat from her little red purse. "No junk food for you either. He's very clever and trained like a whiz to go outside."

If the younger kids had been around, numerous jokes about whizzing would have passed among the boys, but Corazon frowned, her mind obviously elsewhere. "Yes, I worry all the time about Junior getting hurt."

Dean patted her shoulder. "Don't. He has the perfect body for a lineman and great training from the

Rev and my dad." By which he meant that the chubby boy Corazon had overfed grew to have his father's height and his mother's breadth. Not particularly aggressive, Junior's training began when the Ste. Jeanne Parochial students teased him about his weight and he returned home crying. Junior Polk cried no more. He simply mowed down the opposition.

"Say, has Dad covered the pool?" Dean reached for his third helping.

"No, not yet, but the water, she will be cold."

"I think we can handle it. You want to go for a swim, Stace? You did bring a suit."

"You told me to, so yes, I did. It's in my overnight bag."

"Great. Get changed. Meet me at the pool house." Dean snatched a few more cookies as Stacy went for her bag. He consulted a pegboard full of keys and palmed one before going outside after giving Corazon a kiss on her broad cheek. "You are the best," he assured her. So happy with that, the housekeeper did not question which key he'd taken. "Watch the pup for us, will you? He still has accidents no matter what Stacy says. Keep him in the kitchen."

He joined Stacy shortly by the pool. It seemed to be retro day as she wore a bikini bearing red polka dots with perky ties on the side and a full bra top that gave her lots of lift but could have been smaller both top and bottom in his opinion. Stacy dipped a toe in the water.

"Oh, Dean, it's freezing! You aren't going to dump me in there, are you?"

"Fond memories. That's as close as we got to touching during our teen years. But no, that water would shrivel my nuts. How about some sun bathing

153

under the palms? I've got a blanket."

"Sounds good."

Dean opened the gate to the sandy swath Adam Malala donated to Camp Love Letter after saying everyone needed a beach. They walked the smooth and winding path among the palms and still blooming red and yellow hibiscus until Stacy pointed out the crossed trees where she'd once spied on Adam and his now wife making love.

"I wanted to know what adults did and made poor Teddy come with me to watch."

"Yeah, a big punishment for that. Adam thought Tom and I were the ones hiding in the bushes and flashed you good."

Stacy colored clear down her heck and across the tops of her breasts. "He was so big and tattooed all over below the knees, and I do mean everywhere. It's a wonder I wasn't scarred for life after seeing that."

"Adam proposed to his wife under those trees. Seems like a lucky spot to me."

"A lucky spot or a spot to get lucky? Dean, you know this place has cameras all over, one reason that between the surveillance, you, Tom and Uncle Joe, all four of us older girls went to college as virgins."

Dean smiled in a way that reflected his dad at his sexiest if only he could have seen himself. "I got the key to the security building and shut off the screens for this area. Come on. You can compare me to Adam."

He took Stacy's hand and led her through a break in the shrubbery to an open place by the crossed palms. Spreading the blanket, he bore her down with him on the bed of sand and released her perfect white and pink-tipped breasts from the bra top. She pushed back on his shoulders as he lowered his mouth to suckle them.

"Just a minute. Did you do this here with your high school and college girlfriends?"

"Hell, no! Usually kids are crawling all over the place and back then, Knox Polk would have noticed a missing key or a blanked screen within minutes. I just seized an opportunity like I do on the football field. It's all about the timing."

"You did break the speed limit getting here," she agreed.

Dean untied the little bows that held the bottom of the swimsuit and opened her to him like a pretty package. He'd worn a Speedo because he had the bod for it, but the skimpy thing showed his desire a bit too obviously. Stacy rolled it down and gave him a few firm strokes. He returned the favor by doing the same between her legs. She closed her eyes to enjoy but still said, "So this is virgin ground for you and me."

"I swear it is."

"Good." She relaxed as he massaged her breasts and laved her mouth with his tongue. "Peanut butter cookies, not scones," she murmured when he withdrew and took that tongue down the length of her body and used it to test her readiness instead of his finger in that small swatch of light hair. "Better than both," she sighed and raised him up to shade her body and welcome him inside.

Stacy clasped her long legs around his narrow waist and rode with the rhythm he set until she wanted more and faster and let him know with her nails digging into his shoulders and her heels kicking his backside. She tugged on that forehead curl of his, drawing him down into a kiss as she came hard, smothering a cry that might attract attention. He finished with his own big release moments later. As they lay side by side staring up at the palm fronds, Dean made his confession.

"I've wanted to do that here with you since I was eighteen."

"What!" Completely shaken from her après sex lethargy, Stacy leaned her head on one hand and peered down on Dean just lying there with arms linked behind his neck.

"Sure, I came home from college the summer I was eighteen, and you'd gone from being all legs and a pretty girl face to having curves in all the right places. Any man would want you, but it wasn't right. You were only fifteen. I couldn't let my parents down by taking advantage of you, so I took off for Haiti after I made sure that shit, Kent Gonsoulin, wouldn't get to you either."

"You ruined my teenage life on purpose because you were jealous of Kent?"

Dean smirked as only he could when messing with Stacy. "No, I saved your teenage life. Kent might have ruffied you because otherwise you would have fought back hard. I know that. Prince knows that now. He's still wearing the boot, and he got rid of his weave until his scalp heals, shaved his head bald. He's growing a mustache and goatee to make up for it."

Stacy reached over and tweaked his nipple hard. "That's for interfering with my life."

"You should be glad I did. I only wish I'd been able to stop Dr. Rivera from seducing you. I thought you were still too young when you arrived at LSU. There I was a senior football star with a cheerleader girlfriend. What would the team and the family say if I dumped Debbie for my cousin? It still wasn't right. I tried to get my parents to report Rivera, but…"

Stacy pinched his other nipple no more gently. "You told them about my sex life! I'm surprised they didn't call a team meeting to discuss it."

"Unfortunately, no. They said you were at an age when you had to make your own decisions. That hurts by the way." Dean removed her hands from his chest.

"Just another reminder—I am not your cousin. I thought you'd want an experienced woman, and I had nothing to offer. Hugo taught me what I wanted to know. He didn't take advantage of me."

"How about that junior year abroad?"

"I experimented a little, so what." That defiant lower lip poked out.

"Nothing. But it would have been a privilege to be your first, Princess."

"Oh, stop being such a boy scout, or I'll pinch you again."

Dean presented her with a lazy smile. "Just try it."

She did. He rolled her over into the sand with ease and pinned her fair shoulders and the length of her body to the ground. "Tell me, how do I compare to Adam? Then, I'll let you up."

"At nine, I could hardly judge, but I'd say favorably. The tats were rather fascinating though." She gave a small buck to see if she could unseat him. No dice.

"I could get some anywhere you want."

"Oh, then you'd be big, bad Dean. It would serve you right if I said on your penis and balls. I can only say Adam underwent some terrific rite of passage. But no, I like you unadorned exactly as you are." Stacy raised her hands to stroke his back and parted her legs to let him sink between them, a perfect surrender—until he relaxed and she pushed his body over and seated herself firmly on his thighs.

"If you think I am going to throw you off, you are so mistaken, Princess. Go on, have your way with me."

Oh, she did, nipping at his lips and ear lobes, stroking until he hardened again, and she could mount with ease and ride the hell out of him with her blonde hair lashing his chest. Both finished hard and fast. In the distance, car doors slammed and a dog yipped.

They jumped up covered in sand glued to their bodies by sweat. No problem for Dean to cover himself fast with that tiny Speedo, but he did have the grace to tie Stacy's bows and rehook her bra top. Shaking out the blanket they'd long abandoned, they started back to the house, skirting the pool on the way. She should have known not to let Dean get behind her, but evidently, the thought did not occur. With one mighty shove, he sent her flying into the deep end. As she sputtered to the surface, he said, "That's for the purple nurples."

"They aren't purple, just a little puffy! Now I have to dry my hair before we leave for the game, you big lout. Give me a hand out."

"Don't think so. I know that game. See you at the house."

Dean swaggered off. Fuming enough to warm the water, Stacy stroked to the side and caught up to the man who'd finally admitted he'd wanted her since the age of eighteen.

Chapter Eighteen

Stacy sat in the black convertible parked on the Ste. Jeanne d'Arc church lot. She might as well be displayed on one of LeJeune Pommier's cake stands for all the eyes turned her way this Sunday morning. Dean simply had to duck into Pommier's hole-in-the-wall bakery for a sack of beignets before they started back. As good as the ones served at Café du Monde, he claimed.

Of course, she could have gone inside with him, but Mr. Pommier, gone gray but no less of a gossip than ever, would have mixed up a tale about her and Dean along with his famous square doughnuts and carried it to his infirm mother in the nursing home during his Sunday visit after he closed the shop at one. Old Madame Pommier might be toothless, but she sank her gums into any story she thought good enough to tell the aides and Sunday visitors at the facility where she spent her last years. "Not likely to ever die," her beleaguered Mexican daughter-in-law said. "She's a *bruja*, a witch."

Stacy tended to agree. Her childhood memories were of a spare, white-haired old woman always dressed in black relieved only by a full white apron. Rumor had it that Madame donned black the day her middle-aged son married. Her sharp, black eyes demanded that little girls beg for cookies, though she rarely gave a free treat. Fine if Aunt Nell bought a dozen, then she'd make it a baker's by adding one more. Stacy could imagine her cackling to her bingo buddies. "My son saw Dean Billodeaux riding around with his cousin in that black convertible. Doesn't that kind of thing lead to incest?" Madame Pommier would be wrong, that wouldn't stop her.

Stacy didn't bother to cover her head, and the sun shone brightly on her blonde waves. She did retain her sunglasses, not that in a town this size they amounted to any real disguise. The parishioners filing into the church recognized Dean's flashy car and knew her from childhood. A few waved. They'd wonder why Dean hadn't gone to Mass with his Mawmaw Nadine and the other boys in the family despite the kind of pressure the elder Mrs. Billodeaux excelled at applying. Dean merely said, "Not this time, Mawmaw," and gave his grandmother a big hug that lifted her off her feet. "Got to get back to New Orleans. Sorry to miss that great Sunday dinner you always put out." He knew how to get around her with affection and cooking compliments, a skill Stacy had never mastered.

Daddy Joe clapped his oldest son on the back before going into the sanctuary. "Haven't been to confession lately, huh? Been there, boy. Just promise me to be careful."

Dean did promise right there in front of Stacy as if she hadn't caught the comment. Made her glad Aunt Nell raised her Episcopalian like the rest of the girls except for Xochi. She had no need to confess to anyone but God directly. Not that Mawmaw hadn't tried to convert her. "You know the Pope is Polish," she'd wheedled, and at the time the man had been, but not any more. "Polasky, that's a Polish name."

Her deceased parents had rarely felt the need to attend a service of any kind. "No, thank you. I prefer being a Protestant," she'd replied in that precocious way of hers. Mawmaw labeled her *canaille,* tricky, not a favored child in that woman's eyes. Since Mawmaw doted on Dean, she'd freak when she learned they were together. No slouch when it came to being *canaille* herself, maybe Mawmaw already did know. She sniffed these things out like the sheriff's bloodhounds did wanted criminals.

The three recently refurbished church bells, saved from a fire and warehoused for years, pealed, beckoning the stragglers to hurry. A family of five rushed from the back of the lot, a fat, red-haired mother hen of a woman leading three straggling chicks with light and dark heads bobbing. They entered through a side door of the historic Catholic church that sat on a green strewn with live oaks and could have been transplanted from a New England postcard.

The rooster, a blond man with a solid belly pressing against the buttons of a good suit and a strut to his step, took his time bringing up the rear of his gaggle. Stacy glanced away when he stared directly at her. She turned her eyes to Pommier's and willed Dean to reappear. A shadow fell over her from the driver's side of the convertible, not Dean come from another direction, but the fair-haired father. Up close, he seemed familiar, but she couldn't quite place him.

"Why, Stacy Polasky visiting from the Big Easy to grace the hinterlands of Chapelle with her presence. Heard you graduated from college a year early, started your own business, and hardly show up here at all. Can't say as I blame you."

She'd last heard that voice, full of sarcasm and anger, over the phone in her fifteenth year. "You think you're too good for me because you live in a mansion and I live in a doublewide, Stacy Polasky."

"No, Kent, no. My aunt and uncle say I can't date until I'm sixteen. They're standing firm on that. I shouldn't have told you yes to the prom when you called. I am sorry. I mean, gee, who wouldn't want to go with the quarterback of the Ste. Jeanne Flames." A girl who'd never said "gee" in her life had struggled to repair a bad case of wounded vanity.

"I told the guys I was taking you. Why don't you sneak out to be with me?"

"That's pretty hard when you live in a fortress like I do, cameras everywhere, codes on all the doors."

"I heard you're really smart. Think of something."

"I really can't break the family rules."

"Then not that smart. I bet you're a bad lay, too." With her heart pounding, she'd hung up on Kent Gonsoulin. She'd seen him around glaring at her, but never spoken to him again.

Stacy checked the door of the bakery once more. A family of four in church-going clothes emerged with bags, but no Dean. Kent opened the door of the convertible and took possession of the driver's seat. "What, you don't remember me? I'm on the TV all the time. Go, go, go to Gonsoulin's Mobile Homes before they're gone, gone, gone. Does that ring your chimes?"

Stacy plastered a fake smile on her face like bad makeup. "Certainly I remember you, Kent. I heard you have a lovely wife and three children now as well as that great business."

"Kelsey turned to fat right after the first baby was

born and as far as I can tell, all three of the kids are dumb as ditch water."

Considering that the children appeared to be around six, four and two, poor Kelsey probably had little time to diet between pregnancies, an observation Stacy did not share with her unwelcome visitor. Kent hadn't exactly kept his figure either, but he still had a full, square-jawed face some might consider handsome sitting atop a bull neck and a big, white smile just dying to sell a person a bill of goods. Stacy trolled her brain for small talk. "Your children are young. They might be smarter than you think. What are their names?"

Kent compressed his thick lips, not pleased by the direction of the conversation, but he answered. "Kermit—and not after the frog. That's my dad's real name, and he insisted the boy be called after him. Then, Katrina for the hurricane because Kelsey thought that would be cute. She's the only blonde so far. The last boy is Kent Junior after me. The boys favor my wife who isn't a real redhead. Back when, the guys bet me you weren't a true blonde either. I said I'd find out and let them know."

"You can tell them I am. No need to keep them in suspense all these years." Stacy dropped some ice into her voice like cubes falling into a full glass of tepid water. She'd perfected that skill over the years of waiting for Dean. "I need to go see what's keeping Dean. We have to get back to New Orleans. Your wife is probably wondering where you are." Two very elderly women with their hair dyed black and bright red left the bakery with their purchases clutched in arthritic hands and their canes stabbing the sidewalk, but no Dean.

"Hi, Miss Lolly, Miss Maxine," Stacy cried out to them with a vigorous wave for the early Mass goers. Maybe they would return inside and tell Dean his cousin had unwelcome company, but they simply squinted their ancient eyes against the sun and nodded before creaking down the road toward the massive Lincoln Continental they drove hazardously around Chapelle like an aircraft carrier commanding the seas.

Kent kept his seat as if he intended to bask in the sun all morning instead of going to church. "So what's that business you have in the city—teaching Mexicans to speak English, right?"

"No, Xochi and I started an interpreting and translating service. We offer four languages and recently added two more." Stacy reached over the seat to get her purse and woke Mati curled asleep in a white, fluffy ball. He bounded to join her in the front and met Kent's hand slapping him back. "My dog!"

"Jesus H. Christ, I thought it was a white rat. You call that thing a dog?"

Mati whimpered, and Stacy gathered him into her lap. "It was hot in his crate, and I let him out. Here." Trying to keep things professional, she shoved a card for Anchi Services into Kent's hands. "That's our business in case you need our services."

Kent ran a thick thumb over the heavy, pale gray cardstock with the purple lettering as if he caressed a woman's breast. "I remember Xochi. Built, she budded out real early. Pretty if you like those Latina types, but I prefer the blondes and redheads."

"Like your wife," Stacy reminded him. A middle-aged man opened the bakery door and held it for his wife who carried the coffees.

"I could have done better if she hadn't gotten knocked up," said Kent like he had nothing to do with it.

The scent of sugar riding on a waft of cold air signaled the opening of the bakery's door again. Dean stood in the open doorway obviously saying goodbye to someone. Finally, he turned and stepped out with a large, greasy white bag and two tall paper cups of café au lait. Mati sat up and barked eagerly in his direction. Taking his time, Kent slid out of the front seat with his belly rubbing against the steering wheel. Drawing Stacy's attention back to him, he said, "I've been thinking I might expand the family business into Old Mexico, so maybe I will need your services. I have a mobile home show coming up down your way. Maybe we could have dinner and discuss it."

"Make an appointment. My business number is on the card."

Dean approached. Kent sucked in his gut and stood up straighter. He held out a beefy hand and offered a salesman's smile to go with it. Dean put the coffees in the cup holder and slung the bakery bag into the car before shaking with a grip so firm they appeared to be arm wrestling. Dean used his other hand to deliver a fake buddy punch to Kent's gut that made the man drop his hand and take a step back.

"How's my old backup from Ste. Jeanne d'Arc?" Dean asked almost combatively.

"Thriving business, beautiful family. Just getting reacquainted with your cousin who jilted me for the prom." Kent showed all his pearly whites in one hostile grin.

"Believe me, that wasn't her fault. My parents

were pretty strict."

"You always did get the prettiest girls." Kent eyed Stacy as if wondering about the best sales tactic to employ to put her into a deluxe model mobile home.

"I only dated two of them in high school. Plenty left for you."

"Say, was Heather McAvoy a real redhead?"

Kent kept his gaze on Stacy until she blushed. Why was this jerk totally obsessed with pubic hair? She kept hers neatly waxed but enough remained to attest to her blondness.

Dean stepped between them. "A gentleman never tells. Great seeing you, but we have to leave."

Dean took over the driver's seat and started the engine with an aggressive roar. Kent took another step back to avoid having his foot run over as the Mustang left the parking lot. He stood staring after them as they reached the red light by the church and had to idle even though no traffic passed with everyone attending services, out golfing, or gone fishing. Mati snuffled the beignet bag, and Dean dipped into the lumpy pocket of his white shirt to retrieve a little plastic bag tied with leather strip.

"Homemade dog biscuits. Some woman in town is making them, and LeJeune let her put a rack in the bakery."

"Very thoughtful of you." Stacy offered one to Mati who thoroughly approved. "What took you so long? That encounter with my past was really getting awkward."

"Our past. We share a past. The Methodists get out of church when the Catholic Mass begins. LeJeune had his hands full serving the first shift of the worshipers of the beignet cult even with his daughter Selena helping out. I had to shake hands, sign a few autographs. You know how it goes." Preparing to drive south on a brilliantly sunny day, Dean took his sunglasses from the visor and hooked them behind his ears.

"I know only too well. I didn't sense much old buddy camaraderie between you and Kent."

"From middle school on, Kent never made quarterback because I always did. Only year he got to play was after I graduated, and he couldn't get the team to the state playoffs. Some guys never get over high school."

"Okay, I'm going to admit this only once. You did save me from a gross guy when I was fifteen. In that case, Dean knew best." She kept her eyes straight ahead to avoid seeing his told-you-so expression.

"You're welcome," he answered with only the minimum of gloating in his voice.

The light turned green. Dean put the Mustang into gear and made it growl like a beast eager to escape its cage. They tooled out of Chapelle with the breeze tangling Stacy's bright hair and Mati's small ears flapping in the wind.

Chapter Nineteen

With a Thursday night game scheduled in Green Bay, the Sinners practiced long and hard before getting on the plane to Wisconsin. Stacy saw more of Dean on the television while watching him play than she had all week. Bundled up to keep their muscles warm, the players exhaled steam into the cold night air of the outdoor stadium. In New Orleans, the air-conditioning continued to run up the electricity bill, though gradually the summer heat dominated only the afternoons and allowed the mornings and evenings to be mild and pleasant all on their own.

Stacy and Xo watched the game with a big bowl of popcorn set between them on the purple sofa. Occasionally, they refilled Ilsa's smaller wooden bowl since she sat in a side chair. Stacy had invited her out of guilt because the woman seemed a little lonely, maybe even homesick. Ilsa did her job with more call for her Russian skills than for German, but out of jealousy Stacy had let her dangle socially when she should have been showing her around more often. Now secure in her feelings for Dean and his for her, Stacy acknowledged Ilsa as no particular threat. Having to explain the game to her every five minutes, now that was annoying.

"The quarterback, he tells everyone what to do and so makes the big money," Ilsa stated.

"He calls the plays, but plenty of people tell him

what to do. At this level, most of the team makes fairly good money," Stacy answered.

"Tom, he kicks the ball like in German football and makes points, also."

"Yes, one after a touchdown and if the team can't get the score any other way, he can try a field goal for three points. Tom is great at what he does." Xochi fielded that one.

Mati sniffed at Ilsa's toes, then sat down charmingly by her feet and cocked his head waiting for a piece of popcorn to be tossed his way. She nudged him aside. "Go away, doggie. I am not so fond of animals."

Mati took the hint and stationed himself close to Xo, his easiest mark. He caught the morsel thrown to him in mid-air. "Don't feed him junk food," Stacy said.

"We're eating it practically naked, hardly any butter or salt. Besides, dogs are omnivores, right, Ilsa?" Xochi launched another puff of popcorn Mati's way.

"I would not know this. I have the allergies against the dogs and cats."

"Mati doesn't shed. You shouldn't have any problems being here." Stacy spoke in defense of her pet.

"But he pisses in the kitchen when I arrive."

"He still gets excited about guests, that's all. Dean gave him to me," Stace said as if that would shut her up.

"I would not want him to give me a dog, maybe jewelry or something else, like Don Juan offered you."

"Since you labeled Dean a party pooper, that isn't likely to happen. Look, he just scored his second touchdown of the night. A pass right into the end zone.

Come on, Tom. Give us one more point!"

Unimpressed, Ilsa picked up her glass of white wine and sipped. "Tom, he is the more fun one, *nein*?"

Xochi answered her. "Definitely, if you give him a chance. Dean is so serious, always worried about his reputation and not letting anyone down, constantly trying to protect all of us, and there are a lot of Billodeauxs to protect."

"Then, I should give Tom a chance since you say I cannot go out with the clients even though you had dinner with Don Juan. More wine, *bitte*." Ilsa extended her glass in the direction of the bottle sitting on the coffee table.

"That wasn't a date with Don Juan, just a friendly farewell for a sick, old man." Barely taking her eyes from the screen, Stacy gave Ilsa a refill. The Packers inched their way downfield and ran one in on the third down. The Sinners offense claimed their positions with two minutes to go before the half. Dean worked the clock to perfection and achieved a third touchdown with only two seconds left. The announcer proclaimed him as being "still on fire."

As the team left for their break and to make halftime adjustments, Ilsa rose. "I think that is enough of the football for tonight." She stretched her long, slim frame that supported an amazing set of breasts beneath the stunning cowl-necked black sweater that clung to them.

Stacy checked to see if all those Lucky Dogs the woman devoured at lunch each day because they reminded her of German *wurst* were beginning to show. Or maybe New Orleans cuisine had caught up with her, but no. Ilsa must have the metabolism of a hyperactive cheerleader. Her slacks, also black, exposed not a single bulge. She'd also polished off most of the bottle of wine while Xo and Stacy sucked down diet drinks, but didn't sway a bit on her high-heeled leather boots. The woman had to be a robot in disguise.

"The score is still fairly close. The entire game could turn around in the second half. The Sinners don't have it wrapped up yet, and it's hard for visitors to win at Lambeau Field," Xo told her. "Usually, that's when it gets really exciting."

Thoroughly tired of the woman, Stacy said, "I'll call a cab for you. You've had quite a bit to drink."

"No need. I have been drinking wine since I was twelve. I will take the streetcar to my place. It is not that far." Ilsa slung her long, white-blonde ponytail over her shoulder, getting it out of way. It sported a small red scarf knotted at the top, her concession to wearing Sinners colors when her hostesses were decked out in plain black jeans and football jerseys bearing the numbers for Dean and Tom. Ilsa circled wide around Mati as she made for the stairs.

Much as Stacy didn't mind her leaving, she felt compelled to make the offer. "We'll wait with you until the streetcar comes. At halftime, the fans will be out getting more liquor and some of them will be drunk."

"So maybe I will meet someone fun."

Still, Stacy and Xo walked her to the corner, made sure she'd gotten safely to the stop and on the streetcar before they went back inside for the second half. "I thought I didn't like her because of Dean, but I can't seem to warm to Ilsa," Stacy confided to her cousin.

"Any person who doesn't like dogs is suspect in my book. So much for interviewing over the internet. I doubt she'll stay in our employ very long. She'll either go back to Germany because she doesn't like it here, or have too much fun one night and end up marrying some guy because she's got a little Kaiser roll in her oven," Xochi predicted.

"Poor sap," Stacy murmured.

They returned in time to see Dean being blitzed by four big linemen. He threw away the ball but went down hard in a big halftime adjustment made by Green Bay. Neutralize the quarterback. But the Sinners offense closed ranks and protected their man enough for Dean to throw for a touchdown in the third quarter. Still he suffered another sack, and Green Bay caught up to tie at the top of the fourth. As the clock ran down, the Sinners got the ball again, two minutes to go. Again, Dean worked the clock as he moved the ball down the field with short, sharp passes, and on the last play, handed off to his running back to take the ball into the end zone. Final score: 35-28.

As the reporters questioned Dean about his seven game winning streak to which he modestly replied that it felt good but lots of tough games lay ahead, Xochi said, "Really exciting game in the second half. Ilsa should have stuck around."

"Frankly, I enjoyed it more once she left. Dean is going to be so sore tomorrow."

Stacy carried the empty wine bottle and popcorn bowls into the kitchen as Mati pranced at her feet probably hoping to be allowed to lick the butter and salt out of the bottom of the dishes. Instead, he found himself confined there behind a baby gate. "Until you learn not to piddle when company comes."

She put his doggie bed over the top along with the

ruined bra he wouldn't give up and the red scarf Mati had taken a liking to and dragged off her nightstand. She wouldn't play silly tricks on Dean any more and doubted she'd need a red flag to call him to her rescue again. "Goodnight, puffball. Behave yourself."

Nope, no more dumb games to make Dean protective and jealous, but there were other games both of them might enjoy.

****

Dean continued to make management happy by not being seen in public with Stacy. He never called her when on the road or in the locker room, and so she waited, wondering when he would get back to New Orleans and be free to see her in private. Sometimes she wished he'd just cut loose and tell the bigwigs his private life was his own business, but oh no, not Dean. He'd continue to strive to be a good example just as she would keep up a cool professional façade.

Still, behind the scenes both of them had loosened up in a way neither had ever done before. Sure, she'd met Hugo in dark restaurants far from campus, and they went to clubs for dancing where few LSU students and none of the faculty would dare venture, but that didn't compare to her short forays across broad Canal Street in one disguise or another to meet her lover in his condo. Dean Billodeaux, her lover, Stacy savored the words.

Having spent Friday morning at the hospital interpreting for a Costa Rican coffee grower having a procedure similar to the one Don Juan underwent, she'd returned home, shed her business dress for more casual togs, and waited for his call. When her phone rang, she answered eagerly.

"Hey, Princess. I'm home." Spoken with his voice

low and sexy, princess had become her favorite word in the English language.

"Be right over." No need for prolonged conversation when they'd have part of the night together.

She'd prepared in advance to run the gauntlet of paparazzi still doggedly staking out her alley and Dean's street corner. She dressed as a typical tourist in Capri pants, a glittery purple cotton tee with Mardi Gras masks on it, sandals, and a big straw hat to ward off the afternoon sun and cover her hair. Adding sunglasses and a shopping bag generously donated by Mrs. Kim downstairs, she used the inside stairs off the second floor landing that took her into the rear of the electronics shop. Stacy Polasky exited the store as simply another shopper unnoticed by the sentinels of sleaze.

She joined the foot traffic negotiating the double lanes and tram tracks of Canal Street and swung into Dean's building without a pause. Arturo, in on their rendezvous and tipped well for his silence, notified his patron immediately of her presence. Barefooted, he met her in the doorway of his condo. In seconds, she stood in Dean's embrace with her hat knocked to the floor and the shopping bag dropped at her feet.

Stacy refrained from hugging him too hard. "You must be sore from those two sacks last night."

"Some," he replied in his usual stoic way when it came to any kind of pain. Dean's hands ran under her T-shirt to cup her breasts and unhook her bra.

"You know, we're still standing in the doorway. Is Tom home?"

He kicked the door shut. "No." He applied his lips

to hers and started backing them toward his bedroom.

Stacy balked and pushed lightly against his embrace. "Wait. My bag."

"I thought that was just a prop, but we'd better move it. Won't do to have Tom break a leg tripping over it when he gets back from his date with Ilsa."

Stacy snatched her shopping bag from the floor, but stood there stock-still. "Tom is out with Ilsa?"

"That's what I said. She left a message for him at headquarters asking if he wanted to have some fun tonight. He definitely did." Impatient with the lack of forward motion, Dean reached under her legs and pressed Stacy against his chest for a quick carry to the bedroom.

"Where are they going? What will they do?"

"Dinner, House of Blues, dancing and bar hopping afterwards." He lowered her to the bed and went to work stripping off her clothes.

"Xochi told her he was more fun than you."

"If they go dancing, she'll have lots of laughs." Dean stopped in the midst of rolling down the Capri pants with her underwear inside. "Wait, this isn't fun?"

"For you and maybe shortly for me. I really don't like Ilsa. She seems calculating somehow. I'm worried about Tom."

"Grown man, can take care of himself while he's having fun." He disposed of her sandals when the rest of the clothes came off. "Stop worrying."

Nude, Stacy sat up. "Wait."

"Again?"

"I have a treat for you."

"Ah, Stace, you are always a treat." Since she didn't do it for him, Dean stepped out of his jeans and peeled off his T-shirt to reveal several large bruises on his side and back.

"Lie down. I want to give you a massage first. I brought lotion."

Dean turned down the covers before obeying. "If I leave an oily full body imprint on the spread, Krayola will know what we're doing. I sometimes suspect she reports back to Mom."

"I doubt that. Aunt Nell would respect your privacy." Stacy straddled his hips and squeezed the lotion onto her hands.

"Like she did with you and Ugo."

"Stop obsessing about Hugo. I want to make you feel better."

"It isn't perfumed lotion, is it? My sinuses are kind of stuffy from the flight."

"No, unscented. Now just enjoy." A small lie. She'd grabbed her own body lotion on the way out and had no desire to dress again and find a pharmacy to buy another brand. For so many summers, she'd watched as other girls greased Dean's shoulders—bigger than they should have been at his age—as he did lifeguard duty at Camp Love Letter. Their own contact had always been combative—the splash in the face, the dunk to the bottom of the pool. Now, Stacy dug her fingers deep into his shoulders and kneaded the finely honed muscles. Her eyes drifted shut as she rubbed, imagining what came next.

"You know, Stace, the Sinners do have a massage therapist on the payroll. No need to waste time doing this. I'm not that stiff," Dean just had to say.

"Does their masseuse do it in the nude?"

"Hell, no. He's a big hairy dude."

"So I have no competition." Stacy leaned over his back until her breasts pressed against his hot skin. She let her long hair tickle his sides. Droplets of perspiration from her efforts landed on his neck and trickled down onto the sheets.

"Okay, now I am stiff, only not where you're rubbing."

"We'll get to the other side soon. Relax. Let me work." She avoided his bruises and slid down farther on his legs to knead his buttocks so firm under her hands.

"I'm ready for the other side now."

Stacy slapped him sharply on his backside. "When I say so."

Dean folded his hands under his chin, resigned, she guessed, to letting her set the pace. "You know, Princess, the thing I like best about you is that you never expect me to be perfect. You always pointed out my flaws, never let me get away with any crap. Dad, he wanted me to be the best quarterback and a leader. Mom tried to make me ethical, moral, and kind. Lead and protect. I should have that motto tattooed on my chest. Hard to live up to their standards."

Stacy's hands stilled on his thighs. She wanted to tell him he had achieved those goals, but that would only put more pressure on him. As for tattoos, their mention brought back shades of Prince. She obliterated that darkness with sheer sass. "Sorry, you won't get any pity from me Golden Boy, King of the Gridiron, and rescuer of maidens in distress. Don't you dare get a tattoo unless it's a heart with my name inside. Roll over."

He obeyed immediately. "See, I'm stiff, very stiff."

"Looks like that area needs some lotion, lots of

lotion." She ran her hands up and down the length of his hard penis and stroked his balls until they bunched and his short hairs stood on end. "Since you are bruised like an overripe banana, I'll do the work tonight." Stacy settled herself on his fierce erection and began moving over him.

Dean closed his eyes. "Sometimes it is so damn nice to let someone else lead for a change."

"You aren't going to fall asleep after that great massage, are you?"

"Not a chance, Princess."

Stacy started out slow, not taking his length all the way in, but rising up on her knees and teasing the head of his shaft, until he pressed her down firmly all the way. After that, she went long and deep, then faster and faster as she pinned his shoulders to the bed. Dean's groans rewarded her efforts, but he couldn't restrain himself and rose up to meet her with strong, swift pumps of his hips. She gave way before he did, arching her back and crying out. He raised his knees to support her and kept going, doubling her pleasure until he gained his. With her hair making a golden blanket over them, Stacy sagged against his chest.

"I was supposed to be in charge," she murmured as his rapid heartbeat sounded in her ear.

"Sorry, sometimes I can't help myself. I have to take the lead."

"Believe me, no need to apologize—this time."

As they cooled and recovered, the conversation turned to food and what to order in. Starving and too enervated to debate, they settled on a classic pizza with a couple of side salads from Papa's in the Quarter. One thing Dean's refrigerator contained plenty of—beer, wine, sodas, juice, and milk, any of which went fine with the main dish. No doubt about what they both wanted for dessert and served hot later in the evening. Around one a.m., Stacy insisted she had to go home.

"Tom will be back soon, and I have to check on my client in the hospital in the morning."

"Tom won't care, and your patient doesn't know where you spent the night."

"You should get some rest."

"Now who's the party pooper?"

Stacy, getting into her disguise again, said, "You know Ilsa called you that?"

"Tom started it. She picked it up from him."

Stacy balanced against the leather headboard to put on her sandals. Her hand came down on the parrot shirt hanging on the corner. "I don't know why you keep this thing here. You must really love it."

"Yeah, there's something I do love about my parrot shirt. You and Krayola are always trying to put it in the wash. Leave it be. Guess I have to get dressed and walk you home. "

Reluctantly, Dean put on jeans and a dark hoodie that he drew around his face. With his scruff of black beard and his dark eyes glittering, he owned a fairly forbidding look. If the paparazzi noticed him, they'd be fools to approach. But then, some of them were.

They made the crossing without incident, another successful secret assignation. Despite the glee of outwitting the yellow press and the joy of having Dean care so much for her, Stacy wondered if and when they'd go public as she trudged up the stairs to her apartment one more time after the midnight hour. That decision rested entirely with Dean. She would not betray him.

****

Dean sat up replenishing himself with more pizza and a second beer when Tom got in around two. "How did it go with Ilsa?"

"Do I know the way to a *Deutsch* dolly's heart? I took her to Jagerhaus to eat her fill of kraut, red cabbage, schnitzel, and those spaetzle noodles. We had soft pretzels in the bread-basket, a bottle of Liebfraumilch—that's a wine for the uneducated like you. Ilsa said she'd never had it in Germany. Finished off with strudel and German chocolate cake."

"Hey, I have to study the playbook. Only kickers have time to peruse the wine list. Leftovers?" Dean inquired with mild interest. "I did save you some pizza, but I won't fight you for kraut."

"She kept all the leftovers. We skipped House of Blues because she doesn't so much like the blues even though I told her they have other acts. Bar hopped through the Quarter. I tell you that woman can hold her liquor. The dancing didn't go so well." Tom slipped a slice onto a plate and nuked it just enough to melt the cheese and not toughen the crust, another of his brother's strange skills, Dean observed.

"You might be an ace kicker, but you dance like a gigged frog."

"That's okay because I made her laugh until the beer came out her nose."

"Attractive picture."

"Got more attractive later. Turns out Ilsa is quite the athlete. She used to be on a rowing team and does cross-country skiing—well, not in New Orleans, but back home. She showed me her sculling technique. I got to be the boat." Tom grinned from ear to ear, hiding some of his freckles in the deep grooves of his smile. "You have a good time with Stacy?"

"Sorry, can't share that about a woman we both knew growing up. But I do think it's time to take this to the next level."

"A ring?"

"No, we're supposed to be taking this slow."

Tom shook his head with disbelief scattered all over it like his freckles. "Right, right. That's why Xo and I have to stay out of our apartments when you and Stacy are together—unless we're wrong and the two of you are only playing backgammon."

"More like poker, and we haven't shown all our cards yet. I want to go public with her, let everyone know we're a couple. Screw management."

"Bold words, my brother, but I wish you well. Meanwhile, you don't care if I play hide the sausage with Ilsa, right?"

"Not at all. Enjoy."

Tom leaned over Dean's shoulder to collect his plate as he headed for the sink. His pug nose wrinkled. "Flowers, do I smell flowers, lavender maybe?"

"That lotion was supposed to be unscented! Stacy said so. She, um, gave me a massage." Dean rubbed a hand over his shoulder and sniffed his palm. Lavender, damn purple lavender, just what Stacy would use.

"You didn't notice? Good old Stacy, she always could stick it to you."

"You know I have sinus problems after a long flight. Besides, I was distracted, very distracted. I'm going to take a shower. See you in the morning."

Chapter Twenty

With the team scheduled to fly to San Francisco the next Saturday, Stacy counted on being with Dean Friday night. Maybe they could finally go out in public together. Prince Dobbs neared the end of his recovery. He kept his distance from Dean at the home games, always perching on the far end of the bench with his shaved head covered by a black knit Sinners cap and his face glowering out of the frame of a long mustache that joined with a small pointed goatee on his chin. Add a pair of horns poking through that hat, and he could have posed for a sinister devil mascot. Stacy shuddered whenever the camera passed over Prince at a game, but it seldom paused for very long as if to say this wide receiver was on his way out of the state. Good.

Still, she had one onerous appointment to finish for the week. Kent Gonsoulin had called seeking help from Anchi Services in translating a number of sales and loan documents into Spanish. She'd bumped up their hourly rate for such work to discourage him and said he could email the forms to her and she in turn would send the transcribed papers back, no need for him to make the trip to New Orleans. Oh, he was nearby, just across the lake in Mandeville showing a couple of his deluxe mobile homes in the parking lot of a mall along with several other dealers. Could she make allowances for him and schedule a six p.m. meeting? He'd bring the forms along. Maybe they could go out to dinner afterwards and talk about old times. They had no old times but one, the aborted prom date.

Stacy strove to balance repugnance with professionalism. She shouldn't turn down a client willing to pay extra for a service he could perhaps have gotten locally in Chapelle. She okayed the six p.m. appointment and nixed the dinner invitation. Dating clients violated their ethics, she stated primly. By seven, she should be meeting Dean somewhere, his place or hers most likely, when he called. Xochi had already departed with the group of her usual friends. Ilsa, she supposed, would be going out with Tom again. Her German/Russian translator had verified that being with him did qualify as fun. "He is no dancer but makes me laugh." To think she'd once tried to set them up and now wished Ilsa would leave Tom alone and get her kicks elsewhere.

Meanwhile, still dressed in her business attire, she sipped a cup of coffee, strong after being in the pot all afternoon and studied her medical terms while Mati slept on one of her feet under the desk. When the bell rang, she nudged the dog from her shoe and went downstairs to confirm her six o'clock with a glance through the peephole. She had to say Kent filled the tiny view with a vast expanse of flesh, a great deal of face forward confidence, and a wide toothy grin.

Stacy opened the door and tried to forestall him in the small entry. "If you brought the documents, you can just leave them. I'll estimate the cost and send you an email." Not wanting to prolong the encounter, she refrained from mentioning his odd attire: a loud Hawaiian shirt patterned in crimson flowers, Bermuda shorts that exposed legs carpeted in fuzzy yellow hair, boat shoes, and a green plastic lei hanging around his thick neck. Dean might be able to get away with that look, but not Kent.

The plain brown envelope remained clamped under one of his beefy arms just below a sweat stain. "No, I have a few details I want to discuss."

"Very well." Completely aware that Kent most likely stared at her derriere the whole way, Stacy led him up the stairs to the office and offered him a seat on the other side of a stout desk that put some distance between them. "Let's see what you've got"—a bad choice of words for a translator.

Kent grinned bearishly. "You had a chance to do that on prom night and turned it down."

"I've explained that previously. Let me see the documents. I might be able to give you an estimate right now, and you can get back to business."

"Done for the day. November and still hot as Hades in that parking lot. We're doing our Sale Away to Paradise in a Gonsoulin mobile home promotion. Here you go. Aloha." Kent leaned his bulk over the desk and moved the lei from his neck to hers, letting his lips brush her cheek on the way back.

Stacy refrained from scrubbing the moisture off her skin with a tissue. "The documents, please."

Kent leaned back in the visitor's chair that creaked ominously beneath his weight and kept his hand on the envelope. "Must be boring work translating documents. Me, I'm a people person. That's why I'm good at sales. You don't see my family living in a mobile home any more. Moved out of the one my daddy gave us for a wedding gift as soon as my commissions piled up. I don't feel the need to live in the product like he does. Still got the place for rent, though. It's a deluxe triple unit with a Jacuzzi on a wooded acre lot in the country. Lots of privacy. If you get tired of your job and want to move back to Chapelle, we could work out a deal, a very good deal."

"Actually, I own this business. It's not simply a job for me. I find translation mentally stimulating and meet many interesting people when interpreting." Stacy glanced at her watch. Fifteen minutes gone and nothing accomplished. "If I could see the papers?"

"Let me tell you, my throat is dry as a bone and my bone is filled to the brim with piss. You got a cold beer on hand and a john I could use? It's a long drive over that causeway."

Charming. Perhaps the vulgarity helped him make sales with the good ole boys. "I'm afraid I can offer only coffee, Mr. Gonsoulin, and it is rather stale this late in the day. I have some bottled water as well." She lied, not about the status of the coffee, but about the beer. She kept some on hand for Dean, Dixie lager and a few bottles of their Blackened Voodoo brew. It wasn't offered to clients. Ever.

"Come on, Stacy. It's Kent. We're old friends. We could be better friends. Dean is gonna drop you for a supermodel sometime soon just because he can. Me, I believe in loyalty. I'm stuck with my wife till death do us part. Bad for business to divorce in Catholic country, but that's not saying we couldn't have some fun on the side." He started to offer her the envelope, then drew it back as if playing a game.

"Not interested in either of your offers. It appears you aren't serious about needing translation services.

The way out is down the stairs."

"Don't get all pissy with me, Stacy. Just trying to go back to where we left off. Who can blame me? You are one gorgeous lady. Here." He shoved the envelope across the desk.

As if activated by the word pissy or the tension in the air, Mati wriggled from under the desk and popped out by Kent's foot. He raised his leg and peed on the boat shoes.

"Your fucking rat dog just ruined my Dockers!"

Kent drew back to kick at Mati, but Stacy rushed to pull the puppy away in time. From the safety of her arms, her pet issued a tiny growl. Kent's face glowed an angry red that showed even in the part of his fair and thinning hair. Her heart kicked up a notch.

"So sorry, Kent. Let me get you a towel and some water. Mati isn't totally trained yet. I'll lock him up, then you can give me the papers or go if you want." She took the shortcut through the bathroom that adjoined the kitchen and carefully bolted the inner door behind her.

"Bad, Mati," Stacy muttered to the dog but was unable to put any real conviction into her reprimand. She deposited him in his basket by the sofa. With an empty bladder, he wouldn't be likely to make a mess on the rug. If left in the kitchen, he'd only whine and scratch at the door to get her attention. She spied the red scarf Mati had purloined and dragged to his nest as if it were a dead rabbit to gnaw. Shaking it out, she draped the scarf over the curtain rod making sure it showed in the window. Having Dean give her some backup right now wouldn't be such a bad idea.

She got the old towel from a pile kept under the

sink to wipe up accidents and a bottle of water from the fridge and returned to make peace with Kent Gonsoulin if that could be accomplished. This time she bolted the door from the inside as they always did when in the office should a client need to use the facilities. She held out her offerings, not getting too close. "Here, this might help."

"You owe me for the shoes. The scent of urine won't come out." Kent's high color had faded a bit. "I still need to use the john."

"Certainly. Right in there." Stacy pressed against her desk to let him pass, but somehow he managed to rub against her breasts in getting there. He reeked of sweat, puppy pee, and a few beers he'd had before keeping their appointment. Kent slammed the door to express his anger and set Mati to barking in the kitchen. She only hoped Kent wouldn't go through to the apartment and take revenge on her fluff ball of a pet. Stacy dropped the towel over the puddle on the floor and cracked the bottle of water open to wet her dry throat.

Waiting, she removed the ridiculous lei. Mati could have it to chew to pieces later. She opened the envelope and studied a few routine documents. Nothing she and Xochi couldn't handle easily and swiftly, but she had no desire for the job. She waited to hear the sound of urine splashing in the toilet bowl. With all the time he took, she figured she'd have to light the fat, purple lavender-scented candle on the back of the commode once Kent left the premises. The scent of lavender, her body lotion, her hands rubbing it on Dean's shoulders, marking him with her favorite fragrance however unintentionally—tonight they would be together, very soon. The knob in the old door rattled. Hadn't Kent washed his hands? Probably not.

He appeared in the doorway with his shorts unzipped and the bottom buttons of the loud shirt opened to expose a belly bearing the same pale fluff as his legs though it grew thicker around his fully erect penis. "There, I got it all ready for you. Payback for the prom and the dog pee coming right up. Won't take long. I'm about ready to blow. Speaking of which…"

He made a grab for her, but Stacy rolled her chair backwards and escaped around the far side of the desk. Tight quarters to work in since Kent could easily move to block the exit to the stairs. She began pitching whatever came to hand at his smug face: a slim silver vase with sprigs of dried lavender, a cup full of purple pens and pencils with Anchi Services embossed on them, her mug of stale coffee—cold but it made him flinch long enough for her to gain the landing. The rolling pens and pencils undermined his forward charge and sent Kent belly-down on the hardwood floor. He made a grab for her ankle, but she kicked him away and dashed down the stairs. This time, she would not be trapped in her bedroom. She'd seek safety in the traffic of the French Quarter and the prying eyes of the paparazzi always watching her place.

Fumbling with her locks, Stacy burst into the twilight shadows of the November evening and ran directly into the unyielding chest of Prince Dobbs. "Going somewhere? You got a minute?"

Dressed all in black, he wore a Sinners knit cap pulled low. The harsh security light only deepened the lines of his face and darkened the sinister new beard. Stacy pivoted around him, but the man was as quick as everyone said. He turned, too, and had her by the shoulders before she could run any farther. Stacy raised her knee impeded by her slim skirt. If not the groin then the instep again, this time in hard-soled heels, but he shoved her back to arm's length.

"None of that shit now, Stacy. I come to make amends. Doc Funk says I got to, or I'll be freezing my fine ass off in Cleveland."

"Later!" She struggled to get away from his grasp.

Two quick blasts surprised them both. The sound rebounded off the walls of the alley as Prince's good leg folded and his hands dropped from Stacy's shoulders. He sank to the stained concrete adding a new layer with his blood. Behind him, Kent Gonsoulin stood braced in the doorway and held out a snub-nosed black pistol two-handed. He looked for all the world like a cop from the older version of *Hawaii Five-O*. He'd zipped before pursuing her, but with the barrier of Prince out of the way, the weapon pointed directly at Stacy. She raised her hands, stepped aside angling for the street. "No!"

Dean rounded the corner and threw himself at the hand holding the gun. It went off a third time driving a bullet through one of the pretty containers of dusty miller and purple sweet potato vines on the fire escape and sending down a rain of dirt, leaves and pottery fragments into the cul-de-sac as Kent smashed into the doorframe. The firearm skittered away to blend with the shadows like a cockroach running from the light.

"What the fuck, Dean! I just saved your cousin from a mugger or a rapist. I think you broke my wrist. Jesus Christ, it hurts."

"He shot Prince Dobbs," Stacy said, her voice far

more weak and wobbly than she intended.

"That's not Prince Dobbs. He got those whatcha-callits, those little braids all over his head," Kent protested.

Dean didn't answer. He went to kneel by the prone Sinner, checked for a pulse, and whipped off his belt. "Stacy, call an ambulance and the cops."

"My phone is upstairs." Her knees trembled. Do not faint. Just don't!

"Here, use mine." He tossed the cell to her, and she punched in the numbers running on automatic and amazed herself by giving her location and all pertinent details in a crisp, cool voice that only wavered a little as she described the injuries. Dean had the belt cinched around Prince's upper thigh stopping the pump of blood from the leg wound. Immediately after, he began CPR, clearing the airway and delivering a breath before beginning chest compressions.

"Stacy, something to press against the hole in his back."

She stripped off her finely tailored gray jacket without a thought, folded it, and eased the cloth under Prince where the ooze from the wound seeped. All the while, Kent Gonsoulin blathered in the background, "I got a concealed carry permit. Thought he was a mugger, a rapist, a murderer. I mean, I stood my ground."

The little flashes of cameras went off like bug-zappers with photographers arriving way before the police or the ambulance. The paparazzo disguised as the homeless man deserted his cup of change across from the alley, whipped a camera from his many layers of rags, and lay down to get the best angle of the two hunched over the body of Prince Dobbs. The blue and red lights of emergency vehicles illuminated the scene. A cop picked up the prone photographer by a threadbare collar and told him stick around to give a statement. Others pushed back the gathering crowd. The medics took over from Dean and moved Prince to a gurney.

"Will he live?" Stacy asked.

"Can't say. Good work on the first aid, Mr. Billodeaux," the EMT replied.

Everyone in New Orleans recognized Dean. In fact, the looky-loos had started to chant, "Dean, Dean, Dean!" as if they were at a game and he'd just made a first down. Stacy burrowed into his embrace. He wore one of those wonderfully soft cotton dress shirts he had in many colors, this one an olive green that flattered his dark good looks, the kind he put on when he went to Mariah's, never flaunting anything that labeled him as a Sinner. Had he intended to take her out tonight?

Stacy gazed up at those intense brown eyes shaded by such thick lashes. "I am very happy we are together now but so, so sorry I ever started this." Now that the worst was over, the shakes seized her body. Dean held her tighter. The ambulance containing Prince screamed into the oncoming darkness.

"Flirting with Prince you mean? Yeah, you should have known better."

"He said he came tonight to apologize. Kent shot him in the back without any warning. Kent tried to attack me, not Prince. But I mean the whole crazy charade, trying to make you rescue me from Don Juan and Angel so that you'd see me in a new way, Xochi said. I tried to stop it with Prince, but you witnessed how well that went. You truly did save me."

"What's Xo got to do with this?" His hold on her lessened.

"Xochi said I had to stop being your sparring partner and show I needed you. I do need you."

His comforting arms dropped from her shoulders. Dean took a step back. "This whole bit was a trick to get my attention? Stacy, a man might die tonight because of what you started. Like a complete fool I fell for it."

"Don't blame Xo. She wanted to help us—me. I didn't have to carry out her plan."

"That's right. You didn't." The knees of Dean's khakis were darkened with blood. He turned his back on her.

Though the night air still held on to some the warmth of the day a chill washed over her. No chorus of frogs sounded as they would have back at the ranch; only the croak of Kent Gonsoulin as he claimed over and over, "Hell, I stood my ground. I'm not the one should be cuffed. Watch that wrist. Might be broken. Hey, hey, police brutality. You can't cuff an injured man. I want my lawyer." The slam of the police cruiser's door shut him off.

"Anybody see where the gun went?" an officer asked.

"Under the fire escape," Stacy said so faintly she wasn't sure they heard, but the ragged paparazzo pointed in the same direction.

One of the cops stood guard in front of the fire escape waiting for the evidence crew to arrive. Another approached Dean and started asking questions. Stacy's knees wobbled, but it wasn't Dean who rushed to steady her. An officer she knew from the precinct where she and Xochi sometimes went to do interpreting took her elbow and escorted her to another vehicle. The police preferred Xo, thinking her Hispanic looks got better results while a tall blonde only drew lewd comments.

"Sit here, Miss Polasky. I'll see if I can get you some water. Then, we'll take you down to the precinct and get your statement, yours and Mr. Billodeaux's, and the perp in the other cruiser. Get you out of this chaos."

"Thank you, Officer Ancona. If you go upstairs, please be careful not to let my dog out."

"Is that where Prince Dobbs attacked you?" the handsome Italian she suspected of having a crush on Xochi questioned.

"No. Kent Gonsoulin attacked me in my office. You'll see the mess up there—the signs of a struggle. I was fleeing from him when I ran into Prince. Kent shot him with no warning."

"Okay, save the rest for the statement."

He left to speak to the policemen remaining behind and collected Dean, holding the rear door open for him. "Sorry you got to ride back here. Not too hygienic, ya know."

"No problem. Let's get this over with. We—I was meeting some friends tonight, but they'll wait."

Stacy said nothing as she strapped on her seatbelt. They were going to meet some friends? Where? Who? In public?

Dean didn't speak as the sirens shrieked and parted the traffic all the way to the station. Stacy glanced back more than once trying to catch his eye. Staring out at the night turning neon with signs, he sat behind the grill separating them and issued no reassuring words, gave no hint of his emotions. He wore his cold, hard game-face like a mask on Mardi Gras hiding everything.

At the station, they were separated at once and interviewed in different areas. Stacy had the longer tale to tell. Yes, she did want to press charges against Kent Gonsoulin for his actions. She hadn't done so with Prince and now thought if she had, he wouldn't have been shot tonight trying to make amends because Dr. Funk told him he must. There would have been a restraining order and strict instructions from the Sinners management and his lawyer to keep him away. Before leaving, she asked about the man she'd never liked. No word yet. In surgery. Her heart did bleed for his parents.

She searched for Dean. The desk officer told her Mr. Billodeaux had left some time ago. On her own, independent, can-take-care-of-herself Princess Anastasia Marya Polasky held her head high and accepted a ride home from Officer Ancona. On the way, he suggested she summon Xochi and stayed with her until her cousin arrived in a cab. Very solicitous, he made sure both ladies were safely locked in for the night. The police had removed the red scarf from the window as evidence to back up her story that she'd felt threatened by Kent and tried to summon Dean to help. Mati would miss that scarf so much. She'd have to get him another one. Stacy stared across broad Canal Street. No lights shone in Dean's apartment.

Chapter Twenty-One

Dean lay in darkness. He'd called Tom and let him know he wouldn't be bringing Stacy to Mariah's, then out to dinner and over to Paco's for dancing. In the background, he heard Ilsa express some shrill disappointment over the ruination of her fun. He sketched out the story of what had happened to Prince Dobbs when Tom put his phone on speaker. "*Gott in Himmel!*" Ilsa said. He couldn't agree more. Tom asked how Stacy was doing.

"Fine, I guess. The princess always has been able to take care of herself."

"That's cold. She must be really shaken up by this. You should stay with her."

"Tom, she played me. I'll tell you about it later. Go out and have fun with Ilsa. There's nothing you can do to help." Dean disconnected before his brother could say more.

Damn, he wanted to go to sleep and forget all this, but Stacy's lavender scent, clean and soothing, pervaded the bedroom. It clung to his shirt and the sheets of the bed. On his pillow so close to his face, the light aroma blotted out the coppery smell of the blood on his khakis, discarded on the floor and kicked aside to be replaced with jeans.

A woman like her should be required to wear a heavy, dangerous odor like *My Sin*. Did they make that any more? His grandmother owned a bottle of it. A gift from his granddad, she never wore it. The stylish bottle sat on her dresser as a prized ornament. He'd taken a whiff once as a young, horny teen, and it sang to him of sex and scarlet women. He should find a bottle online and send it to Stacy. She needed to have a scent sharp and alluring as a warning, not something simple, sweet, and romantic like lavender. It didn't suit what she was, a deceiver.

Dean stripped the bed in a fury and balled the sheets into the hamper. He showered, washed his hair, shaved, but when he lay down again on clean, crisp sheets, the aroma of Stacy remained. Where? The parrot shirt, the one he'd forbidden Krayola to wash. He ripped it from the leather headboard. It should be burned, but he valued it as a gift from Adam Malala. Into the hamper it went to join the sheets and the bloodstained slacks. He'd get no rest tonight in this bedroom. He went to the living room to watch tape of San Francisco's past games. Concentrate on the game. That was the antidote for everything.

Tom found him there sleeping in the recliner. Not in all that late, around midnight, his brother woke him with a shake to the shoulder. "I'm back. You want to tell me what's going on? I got that Prince Dobbs is in the hospital with bullet wounds because Kent Gonsoulin gunned him down, but why?"

"Stacy said Kent attacked her. She fled and ran into Prince coming to apologize. Kent claims he thought Prince was a mugger, or worse. She'd put up that red scarf in the window, and I came running to her like Mati after she's been gone all day. Saw the gun. Knocked it away. Did first aid on Prince. Then, the medics and the cops took over."

"Sounds like you're Stacy's hero, so why isn't she here?" Tom peered around the apartment as if his cousin might be hiding behind the curtains.

"Because it's all been a sham—Don Juan, Angel, Prince, though she admitted that got out of hand. Who knows? Maybe Kent was part of her scheme, too. Why else would she meet him at her place? To make me jealous, to bring me running to her door? Xochi said Stace had to show she needed me by letting me rescue her. The only person I really saved is Prince—if he's still alive. She made a fool of me, Tom. I need a drink."

"Better make that milk. We leave early for San Francisco tomorrow." To make his point, Tom left the sofa, poured, and delivered the suggested beverage. "You eat anything tonight?"

"No, did you?"

"Ilsa wanted sauerbraten so we went back to Jagerhaus. I promised her dinner and didn't want to trash the whole evening. We chugged a lot of beer, too. Then she wanted to make me feel better or I would have been home sooner. I'm not sure I like the woman, but she's really great at making a guy forget his worries. I figured Stacy would be comforting you, so I stayed a while. You should have called if you needed company."

"I don't need anyone! Stacy set me up to prove how superior she is. A snap of her finger or a red scarf in the window, and I come running to save her from imaginary danger."

His expression must have turned forbidding because Tom moved out of striking range. They rarely fought in any way, not since boyhood and a few teen scuffles. Dean knew he could be broody, mostly about his football performance, but Tom usually joked him out of a dark mood. His sudden movement proved laughter wasn't an option this time. It shamed Dean to treat his brother and best friend this way.

Tom tried reason instead. "I don't think so. Xo wouldn't help her do that. You seemed great together, like the tumblers on a lock finally fell into place and opened a safe. Stacy wanted to change things between you and she did."

"Really? Look at the mess we've got now. If a woman wants you, why can't she just say so without making life complicated?"

"A mystery of the universe, bro. Somehow, I can't imagine Stacy admitting point blank that she loves you."

"Who said anything about love?" His voice had a killer growl to it.

Tom moved far, far away over to the sink. "Not me. Forget I said the L word. You need to eat. I can tell your blood sugar is plunging." He scanned the contents of the refrigerator. "Let's see, Chez Tom can offer scrambled eggs, a ham sandwich, or popcorn."

"Ham sandwich would be good. We got any dill pickles?"

"We do. Cheese?"

"Yes."

Tom assembled the plate as he talked. He knew to use the spicy mustard, a pumpernickel roll, a couple of slices of Swiss, lots of ham, and a bunch of lettuce. He sliced a large dill pickle in half and added it as garnish. "*Et voila!* The Thomas Cassidy Billodeaux special. Should be named after me. Eat hardy and go to bed which is where I am headed right now."

"Thanks. I think I'll watch a little more tape first."

"Suit yourself. Ilsa wore me out. I should sleep well."

"Goodnight." Dean had no intention of sleeping in his bed. The recliner would do just fine for now. Maybe after Krayola cleaned and did the laundry, he'd be able to go back to his bedroom, but not now, not tonight. Tomorrow he'd be on a plane for San Francisco. Stacy wouldn't be in the stands to distract him. He'd do his job, get on with his life, and stop being anyone's hero.

Chapter Twenty-Two

Since the German woman and Tom seemed to be an item now, Stacy felt compelled to invite Ilsa to view the Sunday afternoon game. Fairly sure Dean wouldn't be back to drink it, she offered her the beer in the refrigerator, and her translator polished off one per quarter. Ilsa opened her fourth bottle and put it down long enough to clap. "A first down, that is good, *nein*?"

"It would be if the other team hadn't made it." Stacy offered Ilsa more of the seven-layer dip and the basket of multi-colored corn chips to soak up the alcohol.

Ilsa dug in breaking a chip off in the refried bean layer and rescuing it with another. She bore the beans and sour cream in a lump to her mouth. Incredible, still so thin. Stacy shook her head in wonderment. The woman must have wonderful genes. She had no knowledge of her own ancestry on her Polish father's side other than favoring him strongly. Somewhere in the past, she might have a grandmother who weighed three-hundred pounds, ate tons of sausage and downed it with beer. She certainly didn't take after the small-boned, dark Abbotts, her mother's family.

Sipping diet ginger ale and watching stone cold sober, Stacy knew Dean played a little off his game. He'd thrown two interceptions and been lucky enough that neither resulted in a touchdown. Adam Malala squashed one of them and the other drive petered out on the fourth down. He threw three other long passes that did the job and brought the score to twenty-one for the Sinners. The opposing quarterback, another young phenom better at the running game than Dean, tied it up.

Announcer Al Harney remarked that Billodeaux had lost some of his fire but still had enough heat left to burn the other team in the last quarter if they weren't careful. An injury stopped the game, and Hank Wilkes filled in the time with color. "Billodeaux might be tired from saving a life Friday night. He applied both a tourniquet and CPR to Prince Dobbs already on the injured reserved list when the Sinners' wide receiver was mistaken for a mugger and shot in the French Quarter. The update on Dobbs is hopeful though he is still in critical condition in the ICU. Our thoughts and prayers go out to Prince, son of former Sinner's tight end Asa Dobbs, and to his family."

Wilkes read the prompt. "Dean Billodeaux learned his first aid skills as a lifeguard at Camp Love Letter, Daddy Joe Billodeaux's charitable getaway spot for seriously ill children and their families. Whether he wins or loses here today, he is certainly an all-American hero. Looks like the game is about to resume.

"So exciting Dean saved a man," Ilsa said, sitting her beer on a section of the Sunday newspaper.

Stacy reached over and removed the sports section featuring Dean on his knees giving Prince the breath of life before the condensation off the bottle could soak through to it. She appeared in the photo as only an out of focus blur in the background. The headline proclaimed *Sinner Saintly*. How Dean would hate the notoriety. For three years, he'd managed to stay out of the tabloids and generate only positive news of his charity work and much speculation about which model or starlet would become his wife. Since they'd been together, every other week seemed to generate a sensational article, all her fault.

The ball passed to their team when Adam Malala forced a fumble, then back to San Francisco on a third interception. Neither team managed to score on the other's mistakes. The Sinners had possession at the two-minute warning, and Dean milked the clock until it gave him cream. He set up Tom for an easy last second field goal, and the Sinners remained undefeated 24-21.

"You are correct, the second half is better. I must watch more often. Perhaps at the home game next Sunday. Will Tom get me a ticket, do you think?" Ilsa finished off her fourth beer and prepared to leave.

"I'm sure he can," Xochi told her. "Be careful on the streetcar. You want us to wait with you?"

Ilsa waved away the offer. "I am so fine. The sun still shines. People are in the bars rejoicing. We must go on Monday to Mariah's and celebrate with the team." With her next social event on the calendar, Ilsa clumped her way down the stairs on high-wedged sandals and let herself out without a single weave in her step.

Stacy went upstairs and let Mati out of her bedroom where he'd been incarcerated since Ilsa had no love of dogs. She brought him down hugged against her face. "She can have my ticket. I won't be going."

Xochi nearly dropped the bowl of dip with its now co-mingled layers that she carried to the kitchen before Mati could get at it. "But you must. The whole family will come for the game and expect to see you. What will Dean think?"

"That I'm a big distraction and don't belong there. I've always held myself on the edge of the family and won't be missed while you are an important member of the Billodeauxs. I told Dean you weren't to blame for carrying out the scheme."

"I was! It was my idea in the first place, and it worked, too, up until Prince got shot. You were so good together. I've never seen either of you that happy and relaxed. You swam in violet light. I'll talk to Tom. We can fix this." Mati sat at Xochi's feet and whimpered. "Not for you, puffball." She put the dip into the refrigerator.

"Mati, come." Stacy got the bag of dog treats from the cupboard and gave him one for coming to her. "Stand," she commanded and held another above his nose. Mati got up on his hind legs. She tossed him the treat. "Dance." Stacy held a treat high and made a circle with her hand. Mati followed the morsel on his hind legs. She rewarded him after two turns. "Maybe this is how Dean feels, that I made him come to me and do tricks like a trained dog."

"Perhaps right now. I admit I shouldn't have suggested Prince Dobbs. That man trails darkness behind him like a velvet cloak with an ugly orange lining, but in his own nasty way he brought you together." Xochi caught herself and made the sign of the cross. "May he have a full recovery."

"I hope so, if only for Sharlette and Asa's sake." Stacy picked up the basket of corn chips, dumped the remnants back into a bag and clipped it shut. Game over for today.

Chapter Twenty-Three

Nodding and waving to fans, Dean strode swiftly along the concourse at Louis Armstrong Airport. He didn't stop to autograph sports sections of the Sunday paper bearing his "hero" picture but stayed to the center of the group of Sinners returning triumphant from San Francisco. The word went round: party tonight at Mariah's. He'd have to attend. A ten game winning streak needed to be celebrated even if he hadn't played his best.

Worse awaited him. The tabloids in the tobacco shop near his condo plastered its windows with the CPR shot, but also one of Prince with his hands on Stacy and another of Kent Gonsoulin being cuffed. Lurid speculation from mild to seriously raunchy shouted from the headlines: *Sinner Saves Rival*, *Blonde Boondoggle* and *Three-way Feud?* If the disguised paparazzo still staked out the cul-de-sac, Dean swore he'd drop kick him all the way across Canal Street. Not that he'd be going over there any more. He wondered momentarily how Stacy was taking the notoriety. Not his business. Let her handle it. Team meeting, a hard workout, a party—the best way to get over her fast.

He made it through the day, pulled out a red dress shirt he rarely wore, black slacks and dancing shoes, and made for Mariah's Place where Tom had gone to meet Ilsa an hour before. Stacy wouldn't dare show her face there, but she had guts so she might. He'd manage it if she did. He'd show her how little he cared by finding some other woman to take as a partner on the dance floor.

Plenty of blondes in Mariah's tonight but only one sat in his usual dark corner of the bar. Stacy…No, Ilsa. The neon bar signs cast a scarlet glow over her pale, straight hair. She tossed the strands over her shoulder, leaned against Tom and laughed at something he said. Dean tried to join them quietly, but the team members stood up, raised their bottles and glasses and toasted "To a guy who knows how to run down a clock." Dean waved away his usual Dixie beer and swallowed his first shot of bourbon for the night. He paid for a round to salute Tommy the Toe and downed another. He put away a third while Tom guided Ilsa rather stiffly around the dance floor to a slow tune. If he were out there with Stacy, he would show them how it should be done.

When the couple returned, he said out of the blue, "I can be fun, you know. My dad was a fun fellow. Me, too."

"No, you aren't. You're Dean the Hero. You win games and save lives. I'm the fun guy," Tom reminded him.

"Ilsa, what do you say we go to Paco's and try some hot salsa dancing?" He leaned across his brother to make the invitation. "Tom, you think they still have that piñata we sent over on Friday when I planned to take Stace—when I planned to go there the other night?"

"Probably."

"Good. Com'on, Ilsa. We'll bust that thing wide open and have a good time." Dean made his way around Tom and slung an arm over his brother's date. She wore that red dress with slits up the sides, the one that hadn't tempted him before but looked mighty tasty tonight. Her boobs pushed out of the top like two scoops of vanilla ice cream. Bet they had big red cherries on the top. He'd find out later tonight.

Ilsa transferred her bare arm easily from Tom's and wrapped it around Dean's waist. "I will give you another chance to amuse me."

Halfway across the floor, he called back to Tom, "You comin'?"

"I don't think so."

"Then party on!" Dean addressed the entire club and watched the varied reactions of his teammates from astounded to concerned. See, he could surprise people. He didn't need to be hard-working, reliable Dean all the time.

Before he and Ilsa reached the door, Tom moved up behind them. "How did you get here, Dean?"

"Drove the old truck."

Tom patted him down and took the keys. "Use a cab tonight. Have lots of fun, Ilsa."

"Oh, I think we will!"

Tom stood on the curb until they got into a taxi, and he turned away to reenter the club. Ilsa cozied up to Dean and did nothing to stop him from running his hand under her skirt. Stacy would have stopped that PDA in a backseat instantly because she was a party pooper, but not him. In a pretty deep clutch when they arrived at Paco's under the sign of the tipsy margarita, he had to scrape Ilsa off his body long enough to pay the driver.

The dance club on a Monday night held a light

population of regulars at the bar and merely a DJ in the courtyard playing music for the few who wanted to dance. "Hey, Paco, you still got that football piñata I sent over?" Dean shouted over the music as he scanned the ceiling searching for the one he'd purchased among so many choices, burros and a chicken, even an octopus, but no football. "Which one of you is Paco anyhow?"

"Actually, there ain't no Paco. I am Jose, the manager. The piñata is right over your head." The thin brown man with a worried brow almost blended with the stucco walls. He gestured to the arch leading to the courtyard. A papier-mâché football with red and black streamers hanging from the ends swayed in a light breeze.

"Jose, we're gonna bust that sucker open tonight. But first, a couple of Dos Equis and some dancing!" The beers arrived quickly. Dean chugged his. "You ready to learn salsa dancing, Ilsa?"

"Oh yes, so ready." She gulped the rest of her drink and put out her arms.

Dean led her to the floor and put his hands on her hips while she held onto his shoulders. He felt loose-limbed and light-footed. The song playing was light and poppy, almost country-western, good enough to start, he supposed. "It's about a *chica muy bonita*, a pretty woman," he told Ilsa.

"Yes, this I know. I have some Spanish."

"You are *muy bonita*."

"Yes, I know this also. You are *muy guapo*." She flicked that stupid curl that always fell across his forehead.

"Thank you." He found a Cajun two-step suited the

song better. No sweat, he'd been doing that at weddings and parties since he was a kid, his first dance partner being his Mawmaw Nadine. Still, he couldn't get Ilsa to unbend very much. He did a simple spin out and return. Ilsa executed it awkwardly on her very high heels. When the song ended, he suggested another round to grease their joints. Two more beers down the hatch.

A sultry song began to spin. This time he tried to mold Ilsa to his body, but she simply didn't fit. A leg lift, and Ilsa did have the gams to do it, almost sent them both to the ground. She laughed, having fun, she said. Her only talent appeared to be whipping her head around and flailing his face with her hair, which kept getting in his eyes. He found himself dancing around her as Angel did with Stacy. Now Stacy would have… No Stacy here tonight. She should see all this, see how little he cared, how much fun he could be.

When the music stopped, the place seemed to have filled up considerably. Using both Spanish and English, people talked into cell phones and popped pictures. "We need more to drink—tequila shots!" he proclaimed.

"Off Angelita's belly," someone suggested.

Dean vaguely remembered the chubby waitress from his last trip to Paco's. She rolled up her loose white blouse and stretched herself over one of the little tables. Somehow, the bartender managed to balance four shot glasses on her wobbly flesh. Dean started to pick one up, but that same voice, also a little familiar, shouted, "No, hands behind your back."

Dean peered into the crowd. "That you Angel, old buddy. No hard feelings, huh?"

The slim and almost pretty Hispanic man gave him

a movie star's grin, snapped a picture, and put his phone to his ear again.

"I can do this!" Dean declared. "I am very coordinated." He bent down, gripped the first glass in his teeth, and slowly tipped the contents down his throat. A cheer went up followed by the chant "Drink, Drink, Drink! Chug it!" and Spanish variations of the same. He did, all the rest right in a row. At the end of Angelita's belly where it descended into her short black shirt, he raised his arms in triumph.

"Not a drop schpilled!"

His audience laughed, and he looked down to see wet streaks plastering his red shirt to his chest. "Doesn't matter. I got another great idea. Up, up Angelita, *mi chica muy bonita.*"

"You blind, man," a guy called out. Angelita gave him the finger.

Dean climbed on the small table that wobbled under his weight and pointed to the football piñata. "Let's bust that sucka! Give me a baseball bat."

"No bats in Paco's," the nervous manager said. "We use a stick. See, we blindfold the pretty women and let them have first try."

Ilsa was given the first go and although tall never came near the thing. A few other women lined up, got spun around, made some feeble attempts. Mostly the men enjoyed seeing the breasts bunch and jiggle as the girls took wild swings. He liked that, too, until Xochi showed up and stood in the queue. No one got to leer at his sister's boobies, though she wasn't very dressed up tonight and not much showed.

"Enough!" He seized the stick and beat the hell out of the papier-mâché until the streamers flew off, the crepe paper shredded, and the piñata released its cache of Sinners' souvenirs: little stuffed red devils, key chains displaying the same, foam footballs, and a couple of tightly wrapped T-shirts with his number seven on it. The crowd scrambled. Tables overturned. Bottles broke. Trays of nachos spilled making a greasy slip and slide surface on the floor that sent people falling to their backsides.

"No, no! Now you bust up my place," the manager cried.

"Sorry. Here you go, Jose." Dean opened his wallet and threw a wad of cash into the mix. Chaos increased threefold with fights breaking out as hundred-dollar bills floated toward the floor and cheap souvenirs crushed underfoot.

A small but firm hand took his elbow. "Time to go home, big brother." Xochi towed Ilsa with a tight grip. "Got a cab waiting. Sorry, Jose. We'll pay for damages. Angel, thanks for calling us."

"Well, if some German be-yotch was fooling with my man, I'd want to know, honey." Angel snapped another picture of the three of them leaving.

"What is be-yotch?" Ilsa asked. "We had good fun tonight, *nein*?"

"*Nein*," answered Xochi. "Duck your heads. Into the cab you go. I'll ride up front."

In the backseat, Ilsa taught Dean a German drinking song. He might be able to dance, but he couldn't carry a tune in a bucket of beer. Xochi covered her ears until they arrived at the cul-de-sac where the crime scene tape had come down and only two pots of flowers remained on the fire escape.

"You'd better go upstairs and let us take care of

you tonight, Dean. You can sleep on the sofa."

"Nope, nope. Gotta see Ilsa safely home because I am a gentleman."

"Suit yourself." Xochi took a notepad from her purse and wrote down Ilsa's address and Dean's residence. She prepaid the cabbie enough to get them to Ilsa's and back again to Dean's. "Make sure they arrive there."

The cab pulled onto Canal Street, but Dean had another idea. "Say, I want to get tattoo. You know a good place?"

"The lady said to take you home."

Dean dug out his wallet again. "Would you look here? I still got a hundred, and it's all yours, fella. Best place you know."

The cab made a U-turn and headed back into the Quarter. The passengers stumbled out in front of No Regrets Tattoos that offered a fine display of choices in its window as well as photos of completed projects on bulging biceps, broad backs, sexy smalls, and shapely ankles. Dean squinted at the sign. "I think Prince Dobbs uses this place."

"Then, is good. You get Ilsa printed on your arm, *ja*?"

"*Nein*. It's a secret tattoo in a secret place. Shush now." Dean put a single finger to his lips.

"You want I should wait," the cabbie asked.

"Sure, won't take long."

It didn't, at least it seemed that way as he dozed through part of the process once they got started. Not much business on a Monday. They were the only customers in the place. Dean made Ilsa wait out of view. He told the artist, a lean man with an impressive spread eagle engraved on his bald head, exactly what he wanted. "A heart, a red one with the Sinners devil tail on it."

"Got it. We call that the Joe Billodeaux Special."

"Well, I'm his son so it fits. Inside it I want—guess what? It begins with an S."

"I can't guess, but let me say it is an honor to give Dean Billodeaux his first tat. I'm Cyril, and I guarantee your satisfaction." Cyril offered him a smile defined by many painful piercings and began swabbing the bared backside with alcohol.

"Damn right it is. Come close. Let me whisper in your ear."

"Easy," said the guy whose wife beater bared two full sleeves on his arms filled with red parrots and spotted jaguars staring from a dense jungle for the world to see. He inked and swabbed and finished up with a coat of petroleum jelly and a bandage.

Paying up, Dean said as if it were an entirely good idea, "Next time, maybe a parrot. I rock parrots."

"So do I. Be sure to come here if you decide on that. Here's instructions for aftercare."

"Yes, I will take good care of him," Ilsa assured him. "Maybe someday I get one, too."

The cabbie got off the stoop where he waited while smoking a few butts. "Where to next?"

"*Fraulein* Ilsa's abode."

"Already got the address." The driver stowed his two tipsy passengers in the backseat and belted them in. "No way am I going to be responsible for getting Dean Billodeaux killed in an accident," he explained, but since the couple was making out with lots of tongue, neither answered. He brought them to their destination unscathed, and Dean handed over his last hundred.

"Don't wait. I plan to spend the night."

"More power to ya." The cabbie steered off into the night with a great story to tell.

"This is your place?"

"*Ja*, third floor. We walk. Keeps us in good shape. Ilsa walks everywhere."

He nodded his agreement, but for some reason, he kept tripping on his way up. Ilsa laughed at him and pointed a long, mocking finger. "So much fun."

She roomed in a small apartment with a cranky, rattling window air conditioner and a bathroom possessing stained fixtures he really needed to use at once no matter how unappealing. On his way to the cramped bedroom, Dean stumbled over stray shoes and a pile of discarded clothes while he maneuvered around her modern pale wood furniture. No plants, puppies, or purple in the place.

Ilsa waited already naked and spread out on a bed filling most of the space. Her spectacular breasts were crowned with peaked nipples so red he thought they might be rouged. Maybe she'd pinched them while he took a leak. He fumbled with his shirt buttons until she sat up and helped, deftly discarding his trousers as well. He'd worn low cut red briefs to prove he could be fun, and she dealt with them efficiently. With his ready erection poking him in the belly, he bent and discarded his shoes and socks.

Ilsa pointed to his backside. "You going let me have a look under the bandage?"

"Nope. It's shecret. Gotta be on top tonight. Stacy, she likes being up there. Sometimes we fight over it. Fun."

"Come, come. Ilsa is ready for you. We have more fun." She beckoned with her long nails painted the same scarlet as her discarded gown and ruby nipples.

Her perfume filled his nostrils with a heavy, dangerous scent. *My Sin.* Which reminded him. Dean bent again and searched his pockets for the condoms he always carried. He found one but couldn't seem to get it open even when using his teeth. "Stacy is on the pill. Didn't need one with her. Best sex ever."

"I practice birth control also. Throw it away."

Dean tossed the condom unopened onto a tiny night table bearing a reading lamp that provided the only light in the windowless room and held a stack of erotic novels. "You should have a nicer place."

"I am not so sure I like New Orleans. Is expensive to live here and so hot to me. Stacy does not pay me enough. Maybe later you get me a better flat. Right now, I rent the furniture, but I buy the bed. A good bed is important. Come try it." She patted the mattress covered in ivory satin sheets.

Instead of sliding in beside her, Dean simply dove on top and got down to business. No finesse, no foreplay, just plain fucking, and Ilsa didn't seem to mind. From the start, she didn't feel right. Her sharp pelvic bones rubbed against his and her boobs, spectacular but firm, very firm, disappointed. Implants, he'd come across those before and wondered if she felt anything when he rubbed and nipped them. She made the right noises, but a guy could never really tell. Stacy—soft breasts and so nicely rounded all over, no sharp angles. He must have said some of that aloud because Ilsa slapped him on the rump, thankfully not on the sore side.

"Stacy does that, too."

"No more talk of Stacy tonight. She is the be-yotch. Same as bitch, right?"

"Yeah, yeah she is."

"Have some fun with Ilsa, *nein*?"

"*Ja*!" he said and pumped his hips again.

Chapter Twenty-Four

He must have had fun, lots of fun, because when Dean woke on those stained ivory satin sheets, he found his back scored with scratches and his prick circled in red lipstick. Ilsa had gone to work leaving behind a note stating that fact and anchored by his cell phone which now had her number keyed into the contacts. A pot of ultra-strong coffee waited for him in the miniscule kitchen and not much else to eat or drink, not that he could have kept anything down right now. He passed on taking a shower in the tub that appeared to have a permanent ring around it, but removed the crimson streaks surrounding his lips and on his penis before climbing into the black slacks and tequila-stained shirt. What became of his briefs? No idea. He made his way down the three flights with every step making his head throb.

What Ilsa's place lacked in charm, it made up for in convenience being right on the streetcar line. He kept his eyes closed against the morning sunshine for most of the jolting ride with his only disguise being a heavy morning stubble, an ugly glower, and a deep slouch in his seat—a male version of the walk of shame. No one bothered him. Arturo held the door for his passage into the brownstone building and wisely withheld any remarks except a for a cheery, "Good morning."

"You think so," Dean grumbled.

He collided with Tom coming out of their condo door and leaving on his way to practice. "Look, tell Coach I'm out sick this morning. It's only a home game with Cincinnati. I can afford to miss a day."

"Aren't you the one who says there are no unimportant games?" His brother spared him no sympathy.

Tom's words spoken loudly beat inside of Dean's skull as if someone had locked him inside Ste. Jeanne's bell tower right before Mass. Bong, bong, bong. "Yeah, I guess."

"Then you better get your act together even if you show up late and pay the fine. The team took your order to party up seriously last night. You should have stuck around. Half of them will have big heads this morning. You'll fit right in."

"I told them to party up? Doesn't sound like me."

"That was the new, fun Dean speaking right before he walked out of Mariah's with my date. You're the guy who follows the rules. Whatever happened to bros before hos? You can't handle Stacy so you take my woman?"

Tom tried to push by him, but Dean pressed a hand against his chest, then poked him with a forefinger. "Stacy is not a ho."

"Didn't mean to say she was. Only an expression about disloyalty. You tell me you don't want Ilsa, then you take her. Get out of my way. I don't make your big bucks and those fines add up." Tom swerved to the left but Dean blocked him again.

"I thought you didn't like Ilsa all that much."

"No, but I enjoy what she has to offer. I bet your back is scratched all to hell.

"I admit it smarts along with my hip."

"You injured your hip while out carousing? Great. Management isn't going to like this."

"My hip works just fine, but my behind is sore. Tom, my best bud and true brother, I wouldn't ask this of any other man, but would you take a look at my butt?" Dean didn't wait for an answer but dropped his pants right there in the small foyer.

"Classy. No briefs. Good thing we own the whole floor. You got a big bandage on your rear, asshole." Tom bent closer and ungently tore it away. "And a red heart tattoo with the devil's tail like the one Dad used to sign his autographs in his wilder years."

"Does it say anything inside the heart?"

"Sure does." Tom replaced the bandage with a slap.

"Tell me what it says." He held his breath.

"Mom."

"No!"

"I think I can make out Ilsa if I look real close." Tom stuck his nose in the general vicinity. "Man, you need a shower."

"You're lying, but probably not about the shower."

"Only yanking your chain. It says Stacy."

"I wouldn't, couldn't do that now. I mean we talked about it, but just joking. I'll have to have it removed."

Tom dodged around him and with pants down around his ankles Dean was unable to stop him. His brother stepped into the elevator car with a big shit-eating grin on his freckled face. "Don't panic, Mr. Cool-in-the-Pocket. It reads Sinners. At least you love your team."

"Thank God and all his saints. Please, tell Coach I'm sick. I can't go in this way."

"Make your own excuses, and pull up your pants before Krayola shows up."

"Go on, then. I don't need you. I don't need anyone."

"Until you can't get the ball across the line and I'm called in to make the field goal. You know, I could really screw you over, Dean. Just shank one when you need the points, but I'd never do that because I play for the whole team, not only for you. Go screw yourself."

The door closed on his brother, his best friend, his wingman. Flying alone, Dean made for his own bathroom to hurl the night's alcohol into a clean, unstained toilet bowl full of blue water.

He did call in sick by himself. Dean held the phone away from his ear to avoid eardrum damage as Coach Buck reamed him inside and out. "Sick, my old shriveled ass! You got loaded like the rest of them last night. I would have expected this of your dad before he settled down, but not you. Sleep it off. Be here tomorrow."

A cold shower hadn't helped much, and he felt too unsteady to shave. Krayola found him in the darkened bedroom stretched out in nothing but a fresh pair of skivvies. He scrambled for his robe.

"I gots three grown boys. I know a hangover when I sees one," she informed him with hands on her broad hips. "You done something to your hiney, son? I see a bandage sticking out of yo' briefs."

"It's nothing. I'm okay."

"Sure, you is." She left but returned with a thick glass of tomato juice spiked liberally with hot sauce and bearing a sprig of celery. "You finish this, all of it. When you feelin' a little better I'll make you some eggs and bacon."

Mercifully, his housekeeper refrained from vacuuming or running the washer, but he swore he could hear every swipe of her dust cloth across the furniture. At noon, Ilsa called. Exactly what he needed—her high, often sing-song voice sawing in his ear.

"My Dean is not feeling so well today, I hear."

"Who told you that?"

"I call the Sinners office to make sure you got to work. They tell me you are ill. I be right over with a good cure."

"No, no, that's okay. Krayola is taking care of me."

"That old *Schwarze*? Ilsa can do better. I be there soon."

"No, ah…"

Gone. She'd hung up on him and not fifteen minutes later rang his bell. Where was Arturo when a guy needed him? Krayola ran interference by saying, "I'll see if Mr. Dean is up to having guests."

As soon as she turned her back, Ilsa marched in clutching two Lucky Dogs and immediately spotted Dean hunched over a second Virgin Mary in the dining area. She looked completely fresh in a variation of the Anchi Services outfit, this one a dress in pale gray with short sleeves and cinched with a thin purple belt that showed off her narrow waist. The accent scarf Stacy insisted upon wound blithely two times around her long, white neck. With her makeup subdued, her hair knotted at her nape, Ilsa seemed entirely professional and completely sober.

"You aren't wasted?" he asked.

"What is wasted? Ah, *der Katzenjammer*, the hangover. No, beer is to me like mother's milk, and I have only three, one at Mariah's and two at Paco's. This you have here is no good. Protein is what you need. That and pickle juice," she proclaimed. Ilsa poured out the Virgin Mary, raided his refrigerator, and drained the dill pickle brine into a glass. "Drink! Drink it now."

He tossed it down like a shot, the sooner to get rid of her.

"Now eat. I brought you a plain wurst, but sauerkraut would make it better. You got any?" Ilsa opened cupboards in her search for another cure.

"I don't think so."

"Next, a nice steam bath. Tom told me you have such a thing in your showers, but we did not have a chance to try it."

"Sounds good. I'll take one as soon as you leave for work."

"Ach, some boring legal documents to put into Russian. Can wait. Finish and I will join you."

Krayola blocked the doorway into the bedroom with her bulk and a laundry basket piled high with sheets smelling of lavender and Stacy. Stacy who had deceived him. Stacy who disliked Ilsa so very much.

"Excuse me, Miss Krayola. I'm going to take a shower."

"You already done took a shower. I found yo' wet towels on the floor. What you need another one for?" his housekeeper said to him, but her eyes arrowed in on Ilsa. "And those bloody slacks. You know you supposed to soak them in cold water right away. Just making more work for ole Krayola."

"Yes, ma'am. Sorry. Now, step aside."

"You the boss. Since you have company, I'll be going. Do the wash tomorrow. Leave you in *her* hands." Muttering, "Everybody know tomato juice is the best hangover cure, pickle juice, my Lawd," Krayola moved down the hall with her burden of sheets and towels and bloody trousers.

Ilsa lost no time turning on the taps in the big, glass box of the shower. She figured out how to work the steam jets while Dean threw his robe aside and stepped out of his briefs. "Get in, and I join you soon."

Easier not to resist. Dean entered the stall as the moisture swirled, and leaned back, eyes closed, against the smooth tiles. He knew when Ilsa entered by the small puff of cooler air. She went down on him instantly. He stared at her pale hair grown darker in the mist as it dampened. Her lips were thinner than Stacy's but she knew what to do with them and her tongue and teeth. The urgency of his arousal surprised him. He thought himself incapable this morning and drained dry after last night.

Ilsa rose up on her long legs before allowing him to finish. "I do not so much like the taste."

She mounted him easily in the standing position and braced her feet against the wall. He didn't take long after that. Strange how the woman couldn't dance yet performed so well doing the sexual act. Dean noted the two large hickeys on her white neck as he sank down on a teak bath stool and hung his head. He hadn't marked a woman like that since high school. Talk about regression.

Weak from the heat and coitus, he braced his arms

and heaved from the shower. Krayola had left huge, fluffy white towels behind on the heated rack. Ilsa reached for one and dried him well, patting his scratched back and sore behind and between the legs.

His bandage, peeled away in the steam, lay in the bottom of the shower like a spent condom. "I like this." She traced the red heart with a fingertip. "Only so sad it does not say Ilsa."

He had no answer for that and offered no apology. "I think I can rest now."

"*Ja, Ja.* We both get some sleep."

"Don't you have work to do?"

"Stacy will not know unless you tell her. She is at the hospital again, and I work on my own computer. The job gets done sooner or later."

Dean slept long and deep. Tom's voice sounded in the hall coming straight at them through the open doorway. "You eating dinner tonight or still upchucking?" he asked as he reached the room. Ilsa surfaced from beneath the sheets.

Tom stood there, his long red hair still damp from a locker room shower, a look of disbelief on his face. "Never mind. I can tell you're feeling better. I'm going to eat with Xochi."

"You're taking their side in this?" Dean said still half asleep and barely aware of Ilsa beside him.

"I'm not taking sides, not any more. Remember, you're on your own. Enjoy your evening." Tom left, slamming the bedroom door and more distantly the entry to the condo they shared.

"So, are we ordering in or going out?" Ilsa coiled around Dean.

Chapter Twenty-Five

Stacy walked into her apartment still wearing what Xo called her uptight suit of feminine armor, though she'd given the other two women another fashion option as she'd promised to do. Cutting into a thick pork chop stuffed with cornbread dressing, Tom sat at their dining table. She raised her hands in surrender. "Ignore me. I'm going upstairs. I'll get something later. Enjoy your dinner with Xochi."

"Don't leave on account of me. Dean the Dick is entertaining Ilsa at our place." He buttered a piece of French bread that shed bits of crust on their grape-patterned tablecloth.

"Yes, stay and eat with us. I made a salad, and we picked up entrees from the Palace. I got you the redfish with a crabmeat topping, something rich but light. I'm having the same. You need a good meal." Xochi patted the chair where Stacy usually sat to dine.

"Even the vegetables are good. What am I eating again?" Tom asked his sister.

"A mélange of roasted autumn root vegetables, but yours comes with green beans almondine," Xo explained.

"Yeah, I love when my sisters invite me to dinner since none of you know how to get a meal on the table. Corazon spoiled y'all for cooking and cleaning, but your takeout is always great."

Xo gave Tom a light punch on the arm as she got up and transferred Stacy's meal from a Styrofoam box to their everyday pottery plates also patterned in grapes. "We do our own cleaning, unlike some lazy athletes we know." She pressed Stacy into her chair where a bowl of salad waited before her and a small dish held a hunk of bread.

Because the food was there, Stacy picked up a fork and broke apart the broiled fish fillet. She hadn't much appetite since last Friday. "Thanks for getting me something."

"Thanks for taking the hospital job. You know how going there depresses me. I see illness everywhere. You want some white wine with that?" Xochi held the bottle poised over an empty glass.

"I find I like comforting people, making them less scared as they understand what's going on around them. Who knew I had any nurturing instincts? No, no wine. I'll stick to water." Truthfully, wine reminded her of Ilsa—with Dean right now. Her food stopped halfway to her mouth as she felt a little queasy. As indifferently as she could, she asked Tom, "When did Dean become a dick instead of your best bro, your perfect prince of a man?"

"Get this right. Dean has never been my prince. He achieved dickdom last night when he stole Ilsa right out from under me, then shows up with the world's worst hangover and a tattoo in the morning. He asks me to make excuses for him with the coach like I'm supposed to make up an imaginary illness so he gets off scot-free and rakes in sympathy for being sick. No way. I'm done being Dean's wingman." Tom gestured so emphatically with a deep red baby beet speared on the end of his fork it flew through the air and into Mati's patiently waiting-for-something-to-drop jaws.

"Tom, he could choke on that!" Stacy leaned over ready to perform the Heimlich on her pet.

"Nah, he's chewing it up. Probably good for him. I'd like Dean to choke on it. It's one thing when women walk over me to get to him because I have the face and hair of a leprechaun and I'm only a kicker, but he doesn't encourage that. He said I could have Ilsa if I wanted, then takes her back." Tom stabbed another vegetable.

Stacy stilled his hand. "Tom, don't desert him now. You are well rid of her, and if Ilsa has her claws sunk into him, he'll need your help to escape."

"Claws aren't what Dean is sinking into Ilsa. Sorry, Stace, but they didn't even bother to close the bedroom door. Right in my face, pow!" Tom jerked his hand away and lost a chunk of potato this time. Mati hoovered it up.

"Stop feeding my dog! Listen, from the pictures Angel so kindly sent me from Paco's, Ilsa has made her move on Dean. Xochi went to rescue him as soon as we got the photos. I knew he wouldn't accept help from me. He must have stayed over at her place instead of returning home."

"Yes, he conned me. Ilsa gives off orange vibes like Prince Dobbs. You don't want her back, favorite brother of mine." Xochi sneaked Mati a tiny bit of fish while Stacy was distracted.

"Think of other times when Dean stood up for you. Like when you put the whoopee cushion on Sr. Mary Leo's chair in the fourth grade. Dean saw you waiting in the school office and told the principal you suffered from Jester's Syndrome and couldn't help being the class clown."

"Yeah, Sr. Mary Leo didn't buy that. I had to clean the grill in the barbecue pavilion as my punishment. That's a lot of grease."

"Dean scrubbed the floor in there on his hands and knees for lying because it was the greater sin. He took the heat when both of you got stinking drunk in high school saying he'd bought the liquor."

"No lie. He did buy the booze. I just chipped in for it. It's the red hair and freckles. I always get carded, but Dean looked like a man before he turned seventeen."

"I remember," Stacy said softly.

"Dad took the keys to our truck, parked it in the barn under a tarp, and put a chain around it. I thought the chain was overkill. We had to go to school in the van with you girls and all the babies for the rest of the school year instead of driving ourselves. Took us months to get that privilege, and we blew it—just like Ilsa is probably blowing Dean right now. She's good at it, too."

"I think I'll eat later and take Mati for a walk before it gets too dark. He needs to work off those scraps. Tom, please be there for your brother since I can't."

Stacy covered her plate and put it in the fridge. "Come, Mati. Walkies." She jangled his pale blue leash, clipped it on, and moved out through the living room, but paused to overhear what they might say about her.

"I can't believe you said that at the dinner table, dearest brother. Gross. I'd like to wash your mouth out with soap. You really upset her."

"Sorry. I was out of line. I'm still really pissed at

Dean."

"But spill about the tattoo."

"It's on his butt, Dad's old heart with the devil's tail."

"Tell me it doesn't say Ilsa inside."

"I let him think it did for a little while."

Stacy counted her heartbeats waiting for Tom to continue.

"Only says Sinners, and there's nothing wrong with that."

Not what she would have liked to hear, but far better than Ilsa. Stacy quietly opened the door and led her cherished pet out into the twilight. Lights shone in Dean's bedroom window, but nowhere else in the condo across the street.

Chapter Twenty-Six

Dean apologized to his coach and his team, something his father never would have done, but then he tried hard not to be Joe Billodeaux anywhere except on the football field. Some of the newer guys smirked, but the seasoned veterans seemed relieved at his pledge to be careful of his alcohol intake in the future. He got down to work honing his passes and practicing some new routes with his receivers though they all agreed Cincinnati would be no trouble on Sunday afternoon.

If only the tabloids hadn't come out and rattled him. He'd made the front covers again. No scenes from Mariah's as she would have thrown out the scumbag reporters, but plenty from Paco's, stuff he barely remembered. A long itemized bill from Jose helped him recall the trashing of the dance club. He sent it on to his attorney to be paid immediately, no quibbling.

The worst of the photos showed him slurping tequila shots off a woman's belly under the headline *Daddy Joe's Boy* and beneath it in smaller letters *Like Father Like Son.* Inside, a picture of him dancing awkwardly with Ilsa and the caption *New Blonde in Dean's Life* spread across the page. Another tabloid portrayed him swaying precariously on a very small table as he bashed the football piñata to bits. Some ugly shots captured the mayhem that followed. No one killed. Some injured. He alerted the attorney again to contact those who were hurt and take care of their medical bills before they turned into lawsuits. One paper suggested he had PTSD from witnessing the shooting of Prince Dobbs, which he hadn't actually done. More like Post Traumatic Stacy Disaster if they knew the truth.

The only person involved with any ethics at all turned out to be Cyril who gave a brief interview to the yellow press saying he'd been honored to tattoo Dean Billodeaux whose speech had been slightly impaired at the time, but he was certain he'd given the quarterback exactly what he wanted. As to the nature and location of the tattoo, that remained confidential information.

Dean knew well his father's early history. As teens, he and Tom googled Joe's exploits documented with photos of the now legendary quarterback at the casino with two blondes on his arms and another of Dad offering his infamous black book for the ladies to sign for a sexual assignation. One great shot of the man who would become Daddy Joe to his team later in life offered up a cheesy grin and a black eye from a brawl as well as the quote, "I'm more of a lover than a fighter." At the time, both he and Tom thought how cool. But, losing their driving privileges for heavy drinking and uncomfortable sessions with their mother about respecting women and themselves soon adjusted their attitudes. He'd let his parents down, dredged up his dad's lurid past, and most likely hurt his mother.

This time he called before his parents tried to reach him. He confessed like a good Catholic and promised not to make that mistake again. Mama Nell asked, "What about Stacy?"

"What about her? We broke up after I found out

she'd made a fool out of me and used Prince to do it."

"That's not what Xochi says."

"You mean her co-conspirator. Sure, she'd stand up for Stacy."

"I can see you are still angry. We'll talk face to face on Sunday. The family is coming down for the game. The Rev and his wife will be there, too. He wants to pray over Prince and visit with his parents. He got a substitute minister to fill in with his congregation so he could get away. We will all have dinner together afterwards as usual. Then, we'll go somewhere quiet and work this out." He knew those were orders, not suggestions, no matter how quietly put by his dear mama.

The only way to make up for his behavior and show he'd come away from Stacy unscathed was to play well and win big. He put his mind to it, no drinking, hard workouts. Still, Ilsa kept appearing at his place, and he took what she had to offer because it dulled what he'd felt for Stacy better than booze or drugs. Tom disappeared from his life, pretty hard to do when you shared a place, but he succeeded in leaving his rooms on the far side of the condo early and coming home late long after Dean closed his bedroom door to frolic with Ilsa. He guessed Tom took his meals out or ate with the enemy across Canal Street. The night before the game, he broke his own rule of no sex right before playing, but put Ilsa in a cab well before midnight.

Dean was centered and prepared on Sunday, doing great until he noticed Ilsa mincing in her high heeled boots down the steps of the Dome toward the box where his family sat. Huge Reverend Revelation

Bullock took up the two seats his twin sisters sometimes occupied beside an empty space where Stacy usually sat by Xochi, both of them missing. Ilsa leaned over the Rev's big belly to introduce herself all around. He watched his adolescent brothers eye her high, full breasts excellently showcased in a snug red top with a scooped neckline that exposed more cleavage than the Rev seemed comfortable with as he tried to suck in his gut to avoid any contact. His green-eyed wife, Dr. Arminta Green Bullock, stood up to shake Ilsa's hand and evidently made a suggestion that had the Rev moving over to the end of the aisle and Ilsa taking the seat in the middle next to her. The youngest, T-Rex, oblivious to her sexuality, said something funny and made everyone laugh, even his parents who had slipped behind masks of polite cordiality.

Dean abandoned his stretches and moved over to where Tom warmed up his leg for the kickoff by booting balls into the net. "What's Ilsa doing here? I didn't give her a ticket."

"No, but I did last week when we were still dating. Guess she made use of it, but her seat was definitely not in the family box. Way too soon for that I thought. But maybe not for you. Stacy's out. Ilsa's in." Tom plucked another ball from the pile and kicked it way too hard for practice.

"She's not in. She's just there all the time. Why does Arturo keep letting her come up?"

"Because when I thought we were seeing each other I told him she could visit whenever she wanted. You tell him any different?"

"No."

"Well, then. You going to bobble your first play

like you did when Stacy turned up with Angel?"

"Not this time."

"Because you really don't care about Ilsa, do you?" Tom paused long enough to drill a hard glance into his eyes, Billodeaux brown against Billodeaux brown.

"It's just great sex. You said so yourself."

"Maybe I wasn't done having great sex when you stepped in."

"I apologize. I'll give her back."

Tom shook his head. "It doesn't work that way with women, passing them back and forth like you're practicing pitch and catch. You got her. You keep her. I think you're wanted on the field."

Before the coin toss, the announcer asked for a moment of silence for the full recovery of Prince Dobbs who remained in stable condition and had opened his eyes for the first time that morning. A few cheered. Most bowed their heads respectfully. Some crossed themselves, Dean among them, as thoughts of that night came crowding back. He lost the coin toss.

Naturally, his opponents elected to receive. It did them no good. The final score came down at 42-17. Really by halftime, the game was over. Fans eager to avoid the usual traffic jam on Poydras to the entrance ramp of the interstate left early in the fourth quarter. Although Dean scored four touchdowns, the other two came gratis on interceptions run back for the TDs. The opponents defeated themselves. Still, he wondered if Stacy watched and noticed she hadn't destroyed his game, maybe her intention all along, to take something he held dear and trample it into the turf. Now for the real challenge—to get through dinner and the evening with his parents.

****

Dean arrived at the restaurant late after doing the usual press interviews and dawdling in the locker room. He accepted the ribbing about the new tattoo and the suggestions he get something more manly next time. Adam Malala, heavily inked with traditional Samoan designs from the waist to the knee, simply shook his head. "You call that a tattoo?" Dean planned not to get another in any form.

The family gathered around their usual long table in a private dining area with Teddy on one end in his wheelchair. Some had started in on their salads and the basket usually containing warm hush puppies sat empty. They'd saved him a space near his parents and directly across from—God, no, Ilsa. The absence of Stacy, Xochi, and Tom seemed less obvious with the Rev and his wife filling some of the empty chairs. They, too, must have come late as the Rev was in the process of ordering the large seafood platter. "Make that the broiled version," his wife intervened, always conscious of her husband's health. Feeling a need for red meat, Dean asked for a steak, medium rare, with the usual salad and loaded baked potato.

Ilsa very charmingly regaled him with the story of her meeting the family. "Your little brother, he says to me, 'You talk funny.' I say that is because I am German and my name is Ilsa. He says my name is funny, too. When I ask what he is called, he says, 'T-Rex'. Now it is my turn to laugh, and he makes the claws and growls at me." She reached across the table and gripped his arm with her fingernails painted Sinners red to demonstrate.

The waitress brought the iced tea he'd ordered. He

asked for red wine, merlot, a whole bottle. Mama Nell requested glasses for all the adults. "We'll help you drink that."

"Oh, yes! I do like the red wine. So thoughtful of you to order, Dean." Ilsa smiled as if he'd done this just for her instead of for himself to get through the meal.

The Rev asked for a refill on the hush puppies. Seated in front of a Mardi Gras costume that made him look as if he wore a crown of ostrich feathers, more black witch doctor than AME minister, he hoisted a toast. Out of his official clerical garb, he felt free to drink a little. "To the health and full recovery of Prince Dobbs. I prayed over him mightily this morning, and he opened his eyes to the light. Praise be to Gawd!"

Most of them said, "Amen" before drinking. Ilsa shouted, "*Prosit!*" and clinked her glass against Dean's as well as his parents'. The younger children stared at her amazed. "What? It means To Your Health," she explained. "Also to the health of this prince."

Officially declaring himself tired and hungry, Dean let the conversation flow over and around him as he dug into his sizable steak and mammoth baked potato. The scant glass of wine he'd gotten from the bottle hardly helped at all. Ilsa ate with great appetite and talked merrily until the check arrived. His father said little even though Ilsa flirted with him lightly, calling him a so handsome older man. Bet Daddy Joe loved that. Of course, his dad paid for all after a little friendly give and take with the Rev.

Mama Nell stood. She barely came up to Ilsa's sharp collarbone, but no one intimidated her when it came to her children. "So nice to meet you, Ilsa, but now we must say goodbye. We want some family time with Dean, you understand. Our son will get you a cab." Smooth, Mom, smooth.

"I understand I am not family yet," Ilsa answered casually.

Dean's stomach clenched. He escorted her to the curb. She made a scene of hugging and kissing him before getting into the taxi. Somewhere a paparazzo probably got a shot of it. He simply didn't care. The Rev and his wife also departed for the long drive home to Chapelle. His mom suggested they walk off the meal. Raised to help and be considerate, the younger children assisted Teddy with his wheelchair at the crossings. They entered the privacy of the brownstone building in very little time.

"Now," Mama Nell said. "Kids go into the game room and amuse yourselves while we talk to Dean," which really meant the noise of the foosball game and the X-Box would drown out the grown-up conversation.

"I'm an adult. I'd like to stay," Teddy said, his large blue eyes serious but his fine blond hair, darker than in childhood, still flopping across his forehead as always.

A bad sign, Dean thought. Teddy and Stacy had entered the Billodeaux family on the same day and remained close. Two blondes in a bunch of brunettes they liked to joke. They had to stick together and often still talked on the phone. Teddy would know the whole story, at least Stacy's version of it.

Delaying, Dean asked if anyone wanted a drink and got a universal no except for his father who asked for coffee. "I've got one of these pod machines. What kind do you want?"

"Dark roast with caffeine, nothing flavored. That's

no way to make real coffee, boy."

"I know." But fiddling with the coffeemaker gave him a chance to turn his back and gather his thoughts. "It's quick and easy though."

"Some things in life shouldn't be quick and easy. Do you think it was easy to get your mother to marry me with my reputation?"

Dean delivered the steaming mug to his father. "You eloped to Vegas!"

"Because that lawyer wanted to take you away from me. You needed a mother in a hurry. We asked you to take it slow with Stacy, and now we have this big family rift on our hands. Our team no longer plays together. Three of them wouldn't come to the game or dinner. We have no idea how your twin sisters feel but suspect they'll come down on Stacy's side as usual."

"Her side! What about my side? She and Xochi set me up, making me run around to protect her from imaginary danger like a complete idiot. The princess got in over her head with Prince and Kent Gonsoulin, and I'm to blame?"

"We were very proud of how you handled the situation with Prince. Not so much afterwards. Believe you me, I know how it feels to be taken advantage of by a woman, your birth mother for example. I manned up and made something good come from dat—that."

His dad's Cajun accent came to the fore, not good. Mama Nell quieted his father's hands before he sloshed the coffee since he always gestured when excited. She took up the gauntlet, small but mighty. "Enough. Stacy called us to say the situation is all her fault. She said she's only our ward, not our daughter. She'll stay away from the ranch, the games, and you for the good of the family. She wants you to forgive Xochi for her small part in the plan to get your attention."

"Get my attention! She's had my attention for years."

"How was she supposed to know this?"

"Because girls just do."

"Not really. Stacy cared very deeply for you and took action to show you she needed you. Now, both of you are hurt."

Dean paced, so much like his father when agitated. This way, he escaped his mother's big brown eyes, the ones that always knew when her children lied. "Who says I'm hurt? I'm fine. I have a new girlfriend."

Teddy had been sitting there quietly in his wheelchair like a piece of the furniture. Now, he spoke. "The one you stole from Tom. He says Ilsa is easier than your coffeemaker."

"She's European. That's just the way they are like the Russian models from the Amberello Agency."

"Did you sleep with any Russian models?"

"No. Not my type." Because his type was Stacy. They'd never pry that out of him, not even if they cut him out of the family, exiled him from Lorena Ranch, never came to his games again.

"Ilsa is smart, attractive and very—vibrant. I hope you aren't using her as your rebound girl, Dean. She seems very attached to you already."

His mother, always concerned about female feelings. Didn't guys have feelings, too, not that he planned to admit that, either.

"Me, I'd be worried about more than that when it comes to Ilsa. She reminds me of... Never mind. I hope you are being careful," his dad said, finally getting another word into the conversation.

"She's on the pill, okay?"

Joe Billodeaux raised his dark eyebrows as skeptical as a Cajun could be. "Suit up."

"Can't women take responsibility for anything? Why are you all on my case?"

His mother changed the subject back to her major concern. "We spoke to Stacy earlier trying to persuade her to come with us. She said it wasn't in your best interest. You know, Kent's lawyers have been to see her. They want her to drop the assault charge, saying it's a he said/she said. No one will believe her. He claims he tried to defend her, not shoot her."

"She shouldn't do that. Not again. Maybe he didn't intend to gun her down, but knowing what a douche bag Kent is, he did attack her."

"Not again?" His mother caught that of course.

"She had some trouble with Prince, but didn't make it public for the good of the team."

"For your good, I'll bet," Teddy weighed in. "Xo says she isn't eating or sleeping well because of all this. She's thinking of closing down the business at the end of the year when their contracts are up for renewal and going abroad."

"No. That's not Stacy. She doesn't fold. She fights."

"You should think about forgiving her, Dean," his mother prompted. "She is part of our family no matter what she says."

"Maybe when I feel like less of a fool."

"Maybe when you are less of an asshole. You're breaking her heart, Dean. To think I used to admire you. I'm going to wait in the lobby." Teddy swung his wheelchair wide and ran over Dean's toes on the way out.

"Hey, you could have broken my foot!" Dean wiggled his digits checking for damage.

"Maybe you know how Stacy feels now. Mom, get the door for me. I'll be good after that."

Nell did this small service for her adopted son. "We should all leave. We've said what we have to say. Think about it. Joe, pry the rest of them out of the game room."

Her husband clapped his hands as he moved in that direction. "Come on, hut hut, *allons a* Chapelle."

"You're driving home tonight, Mom?"

"Yes. School tomorrow."

"Be careful on the road. I love you, all of you."

Nell reached way up to cup her eldest son's cheek. "I know. You love Stacy, too, whether you are willing to admit it or not. We care about both of you."

Then her remaining five children filled the living room and flowed out the door with his father herding the smallest of them. Joe paused for a manly shake of the hands, but gave in to a strong hug. "We'll get through this. I know you'll do the right thing."

The second they were gone he missed his family more acutely than he had since moving to New Orleans and getting caught up in being a Sinner. He went to his window and watched them walk toward the parking lot where they'd stowed the van, a small cavalcade with a red wheelchair in the middle, until they went out of sight.

Out of the corner of his eye, he noticed a small ball of frenetic white action. Stacy walked her dog along Canal Street in the coolness of the evening. He noticed something different about her stance, not her usual fierce clip that dared lowlifes to ask for the time and try to grab her watch. Did she look thinner? Hard to tell from this distance. Anyhow, she shouldn't be out there alone. Mati was no real protection. He should... Dean spotted her escorts a few yards behind, Tom and Xochi who urged her to take a seat at an outdoor café. He continued to watch as a waiter brought coffee and two large wedges of cheesecake. Xo shoved a piece at Stacy and insisted she share by placing a fork in her hand. Good, people looked after her. She didn't need Dean Billodeaux to walk her home.

His phone buzzed in his hip pocket. Ilsa's voice flooded into his ear. "Your family is gone? I come over, *Ja*?

"Sure, I can use some company." Odd how alone he felt tonight.

Chapter Twenty-Seven

Dean put two more grueling road games behind him, Pittsburgh and Baltimore, neither of them pushovers. The Sinners won both by a slim margin with the very last score depending on Tom's toe for a fifty-yard field goal. He came through for the team as always. The Sinners winning streak remained unbroken. This was Dean's year in so many ways, but not in others.

Ilsa convinced him that sex the day before the game took nothing away from his playing. She turned out to be right. When he returned home, Isla always waited for him, taking his mind off the other big problem in his life with mind-numbing sex. Having her around all the time didn't sit well with Tom, and he did live in half the condo. It only seemed natural to help Ilsa get a better place to live where they weren't in his brother's face all the time. She'd begin picking up the rent when Stacy paid her more, she said. Dean threw in a wall-mounted TV since Xo and Stace no longer invited her to view the away games at their place, and for her own good he wanted to keep her out the sports bars.

Dean didn't take her to Mariah's Place. Some of the team and his honorary grandmother still disapproved of how he'd snatched Ilsa from Tom. But, he put in an appearance at victory parties, minded his drinking, and took her out afterwards to her favorite German restaurant or another place with good music. A brief but welcome Thanksgiving break came up fast. Since no invitations had been issued to their employee by Xo and Stacy, he felt bad for Ilsa. She hinted broadly that she would be so all alone on her first Thanksgiving in America unless he stayed with her.

His mom would have none of that. He did the kindest thing and got the Mustang out of the garage to transport them both to Lorena Ranch. Mama Nell always said they had room for one more at their table and an abundance of food to share. Breaking all the speed laws and taking the back way, they arrived before Tom who'd been stuck running a family delivery service for his sisters in the SUV. Xo to board in New Orleans, then the twins in Baton Rouge, followed by loading Teddy and his wheelchair in Lafayette after crossing the long causeway over the Atchafalaya Basin. Ilsa remarked she bet Tom was not having so much fun as they did flying along with the top down on an overcast and humid day past fruit stands boarded up for the winter and miles of marsh between towns.

"Yes, my twin sisters are a handful and always late."

"I will meet them, *Ja*?

"Yes, and more of my relatives than you can remember or want to know."

They drew up before the wrought iron gates of Lorena Ranch open for this day of many arrivals, but still under the watchful eye of Knox Polk, ranch manager and retired soldier. Still trim and ramrod straight, his very short hair a white contrast to his light brown skin, he waved Dean in and paused to shake his hand. "You're early."

"Made good time."

"I know what that means. Be careful going back. Lots of drunks on the road on a holiday evening."

"I will. Junior looked good playing for the Flames. He's got the talent. Oh, this is Ilsa, my guest."

"Welcome, Miss Ilsa. I'll let the house know you're coming." Knox pressed the call box on the side of the gate and spoke into it quietly as if he told a secret or played a game of Telephone.

Ilsa took in the long drive lined with ancient live oaks, the white mansion sitting in their midst, and the bayou beyond. "Is like *Gone with the Wind, nein?*"

"I think that was the idea my dad had. His taste is a little questionable sometimes, and he was in the process of building the place before he married my mom. But, we do have a movie theater and a gym I am certain Tara lacked."

"I like it very much." Ilsa squeezed his arm. "You are my Clark Gable."

"No mustache and I have my own teeth," he answered, making her laugh though he'd been quite serious.

Knox had warned the family about the unexpected guest. As they entered through the kitchen door, his mother stepped forward immediately with hands out to take Ilsa's and a strained smile on her face. The air-conditioner ran full blast offsetting heat from the stove where Mawmaw Nadine had taken over to bake her sweet potato and pecan pies after she'd chased Corazon from the kitchen and told her rest for the cleanup. His robust, outspoken grandmother shoved the last pie onto the oven rack and straightened to give Ilsa the once-over.

"How you gonna sit down and eat in that tight dress, *cher*?" she questioned Dean's guest.

"Oh, it is stretchy. I like to eat very much." Ilsa plucked at the electric blue fabric and let it spring back snug against her body.

"Ilsa, this is Dean's grandmother, Nadine." Nell attempted to move the couple along. "I'm so glad Dean invited you, but I warn you things get very chaotic here on holidays. Coffee is on the counter. Cold drinks in the fridge. Help yourself and try not to get trampled. His other grandparents are in the den keeping an eye on the little ones. They tend to get into things. Why don't you join them?"

"We brought wine." Dean held up a canvas sack full of clinking bottles. "Ilsa picked it out."

"Four bottles of good German Riesling. Will it be enough?" Ilsa asked.

"We have plenty of beer and other beverages, so this will be fine. The men just sit around, drink, and watch football all day once they get the turkeys fried."

"Fried turkeys?"

"You have to see it to believe it. Come on, I'll introduce you to Grandma and Grandpa Abbott." Dean deposited the bottles on the counter and steered Ilsa toward the hall.

They didn't move fast enough to completely escape the Mawmaw Nadine commentary. "Another skinny one and a foreigner. Why doesn't he find a nice Cajun Cat'lic girl? You Cat'lic, honey?" Dean's grandmother called after them. Age hadn't made her any more diplomatic, probably worse.

"*Nein.* Lutheran," Ilsa said over her shoulder.

"A Protestant non-Cajun exactly like me," Nell reminded her.

"You turned out okay, *cher*. Gave me lots of grandkids. Besides, Episcopalians are almost Cat'lics. Those Lut'rans tried to wreck the Church."

"Better check your pies. I think I smell something burning." Nell waved her son and his guest urgently away to the safety of the den. "Dean, come back when you get Ilsa settled. I need you to carry the gallons of peanut oil out to the pavilion."

"Sure thing."

The Abbotts, his safe, normal grandparents, small in stature and a little frail with age, nodded benignly when he introduced Ilsa and made no comments. Once he got her seated he asked, "Can I bring you something to drink after I do the peanut oil run?"

"Some wine, *Bitte*."

Dean returned unconcerned to the kitchen. "Mind if I take Ilsa some wine first?" He searched a drawer for a corkscrew and the cupboards for a glass oblivious to the tension in the spice and molasses scented air. "Where's the peanut oil?"

"It's in the pavilion. Your father carried it out this morning. He's there setting up the frying pot. Dean, Stacy is coming. She'll be here any minute. We had to work on her for days to get her to do this. Really, you should have warned me about bringing Ilsa."

"I thought everyone was welcome to Thanksgiving at the ranch." He played it cool but spilled some of the wine he poured.

"Normally true. We'll manage somehow."

Nothing wrong with Mawmaw Nadine's hearing as she often told everyone. "Stacy and this Ilsa don't get along? My, my. Why is that? This handsome grandson of mine involved?" She tweaked Dean's cheek. "Neither one good enough for him."

"Just different personalities," Nell blurted. "Oh, here's Tom and the rest of the gang. Dean, take Ilsa her wine and let me smooth the way." Like a quarterback with no receivers in sight, he took off running.

****

The kitchen filled with young women, Tom, Teddy up on his crutches, and one yapping little dog. "Smells great in here. When's dinner?" Tom asked his mother.

"In a couple of hours. Snacks in the den, but…"

"Come give Mawmaw some sugar." Nadine offered her cheek.

Dutifully, all of them lined up to give Mawmaw kisses and their mother hugs. Nadine did her usual inspection and critique of grown grandchildren she hadn't seen for a while. Nell stood helplessly by unable to get a word in to deflect the upcoming shock of Ilsa's presence.

"Teddy, good to see you using your sticks instead of being in that chair all the time. Jude and Annie, how you expect to meet nice boys wit' all that gunk on your eyes and such short skirts. They think you a whore. Tom, stay out of the sun, and you won't have so many of them freckles. Stacy, you need some feeding up. Them Polish cheekbones is sticking out. That dog housebroken yet?"

"Almost." Stacy edged for the hallway and made her escape before the observations went any deeper. Entering the den with Mati trotting by her side on his leash, she spotted her grandparents first and went to give her kisses. Mati broke into another outburst of yaps and drew her attention to Dean and Ilsa sitting on the far end of the long sofa. Unlike Mawmaw, she did have diplomatic skills honed by her interpreting services.

"Oh, Ilsa. How nice of Dean to bring you. I didn't know myself if I was coming until this morning or I would have invited you."

"*Macht nichts*," Ilsa replied with a shrug. "I am here." She wrapped her arm around Dean's broad shoulders.

"Well, a Billodeaux Thanksgiving is something to behold. Excuse me everyone. I should take Mati outside. He's been in the car for three hours."

She escaped down the long burgundy-tiled hall to the front door and let herself outside to suck in some air. The wind had picked up skirling fallen brown oak leaves into small dust devils. Rain coming. Possibly a thunderstorm with the air too warm for late November. Someone had placed a cypress garden bench near the graves of Titi and Macho. Stacy sank down on the seat and released Mati. "Run, get some exercise. People will be sneaking you food all day because you are adorable."

Whether the wind or her own misery covered Dean's approach, she didn't know. He simply appeared, took the place next to her, and knotted his hands between his knees. Mati ran in frenzied circles around them.

"You know they call that the Bichon blitz. The breeder told me that."

"The Bichon blitz. I like that." He'd coaxed a reluctant smile from her.

"Yeah, football terminology. I like it, too. He's not

a bad dog for a puffball. I'll bet Mawmaw said you needed some feeding up."

"I could stand to lose the pounds and maybe a few more."

"No, you were great as you were. Look, I'm sorry about bringing Ilsa. I didn't think you'd be here. I mean you let her take your place at the game and in the restaurant."

In his bed, she thought. "*Macht nichts.* That means it doesn't matter. Who you bring home to meet your mom and dad is none of my business."

"They already met her in New Orleans."

"It's not the same, Dean. When you bring a woman to a big family gathering it means you are serious about her."

"No, it doesn't. I brought my high school and college girlfriends here, and they were only temporary."

Stacy stopped focusing on the little graves to meet his eyes. She recalled only too well her teen anguish over watching Dean with those girls three years older than her and experienced. "I can't believe you didn't figure out your parents encouraged you to be here with them so they could keep an eye on you."

"I never could do anything under their roof or in their barn or on the beach with all those cameras around. Plenty of other places outside the compound. Not a good day for the beach," he said thoughtfully as if his mind had gone elsewhere for a moment, possibly to the place of the crossed palm trees. She went there in her mind all the time, very unhealthy.

"I just thought I'd invite Ilsa to an American Thanksgiving, nothing serious. But you can't really mean you're going to shut down Anchi Services as hard as you worked to get that business started like Mom said."

"I shouldn't have come to New Orleans and gone to work right out of college." For the wrong reason—because Dean lived there.

"What about Xo and Ilsa? They'll be out of a job. You should think about them."

And about getting away from seeing Dean with Ilsa wrapped around him like a German flag at an Olympic event. "Our contracts come up for renewal at the end of the year. Xo can pick the ones she wants. Ilsa has some clients now she might want to retain, or she can go back to Germany. I'm thinking I should travel to Berlin or Vienna and stay a year to pick up the language, see new sights, meet new people."

"You mean people like Dr. Rivera."

"Why not? Unlike you, I've never had a German. Dean, when you pay for a woman's apartment, she's your mistress, not only an easy lay." That had come boiling out of her like the rumble of thunder and flash of lightning above their heads. Mati stopped running and cowered against her leg. She picked him up and held him close. The temperature plummeted around them as a cold front forced its way in, an uninvited guest for the holiday.

"Ilsa said you put her up in some dump, and she couldn't afford better. It was a dump. I'm helping her out until she can afford the rent."

"Oh, noble Sir Dean to the rescue. She picked the place herself because it was close to the streetcar lines, near the Trade Center and within her means. We didn't force her to live there. I gave her my own bed when she arrived. But, now she has yours, so no worries for poor

Ilsa."

Dean stood up and towered over her. "Forgive me for helping someone who *really* needs it, Princess." He strode back to the house as the first fat raindrops began to fall.

Just like that, they'd returned to their old adversarial role, maybe for the best. Mati whimpered as the thunder rolled again and the lightning flashed nearer than before. Her Aunt Nell stood in the doorway and called over the rumbles, "Anastasia Marya Polasky, get in here before you're soaked."

Stacy obeyed that voice as she had in childhood, but bypassed her aunt as she came indoors. She proceeded straight up the wide, elegant staircase and down the long hallway into the new addition that had housed her and Teddy when they both arrived out of the blue one summer day so long ago and were taken in with kindness and love. Her cream and gold bedroom remained fit for a princess. She sprawled across the queen-sized bed with Mati held tight and bawled in private as hard as she had the day she stumbled across Dean making out, hot and heavy, in his pickup truck with red-haired Heather McAvoy, the second of his high school girlfriends. Nothing changed.

Chapter Twenty-Eight

Nothing stopped a Billodeaux Thanksgiving either. Relatives arrived in high-rise trucks and massive SUVs that defied the flooded roads. Sheltering their covered dishes, aunts, uncles, and cousins waded to the house in their white rubber fisherman's boots or barefooted with their shoes tucked under their arms. The men gathered in the barbecue pavilion to deep fry the turkeys while the women set out the sides on the dining room table in the house since no one would be dining outside today.

The Billodeaux boys gathered round their elders to learn this fine Cajun art. It seemed strange not to have Pawpaw Frank giving the directions, but he'd died one hot day of a heart attack in the air-conditioned cab of his cane tractor, parked under an oak tree and the engine still running. Now, Daddy Joe, hair gone to the color of steel, presided.

As those over eighteen nursed their beers, he gently lowered the fry basket with the big bird rubbed down in Creole seasoning into the boiling oil. "Be careful not to fill the pot more than three-quarters. You don't want any spillage making the propane flare up. Open up the neck so all that oil circulates. In forty-five minutes, we have a moist, juicy turkey. We'll serve this one cold and the next one hot. Now, all we have to do is wait."

Some of the great-uncles organized a card game of bouree. Joe's four brothers-in-law debated the merits of smoking a turkey instead and the best ways to do that. Uncle Charlie worked on getting drunk as usual, summoning T-Rex to fetch him another brew and letting him have a taste of the suds for his service.

Dean stood back a little from one of the screened walls of the pavilion where the rain filtered in and stared at the downpour. His dad came to stand beside him starting off with a general remark that would veer in the direction he wanted it to go like a good quarterback sneak.

"Good thing your mom is in the kitchen with Charlie letting T-Rex drink from his bottle. I still don't understand why your Aunt Lizzie keeps taking that man back." Joe shook his head.

"Habit, I guess. It's hard to break a habit, even a bad one. You aren't worried about T-Rex?"

"I was raised sucking the suds off my daddy's beers. Didn't hurt me none. *Mais* yeah, I miss my old man on days like this. I treasured a quiet day of fishing with my dad away from the five women in the house. One too many women in the household today, huh?" Joe said as subtle as he ever got. "When I went back to get the matches, your mom told me you'd talked to Stacy. How'd it go?"

"Not well. Started out okay, then the princess turned all pissy about Ilsa. I didn't start seeing the woman until after we broke up. It's not her fault Stacy played me for a fool."

"I can't say your sisters are being very welcoming to Ilsa today. Pretty much ignoring her though your date doesn't seem to care. Sorry about that. If she's your choice, we'll work on that, but we'd still like you to make your peace with Stacy."

"Ilsa isn't my choice. She's just a woman I'm seeing right now. Really, I tried to make up with Stacy and told her not to close down Anchi Services. She started in on Ilsa, and then we were right back to being bickering teenagers again. Women, I don't understand them." Dean took a long swallow from his bottle of Dixie and drained it to the bottom.

"You think Stacy made a fool out of you, but you don't have to act foolish because of it." Joe eyed his son's drink, though he had one in his own in hand.

"I swear I'm done overindulging and getting tattoos on my butt. This is my first drink today. Honest to God." Dean crossed himself for good measure.

"There are other ways of being foolish. Be careful. Want to tell me about the tattoo?"

"It's your old devil's tail heart with Sinners written on the inside."

"I'm honored. Look, Tink the Shrink says Stacy is brokenhearted and jealous of Ilsa," Joe said, referring lightly to his psychologist wife. "She's trying to cut herself off from all she loves as self-punishment for nearly getting Prince killed. Deep. We can't allow that, now can we?" Joe threw in a paternal pat on the back with that statement.

"Easy for *we* to say. Maybe I should be the one to leave. I'll be a free agent at the end of this season. The Sinners could get some good defensive players under the salary cap for what I'll cost them. Maybe get Little Joe Bullock out of those snowdrifts up north."

The legendary Joe Billodeaux choked and sputtered on a sip of beer. "That would be heresy! You were born and raised to be the Sinners' quarterback."

"Maybe I was born to do other things elsewhere."

His dad looked too stricken to respond. Dean attempted to lighten up their conversation. "Does Mom know you call her Tink the Shrink?"

That got a grin out of Joe. "Let's keep that between us. No telling what will set a woman off, especially one like your mother. She might find it endearing or maybe not." Joe checked his watch. "Time to get the second turkey started. We want to eat before the first game starts."

Dean stayed where he was contemplating a big puddle growing wider and deeper with every splash of a raindrop. He didn't want Stacy to be heartbroken and pitiful, so maybe it was better they'd gone back to sparring, familiar roles they both knew.

****

Stacy pulled herself together with the help of a wet washcloth and a stash of makeup she'd left behind in a bathroom drawer. About the time she finished becoming presentable, Xo came searching for her. "Thought I'd find you here. Mom says dinner is almost ready. And don't tell me you aren't hungry."

"I'm not, but if I don't eat something Mawmaw will tie me down and force feed me. Dean and I talked. It blew up when we got to Ilsa. She's taking advantage of him, and he just doesn't see it." Stacy ran a brush through her wind-tangled hair until the waves fell perfectly around her pale face.

"The way Mama Nell raised him he'd never keep a mistress. I think he really believes he's only helping her out temporarily, but Ilsa made sure we all knew about her big move and who funded it."

"She really rubbed it in. He's rationalizing."

"I guess you're right. Still, I'm worried about both

of you. His bright light is muddied, and your purple is fading to gray." Xo gazed at her own image in the mirror and quickly looked away as if she'd seen something she disliked.

Stacy shook her head over her assessment. "I'm going to miss you and all your woo-woo stuff when I leave. I never thought we'd be this close. Admit you didn't like me at first."

"No one liked you at first. You were the worst snob, so superior to everyone. You won Lorena over with Titi and Jude and Annie with your style, but not me. I was too tough for that stuff. When I moved down to this end of the hall and painted over the gray and white so I could still have a yellow room with a red rose border, you said the place looked like a fiesta in there."

Stacy nodded. "Add a few piñatas and you would have had Paco's of Chapelle. It grew on me, all that glaring color glimpsed through the bathroom we shared. I used to think the bathroom fixtures in here were real gold as befitted a princess not just gold-colored. We both landed in a good place after our parents' deaths, but I didn't appreciate it for a long time. I'm going to miss Lorena Ranch and Anchi Services and you."

"I don't want to do without the cousin who rushed through that adjoining bathroom when I screamed in the night and couldn't find my gris-gris bag to calm myself. You never told Mom and Dad that you stayed with me when the bad dreams came. I didn't want them to know. I was too old for all that."

"Since Titi ate the bag, I felt responsible. Good thing those herbs weren't poisonous. Remember how we got Mr. Polk to drive us to the *traiteur's* place to get another, and I put my allowance money under a rock for the Virgin Mary."

"That's when I began to like you. Don't go to Europe!" Xochi embraced her hard and finally drew away. "We'd better get down there. Ilsa's telling everyone next time she'll bring the sauerkraut. It's enough to kill my appetite, too."

"Should I lock Mati up here? He'll beg and get in the way."

"No, they couldn't set up the bouncer and the outdoor games for the little kids. They'll enjoy him. Mom says she'll have to put on a movie for the children in the theater, and the men must make do with watching football in the den."

"Big sacrifice with the size of Uncle Joe's TV."

"Speaking of sacrifices, we'd better get going."

With Mati at their heels, the young women took the shortcut and rode down in the elevator Teddy used when in residence. Plenty of food remained to fill their plates with the long dining room table sporting all its extra leaves and weighed down with the abundance of Cajun starches—potato salad, rice dressing, cornbread dressing, French bread and rolls, mac and cheese, and baked beans—on one side. A colorful narrow aisle of green beans with bacon, candied yams, glazed carrots, slaw, and salad held the center. At the far end, the elderly Billodeaux butler, stiff and stately, expertly carved the two turkeys, a large ham and a seasoned pork roast. Brinsley's wife, family nurse, and former nun, waited to treat the tummy aches, skinned knees, and bruises sure to occur with so many children running around inside as well as any possible heart attacks among the elders.

Stacy ate enough to please those who watched her

every bite but held off on dessert until later, as many did. She derived some satisfaction from noting Ilsa's hipbones weren't quite so jutting any more. The German woman had succumbed to Louisiana cuisine at last. Probably no one else noticed since Ilsa had chosen to wear a tight bandage dress in varying shades of blue that intensified her light eyes. That bit of a belly hid beneath the shadow of her deep cleavage. Every male over the age of twelve tracked her with their eyes and envied Dean. Nothing Stacy could do about it but tamp down her jealousy and be polite.

Xo said she'd faded and inside that was exactly the way she felt. She'd worn a simple gray cotton sweater with black slacks and flats because it suited her mood. No one dressed fancy for a Billodeaux Thanksgiving, which ran toward elastic waistbands and loose tops. No high heels because of all the running back and forth to the kitchen and buffet table. Dean hadn't given Ilsa the dress code evidently. Most likely it never crossed his mind.

Instead of brooding over what she couldn't change, Stacy rummaged through a deep closet where the kids kept their sports gear and found an old hula-hoop. She got the dog treats out of her purse and summoned Mati from a group of adoring children to put on a little show for them as the men gathered in the den for football and Nell set up a movie. Mati, a natural ham, happily did his dance for the audience. He sat on his haunches with a treat on his nose until his mistress gave the command for him to flip it up in the air and eat it. She had little Edie hold the hoop down low for the dog to jump through, holding it a little higher each time. "How high can he go?" she asked the kids. They held their arms up sky high.

A deep, masculine voice from the back of the group said with a hard edge of sarcasm, "Stacy is great at training hoop jumping."

"There's a big lout in every audience. Why don't you go criticize the Lions in the other room, Dean?"

"Your wish is my command, Princess." He made a mock bow, slid his arm around Ilsa's waist, and took her away with him.

Her next career should obviously be dog training. With time on her hands in the evenings, she'd lavished attention on Mati by teaching him simple tricks. He finally refused a waist-high hoop and began to sniff the rear seats in the theater. "No, Mati!" Gathering him up, Stacy headed for the theater exit. Still pouring outside, and oh, how Mati hated to pee or poop in the rain, she stood there holding an umbrella and waiting for him to do his business.

With that out of the way, she sat through two movies involving animated cars and planes, though she would have rather watched football with Dean and Joe shouting advice to the officials and both quarterbacks, a part of their holiday tradition. Ilsa sat between the two men when Stacy moved to the dining room to make a turkey sandwich and get a piece of sweet potato pie for dinner. As the second game ended, Tom and Teddy grabbed a bite to eat and began making noises to leave in order to catch as much as they could of the third game at their apartments. Fine with her that this endless day was coming to a close.

Corazon had stowed a basket of leftovers for each of them in the SUV, enough to survive on for a week if they took a wrong turn and got lost in the Atchafalaya swamp. None of "her" children would ever go hungry. Mama Nell insisted on a group hug and usual farewell. Dean slipped into the circle beside Stacy, his arm around her waist. "Love y'all," everyone said. "Love you," Stacy repeated.

Dean and Ilsa departed in the Mustang, top up, going in one direction. Tom, Stacy, and the others moved out in another. The rain had stopped. Cold, clear air dominated a frigid starry night.

Chapter Twenty-Nine

Dean burned up the field with his post-Thankgiving performance and led the Sinners to three more victories before Christmas. Their perfect record stood with one to go, Atlanta away, just before New Year's Day. Stacy turned off the TV after the last night game before Christmas concluded. "At least, I didn't destroy Dean's talent. Prince may never play again, but there is that. I guess I'll turn in for the night. You want the Christmas lights on?" she asked Xo.

"No, I'm going upstairs to read." Xochi began clearing away the popcorn bowls and drink glasses.

Stacy unplugged the white lights on their artificial tree all decked out in silver ribbons and clusters of purple glass grapes. Another difficult holiday lay ahead with no way to get out of it. Her shopping completed, two large bags of wrapped gifts waited for transport to Lorena Ranch, including a special parting gift for Dean and a "being a good sport" present for Ilsa, a gift certificate to her favorite German restaurant. Christmas at the ranch meant only immediate family, though others might drop in for a short time and partake of Corazon's cookies and a glass of cheer.

She'd dealt with all the clients. Xo would keep the police contract for now and any others requiring French, Spanish, and Portuguese at the Trade Center as well as staying in the apartment, possibly with a new roommate. Ilsa had no interest in continuing the translating and interpreting trade but hadn't confided any other plans to Stacy even when offered air fare home. Her sole regret other than losing Dean remained her hospital work, which she found satisfying and hated to leave. Maybe if and when she returned from Europe, she'd specialize in medical translation services.

With that on her mind, she said to Xo, "Say, did I tell you I ran into Prince Dobbs going into physical therapy? He says he's a changed man. He saw Jesus when he came near to dying."

"They do give out some pretty strong painkillers," Xo said, unimpressed.

"This from a woman who sees auras. Anyhow, I asked if maybe he didn't mistake the Rev for Jesus since he prayed over him several times. No, he said. Jesus is a black man darker than himself but lighter than the Rev, long dreads and a beard, white robe, bright light, and way thinner. Christ told him he'd gotten shot because his apology to me was insincere and done only for his own ambitions. Then, Prince said he'd get on his knees to beg my forgiveness if he thought he could get up again by himself. Sounded pretty serious. According to him, in apologizing to me, he did the same for all women he'd treated badly."

Xochi shrugged and picked up her book, another of her Spanish novels. "I doubt those college girls would accept that. I'd have to see Prince to believe him. He's probably still taking drugs to get through therapy."

"If it lasts, it will be a nice change in his personality. He's determined to play again next year. I wonder if I'll be able to catch any of the games in Munich. Visit me, okay?"

"Stay here and we'll take our next vacation there," Xo answered.

"Too late now. Goodnight."

Stacy went upstairs trailed by Mati who dragged along the red replacement scarf she'd gotten him in lieu of the one the police had taken as evidence. Clearly, he hoped to get a game of tug going before bedtime. Her plane ticket lay on her dresser. Initially, she'd saved every extra cent earned in the business to plow into expansion. Hiring Ilsa had been her first move in that direction. Now Dean used Ilsa's services. She'd split the bank account with Xochi and used her portion for air fare, warmer clothes, and the down payment on a rented flat in Schwabing, the student district of Munich, once very Bohemian. Near two universities where she could take language courses and the vast English gardens for activities, she considered the location ideal for her purposes of acquiring a new language—and staying away from Dean and all that reminded her of him. Mati didn't know it yet as he gazed at her expectantly with his dark button eyes and the ratty red scarf in his mouth, but he'd be wearing a blue bow on Christmas when she gave him to Edie.

What if she took that scarf right now and put it in the window? Across the way, no light shone in Dean's condo. The team would fly in tomorrow morning. No chance he'd see her plea until afternoon. Suppose she waited here for him? Would he cross Canal Street which now seemed as wide and deep as a real waterway, and just as difficult to traverse since their breakup? Or had she cried wolf one too many times and now must be devoured by her own regret?

What would she say if he ran to her rescue again? I

need you, Dean. I love you. That's the emergency. Dumb idea. He'd be with Ilsa who had slacked off on her duties since she latched onto Dean. Stacy took up one end of the scarf and played with Mati until he settled down for the night. If only going to sleep would be as easy for her.

****

Dean Billodeaux arrived at his condo, stressed, exhausted, and in need of sleep being too wound up after the game and unable to nap on the plane with any success. His phone buzzed again. Ilsa had no conception of the strength and energy expended during a season of football. Throw in the tension of trying to keep the Sinners undefeated, a feat his father had never accomplished, and more sex with her simply seemed like a waste of vitality needed elsewhere. He'd specifically asked her not come to his place out of consideration for Tom. The apartment he'd gotten for her wasn't all that far away. He'd go when he felt like it, and her incessant phone messages didn't encourage him.

In the past, he'd let his girlfriends break up with him, lack of commitment being their number one reason. Since arriving in New Orleans, he hadn't dated anyone long enough for it to be a problem. This time, he'd have to take the initiative. He planned to tell Ilsa that he'd be going to Lorena Ranch for Christmas to spend time with family and say a difficult farewell to Stacy. He wanted to make things right between them before she left. His mother had asked that he not bring Ilsa, maybe later on New Year's Eve after Stacy was gone, but he wouldn't blame this on his mom.

Ilsa might be put out and maybe not put out in

other ways. He didn't care. Her anger would be appeased by an expensive gift, he was certain, and he'd offer to get her on a plane to visit her own kin for the holidays. She had hinted long and hard that she wanted jewelry for Christmas. He'd gone to an expensive and reputable shop only blocks from his condo and purchased a diamond tennis bracelet with good-sized stones. The prissy male clerk with the neatly trimmed silver mustache suggested that tennis bracelets might be a trifle out of style and perhaps he should consider a more complex custom design with colored stones.

"Just put the receipt in the box. She can return it later if she wants something else," Dean told the dapper little man who muttered *tres romantique* before wrapping the item in their signature black box and gold bow.

He checked the latest text message. "I have something wonderful for you, *Liebling*. Come quickly to me." Probably another sexy nightie to model or erotic oils to rub into his skin. That the idea didn't titillate but only made him weary told him something. He was tired of Ilsa and often wondered if he'd wanted her for any other reason than to irritate Stacy. After the holidays but before the playoffs, he'd tell her they were done, quick, clean, and honest the way such things should be handled. *Ilsa, you are a beautiful and intelligent woman, but I don't love you.* By that time Stacy would be in Germany, unless on Christmas day he could convince her to remain here.

The phone buzzed again. This time he chose to answer with one short phrase. "On my way."

As he'd anticipated, Ilsa opened the door and displayed herself in a very festive red lace naughty nightie and a jaunty Santa cap perched on her pale blonde hair. The apartment was dim and lit by dozens of fat candles set on mirrored surfaces as if she'd prepared for the meeting of a secret cult. Christmas carols, sounding very much like the von Trapp family singers played in German. She'd set a special scene for him amid a better quality of modern furniture than she'd rented in the past.

Dean forced a smile as she kissed his cheek marking him with red lipstick. He rubbed it away with his thumb and thrust the jewelry box at her. "Sounded like you wanted to exchange gifts early so here you go."

Eagerly, she tore off the wrapping and held out her thin, white wrist to allow him to put on the bracelet. Turning her hand, she made the diamonds flash in the multicolored lights of a tall Christmas tree obviously custom decorated by a florist and standing in a corner. "Oh, I love it, and I love you so much. Come sit beside Ilsa and let me show how much I like this present." She arrayed herself on the white leather sofa and patted the cushion beside her.

"Not now. Look, I have to go to the ranch for Christmas. It's going to be just Mom, Dad and my brothers and sisters. We're having a farewell party for Stacy only for the family, so I thought you might want to fly home and spend time with yours. My treat." Maybe, just maybe, she'd stay there and that would be the end of them.

"I think you will not want me to go away. Here, open your present." She handed him a tall and heavy box sitting on the genuine teak coffee table.

Dean drew out a large beer stein traditionally

decorated with a merry couple garbed in lederhosen and a dirndl on one side, a castle on the other all wreathed in edelweiss, and an engraved pewter lid—"To Dean with love from Ilsa" and the date. Except for the inscription, he'd seen plenty like it, but thanked her politely. "This will look great in my game room. Thanks."

"Every time you see it you will think of Ilsa and what fun we have, but look inside."

Cautiously, he raised the lid and put his hand in deep, really expecting something along the line of edible underwear or penis rings. He fished out a piece of paper from its depths and unfolded the note—maybe like one of those homemade certificates for hugs and kisses kids made, but in Ilsa's case sure be some exotic sexual pleasure.

"Read!"

"Congratulations. In July you will be a Papa. Huh?" Not a good time for his throwing hand to develop the shakes.

"*Ja, Ja*, we have a baby next year. Now we celebrate. The doctor says is okay, but nothing too rough."

"How long have you known?" He seemed to be losing his wind as well since the words barely came out.

"I am almost two months, but Ilsa is so healthy, I do not have the vomiting. I am not so sure until I have my appointment this morning."

"I thought you were on the pill."

"Ach, *nein*. They make me swell. I use the diaphragm. Sometimes, we have such a good time I forget to put it in. *Macht nichts*. Now we get married and have a beautiful child together."

Dean found himself using the words planned only an hour ago. "Ilsa, you are a beautiful, and intelligent woman, but I don't love you."

The Merry Christmas in Bavaria act stopped right there. Ilsa's eyes turned cold as only light blue eyes can. "You want to pay me to get rid of it."

Was that a question or a suggestion? He didn't know. "No, I may not go to church very often, but I am Catholic. I'll see you and the child are well taken care of. I want to be a part of its life and a good father, but I will not marry you."

"Fine, then. You take care of me. You want to have sex now?"

"No, I believe we are done with that. My lawyers will get in touch and draw up an agreement for support. My mom can recommend an obstetrician. She's had plenty of experience. No drinking alcohol and you eat right, okay?"

"This I know. I am not a *Dummkopf*."

"No, but I am. Merry Christmas, Ilsa." Dean moved toward the door seeking escape as if he were pursued by three tackles.

Ilsa followed close behind and shoved the stein at him. "You forget your other gift."

"Yeah, thanks." He walked out with the tall stein in the crook of his arm. It stayed there until he turned into his brownstone and gave it to Arturo instead of a tip. Numb, he took the elevator and arrived at his condo, quiet, empty, Tom nowhere around. If ever he needed a brother, best friend and wingman, it was now, but Tom had been cool to him since before Thanksgiving. They'd had words when he returned from Ilsa's place after doing more than dropping her off.

With the Seahawks playing in the background, Tom had said, "Look, I'm over the way you took Ilsa. Who needs woman so fickle she'll drop you in the middle of a date? But did you have to rub your mistress in Stacy's face at a family gathering?"

"Isla is not my mistress. I'm helping her out with rent is all."

"Believe what you want to believe. You better sit down and watch this game. The Seahawks are young and rough. I'm willing to bet it will be us and them in the Super Bowl." Dean fell back into one of the recliners, but Tom had gotten up from his and headed to his room. "I'm only the kicker. What do I know?"

Where was his brother now when he needed him? Tom had iced him out saying he had things to do and not ridden back to the condo with him. Maybe they'd see each other at Mariah's later. Not likely now as he had no desire to go there.

Dean sat in the oncoming darkness without turning on a light. He'd let down the team, his fans, his family, and most especially his mother. Daddy Joe would understand, but how many times had he told Dean to be careful—a hundred, a thousand? And Stacy, he'd left her for making him feel foolish and being deceptive. Her early attempts at getting him to notice her in a new way seemed almost laughable now. He really had saved her from Prince and maybe Kent, though that would be debated in court. Who had made the greater fool of him? No question about that. In a case like this, who rescued the rescuer?

Dean moved through the apartment and flicked on his bedroom light. He rooted though his clothes finding the parrot shirt washed clean of Stacy, then what he really wanted—a red Sinners jersey. He opened his drapes, hung it over the curtain rod, and waited.

Chapter Thirty

Stacy finished her obligations early. Most of her business clients had gone home for the holidays but not before showering her with small gifts of candy, wine, gift cards, and in the case of Don Juan, some pretty costly perfume that she would probably never use. She placed these offerings gathered from her office under her purple and silver-ornamented tree and plugged in the lights. Might as well make a try at being festive.

Indulging in a bad habit, she raised her shade to see if Dean had gotten home. A light burned in his bedroom window. Wonderful, he probably entertained Ilsa right now, or more likely the other way around. Strange that he'd left the drapes open. Fearful of paparazzi with long lenses, he never did that. Odder still that he'd slung something over the rod. In the lowering light of December, she made out his number seven on a red jersey. Dean did not self-aggrandize. No matter how much she tweaked him about it, he lacked Prince Dobbs' huge ego.

The wrongness of the view bothered her deeply. Mati snuffled at her feet. She picked him up and showed him the scene. "What do you think? Is Dean in trouble?" Mati yipped twice. "I'll take that as a yes. Be good. I have to go over there."

Last minute Christmas shoppers and employees getting off work clogged the sidewalks in the chill, damp air. The lights on Canal Street took forever to change, and drivers in a hurry to get home took chances making rash turns into traffic. An overburdened streetcar blocked the crosswalk momentarily. At last, she reached the other side as fast as she could move in the straight skirt of her gray suit and hurried to the entry of the brownstone building. Arturo opened the door, but stopped her before she could pass.

"Miss Stacy, would you return this to Mr. Billodeaux? It seems to be a personal gift and, well, I'd appreciate a small gratuity more. Shall I call to say you are on your way up?" He handed over a large beer stein.

"I think he knows." She read the engraving on the lid. Dean had given away a gift from Ilsa? Great, they'd broken up, and now he expected to rebound back to her, making her come running to him. Furious, she got on the elevator and stalked to his apartment the second the door opened. Her sensible business heels struck the marble floor of the small foyer with a staccato like gunfire. Stacy raised her hand to knock, but his door opened. Dean lifted her off her feet in an embrace and twirled her inside. "Thank God, you came. I've never needed anyone more."

How long had she waited to hear words like those? But Stacy steeled herself. She held out the stein when he set her down. "Here, Arturo would rather have money. I take it you and Ilsa are finished."

Dean put the stein on a side table and drew her to the brown velour couch. "Sit down because I need to. Ilsa and I are finished dating but not with each other. Ah, Stace, I screwed up big time. She's pregnant." He stared into the fire of the glowing gas logs, the only light in the living room, and did not meet her eyes.

Stacy's mind went in the logical direction. "And because you are such a white knight, you are going to marry her regardless of how you feel about her." Suddenly, being Dean's rebound girl seemed preferable. No chance of that now.

"No. I can't do it. I'll take care of her and the child. I'll be a father to it as my dad was to me, but I don't love her." He gripped both her hands as if she might try to escape and hung his head. "I'm a big disappointment to everyone including you."

"Not to me. You're only human, Dean. The team expects you to be your father on the field. You act out one time, and they come down on you. Aunt Nell may never admit it, but you were the first and, she thought at the time, only child to come into her life. I think she still sees you as her perfect baby boy."

"Hey, she never let me get away with anything."

"But being the first, she always expected you to take the high ground. That's hard to maintain."

"Thanks. You're letting me off easy. Stacy, I held back my feelings when you were growing up. I still denied them when you were right there waiting across the street. You took the first steps to bring us together when I couldn't. We were so right together, then I threw it all away like a bad pass, so full of myself, so self-righteous."

Stacy freed a hand. "Damn right. I've always said you weren't perfect."

"Would you let me finish? This is hard. I used Ilsa to get over you and probably just to annoy you. She used me, too, evidently as an ever-lasting meal ticket. She said she practiced birth control."

"Dean, you might be a brilliant quarterback, but

when it comes to women, not so much." She twisted her other hand free.

"Please, don't go. I'm trying to make a point."

"Another big score?"

"Maybe, it's up to you. Listen, I know this is a rotten time to say I love you when Ilsa and the child will be in our lives forever. I don't know if you can live with that. But, Princess, you are the only woman I want to marry. Rescue me."

Stacy smoothed away that curl that always hung down on his forehead. "Yes, far from perfect, but no one is. I always imagined I'd make you grovel at my feet someday while offering me a diamond fit for royalty. Then, we'd be married in a huge white wedding in June. I don't see that happening now."

"I can grovel, get you a big honking diamond, do whatever a white wedding is in June. I need you so very much to see me through this mess." He took her hand again and started to slide to his knees on the floor.

"Get up! You are really bad at this."

"I admit I'm no Don Juan when it comes to proposals."

"Oh, you're going to throw him in my face and still expect me to marry you?"

"No, I only wish I were that suave. Stacy, will you marry me—without groveling or a big ring in my hand—but whenever you want, wherever you want?"

As usual, her mind worked on the details. "It wouldn't be right to do anything before the baby is born. I should go to Germany as planned and return in September. We could quietly get engaged then and have a small wedding the following spring."

"Stace, that's two Super Bowls away, but did I hear

a yes buried in there somewhere?"

"Considering that I planned to marry you since I was fourteen, it is a yes."

He smirked. "I knew you weren't telling the truth when you said it was only a crush."

She bombarded him with several of his little multi-colored throw pillows until he grabbed her wrist. "I'm feeling better now. Bad enough that I conceived a child without any forethought on a woman I barely like, but I thought I'd lost you, too. If you hadn't seen my plea for help in the window and come over here, I don't know what I would have done."

"Hopefully, crossed the street for me, you big lout."

"Anytime from now on, Princess. Come here."

Their long embrace had reached the urgent need to go to the bedroom and undress phase when someone punched in the key code. They didn't stop.

Tom looked at the Anchi Services scarf draped over the back of the sofa, Stacy's unbuttoned suit jacket, Dean's open shirt. "That's right, it's only me. Hi, Stacy. Appears you two have made up." He wandered closer. "Nice stein."

Dean leaned back but kept his arm around Stacy as if she might change her mind and run off across four lanes of heavy traffic. "You are welcome to have it."

Tom peered at the inscription. "No, thanks. Have you told Ilsa that you and Stacy are back together?"

"No. She's pregnant."

"Stacy?"

"Ilsa."

"Oh, I saw that coming." Tom casually flipped the lid of the stein open and shut a few times.

"I'm beginning to believe I'm the only one who didn't. Say, do you think it could be yours?" Dean's face turned hopeful.

"No way. I suited up, worn my rubber raincoat every time. I might be your wingman, but I won't marry Ilsa for you." Tom backed hands-up toward his half of the condo.

"I wouldn't ask you to do that, but maybe you'd be best man in my wedding to Stacy whenever it takes place."

Tom looked from one face to the other. "You are one forgiving woman, Stace."

"Oh, we've been working up to this for years and years."

"I guess you have. If you can tolerate Ilsa and her child in your life I suppose you can handle all the jokes the team will make about Cajuns marrying their cousins."

"We're not cousins!" they said in unison.

Chapter Thirty-One

Ilsa took the offer of a first class ticket to Germany where she would tell her family about the baby and the man who fathered it, as well as celebrate the holidays. While Dean drove her to the airport, she chattered gaily about German Christmas customs. He hoped she'd get her fill of *stollen* and *pfeffernusse*, but made it clear that if she wanted a settlement she must return directly after January first to undergo prenatal DNA testing for paternity and sign the legal documents if he proved to be the father. Just what he needed with one game to go and playoffs on his mind.

"But of course, you are the papa. You are angry with Ilsa right now for her little mistake, but later you will see our beautiful baby and be happy." The tennis bracelet glittered on her arm as they parked, and Dean took her bags to check-in. "Will you wait with me for my flight?"

"No, I have a lot to do. Christmas at the ranch, remember?"

"*Ja*, next year I will be family, I think."

"I'm sure you and the baby will be welcome—next year." He wondered if she thought he'd marry her once paternity was proved or perhaps after the baby came. No way. But Ilsa didn't know he'd reconciled with Stacy, and he certainly wasn't about to tell her in a crowded airport. The way those two women disliked each other she'd create a scene that would end up with him spread-eagled against a wall and in the tabloids the next day touting some bogus charge.

After receiving Ilsa's lavish goodbye kiss, Dean sped from short-term parking and back to New Orleans. No way would he let Stacy trot off to Germany, too, without an engagement ring on her finger. He sought out the same jewelry store where he'd gotten the bracelet and unfortunately drew the exact clerk he'd had the last time. Not one to waste time, Dean got right to the point. "I need an engagement ring."

"Ah, the lady was pleased with her bracelet."

"I guess. She wore it this morning. The ring is for someone else.

"I see. We at Schifferman's guarantee absolute discretion," the immaculate little man said, though his gray brows, so shapely they might have been waxed, rose.

"I need a big honking diamond, a good one."

"Would ten carats do?"

"Is that honking size?"

"I would say so, sir." The clerk went to the back and returned sometime later with a tray of four rings displayed on black velvet. "The first is a ten-carat, blue-white diamond solitaire with…"

"No, I need something special. What about the one on the end?"

"A square princess cut diamond, fancy intense yellow in color with fifty-eight facets and extra cuts on the chevrons for added sparkle. The eighteen carat gold band is set with fourteen round brilliants…"

Showing his ability to make snap decisions much like his father, Dean said, "I don't give a fuck about the band. This is it. Made for a princess. Put it in a box. I need to meet someone pretty soon. "

"Perhaps, we should discuss financing first?"

Dean whipped out his black AMEX card and shoved it across the counter. "It's good."

"Excuse me, but I do have to check." The clerk scooped up the card and his tray and disappeared into the backroom again. He returned quite soon with an obsequious smile on his face and the ring in a black leather box. "Your charge went through with no trouble at all, Mr...ah."

"It's pronounced Be-yo-doe. I'm the quarterback for the Sinners."

"Oh, yes! I knew the name was familiar. I don't really follow sports, but Prince Dobbs buys all his gold chains and pinkie rings here, one of my favorite clients. He hasn't your superb taste, but does know what he likes. How is he doing since his unfortunate accident?"

"I understand he's found Jesus. That might be bad for your business."

"I'm very afraid so. However, the next time you require the finest in service, please ask for Leslie. My card." He slipped it across the counter along with the ring in a tiny bag and the credit card. "Merry Christmas and good luck with—whoever." Leslie's hand twirled in the air.

"Same to you." Dean shoved the ring into his pocket and walked to the parking garage to get the Mustang and take Stacy home to the ranch.

****

Stacy had her own last minute shopping to do while Dean took Ilsa to the airport. She drafted Tom to drive her to the nearest animal shelter and walk the rows of cages looking for the right dog. Mati on a leash trotted along with them slowing their pace as he tried to make friends with all the captives thrusting their black noses against the wire. The matron at the desk of doggie prison had asked if the Bichon Frise was a surrender dog. "We get them sometimes because they are hard to housebreak."

"He almost has the hang of it. Soon he'll be outside more. Could we see the animals, please?"

"You know, you shouldn't get anyone a dog for Christmas without asking first. You'd be surprised how many half-grown pups we get here in the spring," the gray-haired volunteer with a nametag reading Maude said as she unlocked a metal inner door. Immediately, the air filled with the sound of desperate barking that seemed to say, "Get me outta here. Pick me! Pick me!"

Stacy took Tom's arm. "So many of them. It's sad. I thought about looking for one like Macho."

Tom shook his head. "Macho was one of a kind. You can't replace him. He came from Texas, a good ole boy, not slum dogs like most of these."

"Tom, I'm surprised at you. None of us can choose where we are born."

"Sorry, just being loyal to Macho, I guess."

"We get purebreds here, too," their guide said, offended. "But there's nothing wrong with an animal without a fancy pedigree. They all have lots of love to give."

"What's the hardest type of dog to place?" Stacy asked, overwhelmed by the sheer number of choices.

"Old ones and your generic big black dog, Lab mixes most of them, good-natured, large, and ordinary looking. People want cute little pets like the one you got. We have six bbd's in the shelter right now."

"Show them to us, but, I'm sorry, no old ones. This is for an active little boy who will want to play."

That narrowed the choice to four. One bristled and growled when Mati made an advance. Another cowered in the rear of the cage afraid to come forward. A third still nursed a litter of puppies abandoned along with their mother. "She and the pups will be available in a few weeks, and we'll spay her before adoption," the volunteer offered like a good salesperson.

"No, I'll be out of the country by then. I need a dog now."

"Last one, Diamond Lil we called her for that white patch on her chest. About six months old and found wandering the streets. She's been spayed, has all her shots, a sweet one, aren't you Lil?" The woman reached through the wire and scratched behind one of a pair of perfectly folded black ears.

Mati pushed forward to rub noses. Lil lay down to accommodate his short stature and give him a good sniff. "Could you let her out?"

"Sure, but get ready. She's got lots of energy." Diamond Lil plunged and jumped and fawned and licked on the end of a tight leash. Mati danced with her. "I admit she needs training," Maude confessed.

Stacy opened her purse and took out two dog treats. "Sit, Lil," she said meeting the dog's large black eyes. Mati sat at once and waited in anticipation of a snack. Lil hesitated, then plunked down beside him, her butt still wiggling. Both got their reward. "We'll take her. I have a little time to work on training before I leave."

As the pleased volunteer led Lil to the office to

complete her paperwork, Tom said, "Why leave now when you and Dean are back together?"

"I honestly can't stand the thought of being here when another woman has Dean's child. I'm giving Mati to Edie because I can't take him with me. Anyhow, I can't give Edie a dog and not get one for T-Rex. Besides, she'll be company for Mati. I don't want him to be lonely."

Tom scrunched his freckled forehead. "So you're giving Dean to Ilsa? Sure sounds that way to me."

"No! I'm shattered over leaving him and Mati. Don't you dare tell your brother that. He has enough problems. Let's go. Dean must be waiting.

Chapter Thirty-Two

Dean was waiting, parked in the cul-de-sac deserted by paparazzi since he failed to come here any more. Instead of "Merry Christmas, Princess" or greeting Stacy with a kiss, he said, "Another dog?" as Lil bounded at his feet wearing a new red studded collar around her black neck.

"For T-Rex. I'll explain later."

"Tom, is the dog riding with you?" Dean asked.

"Heck, no. I already got the three sisters and Teddy to pick up. Diamond Lil is all yours to transport."

Dean eyed the leather seats of his Mustang GT. "Got a blanket we can put down, Stacy?"

"I have one in the back of the SUV." Tom handed over an old army blanket.

"What would I do without you, bro?"

"Pretty bad. We both know that."

Xochi appeared with her overnight bag in-hand. Tom stowed it and her in the SUV. "One down, three to go. See you in Chapelle." They started home for Christmas.

Dean retraced his Thanksgiving trip with Ilsa, the landscape being bleaker now with most of the cypress trees bare except for an occasional holdout still bearing leaves of rusty orange as they crossed the swamps. The small towns along the way made up for this with crèches in front of their churches and brightly lit wreaths, bells, and Santas on their lampposts. Finally, they arrived in Chapelle, passing the live oaks on the square, which hosted a frenzy of angel figures in their boughs. The gates at Lorena Ranch wore two large evergreen wreaths with red bows, and the oaks bore white lights strung along their branches lighting the way to the house.

The barking of two excited dogs brought the youngest Billodeauxs to the kitchen doorway. "Mati!" Edie screamed and held out her arms for the Bichon Frise to launch himself into her embrace.

"T-Rex, I brought the other dog for you," Stacy said as the rest of the family spilled out onto the lawn.

Dean's smallest brother took a good look at Lil quivering with good will. He'd lived on a ranch his whole short life. "It's a girl," he said with disgust.

"Would you rather have a dog like Mati?" Stacy asked him.

"Jeez, no. I want a big one." T-Rex held his arms wide to give a measure. Lil took that as an invitation and jumped against him, knocking the boy to the ground and licking his face until he laughed. Sitting up, he said, "I guess she's all right."

"Her name is Diamond Lil, and she's more than all right. Someone get me a tennis ball. She's supposed to have Labrador retriever in her."

Trin raided the sports closet and returned with the ball. T-Rex threw it hard as he could, not a bad arm for a seven-year-old. Lil raced off after her quarry leaving poor, short-legged Mati way behind in the chase. She returned eagerly to T-Rex but engaged in a tug of war for her prize. Stacy took the ever-handy dog treat from her purse and commanded, "Drop!" while holding out the morsel. Lil cocked her head debating whether to keep the ball or go for the treat. When Mati sat on his haunches to beg, she gave in and deposited the slobbery orb at T-Rex's feet.

"Oh, cool! I'll keep her." He pitched the ball again and sent Lil racing.

"Might have been nice if someone asked before getting him a dog," Nell said.

"She's a rescue dog, Aunt Nell. Should I take her back?" Stacy said, knowing the answer in advance.

"Right. Hit me in my soft spot. She's here to stay."

Stacy turned over the snacks to Dean's little brother. "Here, she isn't allowed one until she gives you the ball. Keep practicing. Someone see if we have another ball for Mati so he has a chance, too."

Dean stood there watching Stacy persuade people to do what she wanted them to do in a subtle sort of way, not bossy like she'd been in childhood. He studied her technique—the special object, the tender plea—and thought he could pull it off without getting into an argument. Moving to where his parents stood, Joe with his arm around Nell, he asked, "Could you keep the horde out here for a little while? I want to talk to Stacy in the den."

"Good to see you must have made up if she rode here with you," his mom said.

"That's right, son. Go talk it out. Do it better this time," his dad directed as if coaching him in handing off a football.

"I'll try." Dean hefted Stacy's shopping bags full of presents. His offerings ran more to generous gift cards. "Stacy, let's go have a look at the Christmas tree."

"Isn't it the same as always?"

"Maybe not. We should put the presents under it."

"Okay." She followed him into the den where a fire burned brightly shining on Joe's football trophies and awards. A towering tree scraped the high ceiling in one corner making the angel on top hunch over a bit. Covered with the usual gleaming balls, garlands, and strings of lights, its boughs harbored every homely Christmas ornament ever made by the Billodeaux children. A cascade of gifts sat under it because last year T-Rex and Edie had declared they knew Santa wasn't real. Dean left the sacks beneath its boughs without unloading them.

"Looks the same to me," Stacy said, standing back a little."

"Sit. Look harder."

While she did, he got down on one knee, not groveling but more like a player waiting to be called into the game, and took out the ring. Her eyes turned back to his. "Stacy Polasky, will you wear this ring as a symbol that you will marry me?"

She took the ring and held it up to the light. "It's breathtaking—as if it holds crushed ice and fire inside at the same time."

"That's called a fancy yellow princess cut," he said showing off his newly acquired knowledge. "Is it honking enough?"

"Absolutely. But I can't accept this now. I'd get mugged in Schwabing with this on my finger—which doesn't mean I don't love it."

"If you think you're going abroad without an engagement ring on your finger, you are completely mistaken. The world is full of Dr. Riveras."

"Dean, since I've been in New Orleans, there has been no one but you. If it would make you feel better maybe we could go to LeClerc's in town and get a little promise ring."

Dean shook his head. "Like the one Heather McAvoy wanted from me? No way." He got off his knees and sat beside her on the big brown leather sofa battered by children and dogs over the years. "Stacy, don't go to Germany. Stand by me." He put the ring on her finger.

"My plans are all in place, I—"

"You need to make a halftime adjustment. I want you to come to the next game and see if I can make it a perfect season. I want you sitting in the stands at the Super Bowl because I'm taking the Sinners there this year."

"Won't it be crowded with both Ilsa and me in the family box? Dean, do you remember when you said you wished you'd been my first lover? Well, I wish I was the one carrying your child. I don't believe I can bear to stay around and watch her grow big with your baby."

Dean grinned with soupcon of his father's old wickedness. "I can be a good Catholic. We'll start a family as soon as we get married."

"Not what I had in mind. Think of the scandal if we rush this and you have a fiancée and a pregnant girlfriend at the same time."

"Okay, I can handle it, but if Princess Anastasia Marya Polasky can't, give the ring back." Oh, he did know her weaknesses and played upon them.

Stacy clenched her fingers into a fist when he tried to take the ring. "I was thinking of you and the family. Of course, I can handle it. My classes don't actually begin until April, and I must be here for Kent Gonsoulin's trial, whenever that takes place. I only wanted to get away from your being with Ilsa."

"So you'd be willing to stay until after the Super Bowl and see how it goes?" Dean negotiated.

"Maybe, I guess. But, I was going to give Mati to Edie for Christmas because I couldn't take him with me. That's why I got a dog for T-Rex, too, so he wouldn't be jealous."

"I'll buy her another from the same breeder. Print out a picture of a Bichon Frise, put it in a box with a note that says she's getting Mati's brother. Problem solved. If you must go in April, Mati can visit here at the ranch until you return."

Stacy cupped his face in her hands and used a forefinger to push back that wayward curl on his forehead, a gesture becoming a habit now that she'd touched him so often. "I'll stay."

"Finally." He went in for the big, dramatic kiss, but the first of the horde of Billodeauxs swung into the room searching for provisions.

"Hey, you done in here? All the snacks are on the coffee table. A man could starve waiting on you guys to move," Mack complained, expressing the outsized appetite of a seventeen-year-old boy.

"By all means, gorge yourself. We're done here." Dean took Stacy's hand to help her from the sofa.

As they left his corn chip-crunching, salsa-dipping brother who'd flopped next to them, she stared at the Christmas tree again. "I still don't see what's so special about the tree."

"I just gave you a honking big engagement ring in front of it, Stace. That's what's special about it. Must I do all the work?"

"Yes. I think you must."

****

At seven with the entire family in attendance, the Billodeauxs sat down for a formal Christmas Eve dinner, one of the few times a year when the silver and good china made it out of the closet. Brinsley moved around the table ladling seafood gumbo into each gold-rimmed soup bowl already containing a mound of rice.

No one dipped a spoon until Nell offered a simple grace. "We thank God for another year of health and prosperity, but most of all for the family gathered around us. Amen. Would anyone like to add anything?"

Dean stood up and got moans from the teen-aged boys poised to eat. "I have some news. Stacy and I are engaged, and Ilsa is having my baby." Spoons fell into the gumbo splattering the Irish linen tablecloth Brinsley had personally ironed. The clink of the heavy silver ladle dropping against the tureen sounded like the tolling of a bell in the stunned silence.

Mama Nell got it together first. "We are so happy for you and Stacy. Our first grandchild, wonderful."

Daddy Joe chimed in with the practical advice. "Use my attorneys. Back in the day, they kept my DNA profile available and had a template for a paternity agreement. Lots of experience fighting off these suits. Dean, you were the only one proven to be my son, but look how well that worked out. It couldn't be anyone else's kid?"

"Maybe Tom's, but Ilsa is fairly certain."

The triplet teens suddenly took more interest in dinner conversation than they had in years. Tom turned the brilliant color reserved for embarrassed redheads.

"Not mine. I listened to Dad. Mack, you'd better, too."

Trin pushed his heavy, black-framed glasses back to the bridge of his nose and said, "Why do you assume I can't get a girl?"

"Because you're a geek." Mack, sitting beside him, messed up the dark curls hanging in his brother's eyes.

"Aw, leave him alone or I'll run you down with my chair," Teddy said. He had plenty of claims to geekdom, too, plus being in a wheelchair much of the time.

"I don't understand. If Dean is marrying Stacy, how can Ilsa have his baby?" Edie asked, her big, brown eyes perplexed in her elfin face.

"Because people are just like dogs and horses. You don't have to be married to have babies," T-Rex said, happy to share his knowledge.

"That's not what Mawmaw Nadine says. I'm going to ask her again at the hymn service," Edie answered. The much older and wiser Lorena snickered.

"Don't do that! We'll talk later, Edie," Mama Nell exclaimed. "We are celebrating the birth of Christ and a very special engagement that will make Stacy an official Billodeaux. Next year, we will welcome a new child to the family. Now eat your gumbo before it gets cold."

"Ahem," Jude said, not afraid to defy her mother, which she did far too often. "We haven't seen the ring yet. The way Stacy has been walking around with her hand in her pocket all evening, I thought she had a contagious rash."

Stacy, who had remained silent, finally revealed the ring and passed it around the long table. "You know I might want to keep my own name."

"No way," Dean replied.

Gentle Annie attempted a suggestion. "You could hyphenate, except Polasky-Billodeaux sounds terrible and no little kid could print it on a form."

"They will settle that later." Nell admired the engagement ring, then passed it to her daughters.

Jude studied the diamond and held it up to the light of the candelabra. "Who would have thought my big brother had good taste."

"I don't, but someone named Leslie does."

"Figures."

She passed it to Lorena who said dreamily, "I want one just like this," and tried it on her finger.

Xochi nodded her approval. "Beautiful, but an amethyst might have been better."

With hardly a glance, the guys passed it back to Stacy. Brinsley offered to re-heat the soup.

"No, they'll eat it as is or not at all. Please bring out the turkey, or we'll never get to church," Nell said.

They ate a wonderful dinner beautifully served right down to a plum pudding Brinsley had imported from England and flamed with brandy in the darkened dining room for special effect. Leftovers tomorrow so that he and Corazon could be with their families.

Adjourning to the den, each person picked out one gift to open, a custom that had stopped a lot of wheedling and whining over the years. The rest would be saved until morning.

Stacy insisted Dean open her gift first. He held up a gold foil-wrapped object suspiciously shaped like a football and shook it next to his ear as if the contents would rattle, making Edie laugh. "I have no idea what this could be. Maybe it's made of chocolate."

"That would be so cool," T-Rex agreed enthusiastically. "You'll share, right?"

Dean peeled off the paper. "Sorry, kiddo. It's a real football. I really needed one of these. Looks like a used one, and somebody's dog gnawed it. Give a diamond to a person and this is what you get in return."

"It's priceless, you big lout! That's your game ball, the one you used to score the touchdown. I wouldn't let Angel keep it, and yes, Mati did get at it since it was under my bed. Sorry." Mati raised his weary head bedecked with a stick-on red bow by Edie at the mention of his name and lolled happily at Dean.

"Best gift ever even with the teeth marks."

Edie squealed and held up a tiny photo drawn from a large box. "It says I'm going to get Mati's brother as soon as he is born."

"I already got a dog," T-Rex countered. "She's big."

"She's undisciplined. That's why she's staying in the kitchen tonight," Nell said.

"Can't she sleep in my bedroom?" her youngest son begged.

"Fine. That's your gift. Everyone go spruce up for church. No Cajun casual this evening. And not a word to Mawmaw about the news when we see her tonight. Dean and Stacy will visit her tomorrow." Dean and Stacy gave Nell a not too thrilled with that idea look, but they would obey.

Though Nell held to her Protestant beliefs and raised all her daughters Episcopalian except Xochi whose deceased mother had begun raising her Catholic, she kept to a Billodeaux family tradition of attending the eleven p.m. hymn service at Ste. Jeanne d'Arc. At midnight, each person lit a candle and sang *Silent Night* with the lights low and the scent of the pine boughs around the poinsettias on the windowsills perfuming the air. A sense of serenity prevailed as they filed from the church after the service under a cold night sky filled with stars and past live oak trees bearing glowing angels. Edie nodded in Nell's arms. Joe hauled T-Rex, much heavier than his twin sister, back to the van.

"Peace in Chapelle—at least for tonight," Nell said as she led her brood home.

Chapter Thirty-Three

Knowing the sportscasters up in their booth were probably comparing him to his daddy right this minute, Dean Billodeaux paced the sidelines in the fourth quarter of the Atlanta game, the last of the regular season. Coach had taken him out at the half after he'd scored two touchdowns and suffered an equal number of sacks. Atlanta put one TD on the board, not much safety in those numbers. Dean wanted the perfect season more than he did a Super Bowl ring because the great Joe Billodeaux had never accomplished that—and for exactly the same reason.

"We already sewed up the best playoff spot, got home field advantage, and a week off while the wildcards duke it out. You need to be healthy and ready to go then. Nothing more the Falcons want to do than ruin your perfect season, and they are out for blood today. You're benched, son," Marty Buck decreed.

"I thought there were no unimportant games, Coach."

"That's true, but some are more important than others."

In went Dean's adequate but not brilliant backup, a guy named Leon Davies at the end of his career. He'd get the only Super Bowl ring of his life if the Sinners went that far. Davies had experience and could take his lumps, but he failed to put any points on the board the entire second half while Atlanta brought in another to tie the game. His final march down the field stalled at the sixty-yard line with under a minute to go. Out came Tommy the Toe who swung his leg a few times, cool and oblivious to the noise the home fans sent up to distract him, and prepared to kick a field goal. As usual, their opponents called a time out to put the freeze on him. Tom simply did a few stretches as he waited, then got back into position, ran his three paces and booted that ball over the goalposts with maybe three inches to spare and a slight shank to the right, not his prettiest kick, but it did the job. The Sinners surged onto the field, but Dean got to his brother first with a bone-crushing man-hug. Tom said simply, "You're welcome."

Both looked into the stands where the rest of their family sat, all of them on their feet, even Teddy who had pushed up on his braces. His father beamed with a pride fit to bust the buttons of his Sinners' blazer. Their mom, who always said football wasn't the most important thing in life, smiled and clapped. T-Rex jumped up and down undoubtedly claiming he'd do the same someday. Best of all, Stacy, wearing his ring, sat next to Xochi in her usual place—and Ilsa remained in Germany. The end of a perfect season and a not so perfect year.

****

Ilsa returned shortly after the start of the New Year, and being no *Dummkopf*, immediately retained her own attorney, one who specialized in divorce settlements. She underwent amniocentesis with an alacrity that said she felt sure of the results and waited a week for the results. The child proved to be both

Dean's and a boy. Negotiations began. Taking care of Ilsa's medical bills was a given, the rest not so easy. They worked on an agreement as the Sinners worked through three playoff games. At the first meeting, Stacy sat beside Dean at the wide boardroom table.

"What is she doing here?" Ilsa asked, radiating hostility.

"Because I want her here." Dean had his game face on, cool and hard, strong and focused.

Stacy doubted if Ilsa had ever seen that face before, being more accustomed to a visage of drooling lust, and it threw her off a bit. "Nice ring," she commented to Stacy as she jingled the diamond tennis bracelet on her wrist.

"Thank you. I like it very much." Their engagement had not been announced, but speculation ran wild about the ring in the tabloids and more reputable magazines. Stacy didn't plan to give Ilsa the news, but she dearly wanted to.

Isla appeared more well-fed than usual but not obviously pregnant. Stacy wished enormous weight gain and stretch marks on her, but considering the woman's tall frame, would most likely not get that satisfaction. All the better because the secret could be kept a little longer. The first thing Dean wanted was a non-disclosure agreement forbidding Ilsa to talk to the press.

"How am I to make enough money while I am pregnant if I cannot tell my story?" she asked. She parlayed that into a house in the garden district with a nice living allowance.

"To remain in my name if I'm paying for it," Dean said.

Stacy shook her head. "No, let her own the house because otherwise…" She didn't need to say if he kept the house Ilsa would appear to be his mistress.

"Okay, I get it." Dean conceded that but wanted some of his own demands—the child to be born and raised in south Louisiana with thirty days allowed each year for him to visit his grandparents in Germany or travel abroad with his mother. Otherwise, the boy stayed at the ranch if Ilsa chose to roam without him. If she violated this, her living allowance, which might as well have been alimony, would cease. She agreed.

The child support was liberal, but Ilsa's lawyer tried to attach a clause having it go up whenever Dean signed a new contract. Unlike Leslie at the jewelry store, he did know sports. Dean would be a free agent at the end of the season with really big money rolling in if the Sinners wanted to retain him. Dean's attorneys fended that off. So it went, more hard fought and stressful than the three playoff games where the Sinners rolled over the wildcard team, easily took their second game, but practically fought to the death in the third round home game that made them winners of the championship. With that, Ilsa made one more demand. She wanted and got a ticket to the Super Bowl to sit with the family.

Chapter Thirty-Four

The Seahawks it was, exactly as Tom predicted. The venue, Levi's Field in Santa Clara, California, home of the Niners, still had its new stadium smell and all the cultural amenities the Silicon Valley could offer: fine art on the walls, a gastropub using herbs grown on the rooftop near the solar panels, and food ordered by smart phone delivered directly to the seats. The place practically came with a good weather guarantee far from the fogs and whipping winds of old Candlestick Park and featured a sod field kept green with reclaimed water and open to the sun.

Ordinarily, the Billodeaux family preferred being close to the field, but considering the delicate circumstances, they rented a luxury suite with enough room to keep Ilsa and Stacy a fair distance apart. Just before signing the final agreement, Isla had again challenged Stacy's presence and gotten pouty to the point of a refusal to cooperate. She voiced her intention to tell her story to the world in a soprano voice worthy in range and volume of a Wagnerian opera singer complete with horned helmet. Stacy laid claim to Dean loudly and clearly announcing their engagement to the woman, which had gone down like sour pickle juice after a hangover. Isla signed the papers, too smart to throw away what had been won, but no one knew when hostilities would break out again.

Arriving in California a week in advance of the game, Dean enjoyed a relatively peaceful round of press interviews and photo ops. Word of Ilsa's condition remained a secret within the family, but wouldn't for long even though she bore her pregnancy like a movie star with a baby bump so discreet going into the fourth month it left people guessing.

Mawmaw Nadine fussed about low birth weights and young women who cared more about their figures than a healthy baby. All things considered, she'd taken the news well with a sad shake of her head and the comment, "Why you always go for the foreign blondes, Deanie?"

Stacy with her Polish ancestry and no blood connection to Mawmaw knew herself to be included in that list, but Dean replied, "I take after my daddy before he met my mom, I guess." That put a stopper in the old woman's gob. "You and Stacy are legal since she don't have no Billodeaux in her," Mawmaw conceded with a great heaving of the ample bosom that had nursed five children. "I be praying for y'all and that *cher bebe*."

Remembering his mother's second and third pregnancies well, Dean worried about the small size of the baby bump, too. Nell squeezed his arm. "Thanks to the wonders of modern medicine, I never had a normal birth, always twins and triplets. Short as I am, I looked like a full moon rising from early on. Don't fret. I'll keep an eye on Ilsa and her diet at the game. I think she wants attention and acceptance. I can give her that much. I'm counting on Stacy to keep her cool." In other words, his mom would take care of everything. He left it her hands and turned his attention to the big game.

Dean swore his dad kept his nose pressed against

the glass of the luxury box for the entire event as he yearned to be nearer the field. Anyone who shelled out a thousand dollars plus per ticket got their money's worth this year. A rough and tumble first half brought the score to 21-21 going into the locker room, still anybody's game. Seattle took advantage of holes in the Sinner's defensive line, and Dean and his receivers made up for that with long spirals thrown and fantastic catches far down the field. Nothing much to discuss at the half except for the ass-chewing the defense got from Coach Buck. Both teams came back ready to rumble.

Dean took a hard sack late in the third quarter and spent some precious minutes out of the game. Leon Davies lost the ball and let Seattle score again. The Sinners came back tough and answered that one at the top of the fourth. Still tied, the clock ticked off the final minutes of the Super Bowl, and Seattle had the ball. Helpless, Dean paced and shouted support to his defense. Redemption came from their aging Samoan cornerback, Adam Malala, who stripped the ball from a receiver and ran it all the way back for the final touchdown. Seattle had run the clock down so far they had no chance to retaliate. After a ten year drought, the Sinners claimed another ring, Adam's second since he'd played a similar role in Joe's final victory.

Dean hardly cared about sharing the glory and would have preferred that Adam be MVP instead of him. He voiced that thought after he accepted the trophy with his family lined up behind him on the dais. Daddy Joe kept a firm grip around Ilsa's expanding waist, keeping her from being jostled in the crowd and looking out for his future grandson, possibly another Sinners quarterback still in the womb. He also held her back when Dean called Stacy forward and announced their engagement to the world. The Billodeauxs did know about teamwork.

Unfortunately, this led to some ugly fabrications in the gossip rags that Joe Billodeaux suffered from a mid-life crisis and had abandoned his wife and many children to start another family with a tall, blonde model. Dean stepped forward the following week at a press conference acknowledging the child as his conceived during a brief break in a his relationship with his fiancée. He answered no questions, but with the truth out, he did ask Stacy not to go to Germany at all. He had mastered running down a clock. At least, he thought he had.

"Look, sure, the baby is due in July, but we could have that white wedding thing you want in late August during preseason when I won't be playing much. I know it's hot and sticky then, but June in Louisiana isn't any better. Princess, I don't want to wait another season for you to be my wife."

"I don't know, Dean. I really should learn German and find out what Ilsa is calling me when she gets mad," his fiancée said with a perfectly straight face.

"I'll get you one of those language courses on CDs if it means that much to you."

"Oh, you can't really learn the vernacular from those." Stacy shook her head sadly as if he should know this already.

"Maybe early August then. I can probably carve out a week from training camp and take you to Munich where you can pick up all the curse words you want in the beer halls." He threw in that charming Billodeaux smile inherited directly from his daddy and hardly ever used on women by Dean.

"It's going to be hard to get a big wedding together that quickly. We should wait a year."

"I know having a wedding fit for a princess means a lot to you, but we've been waiting half our lives for this!" That damned curl of his flopped in his face.

Stacy pushed it away. Her radiant smile broke through. "I'm teasing, you big lout. That kind of wedding was a childhood dream. I've outgrown it. We can get married by a justice of the peace next week if you want."

"No, you are going to get the biggest, most honking wedding I can afford, maybe in the middle of July." He'd inched the date as far forward as he could go and just had to convince Stacy to run with it.

"Maybe if you get your other hind cheek tattooed with Stacy inside a heart for Valentine's Day, I might consider the end of July."

He'd lost some yardage and hadn't foreseen the trick play. "You're joking again, right Stace? You don't really want that, huh?"

This time her smile was unreadable. He'd never understand women as well as he did football.

Chapter Thirty-Five

Many hurdles had to be leapt between Valentine's Day and the last Saturday in July. Dean soon learned planning a big wedding was more complicated than his playbook. They went through the rigmarole of getting permission from the Episcopal priest in Chapelle to allow them to marry in the gothic cathedral on St. Charles, a building every bit as grand as old St. Louis on Jackson Square. He went through the pre-wedding interview, no sweat, figuring the Catholic version would have been worse. They tasted a dozen samples of cake, all white with different fillings, sweet! He thanked Jesus, Mary, and Joseph that he'd been banned from wedding dress shopping.

In the midst of the preparations, Kent Gonsoulin came to trial. Dean sat in the courtroom while Kent's high-priced lawyer grilled Stacy on the stand, implying that she'd lured the man to her office with the intention of having sex. Wisely, she'd dressed for court in one of her gray Anchi Services suits, the exact sort of ensemble she'd worn the day Prince got shot and told this to the jury. While she looked great in it, the outfit did not ooze sexual appeal. Coolly, she said Mr. Gonsoulin had asked to use the bathroom and returned exposing himself to her. She'd fled.

The defense asked if maybe his client had simply forgotten to zip up. "No, he let it all hang out." Stacy drew laughter from the audience. "He said he'd gotten it ready for me. I needed to pay for jilting him for the prom and letting my dog pee on his feet. He was ready to pop." Dean watched the back of Kent's neck go red, well, redder than usual. His lawyer made Stacy admit that Mr. Gonsoulin never actually touched her.

"I kicked his hand away from my ankle after he fell on the spilled pencils."

"Perhaps, he sought your assistance in getting up."

"He'd already gotten it up by himself before he slipped," Stacy replied. "I had no intention of joining him on the floor." More laughter. Way to go, Princess.

She told of running into Prince Dobbs and what ensued. No, she could not swear Mr. Gonsoulin intended to shoot her and had to confess he might have been trying to save her from a mugger. Stacy recounted Dean's arrival, summoned by a signal of putting a red scarf in the window, because she'd feared trouble with Kent. To hear her tell it, he'd been the unstained hero of the night. Remembering how he'd treated Stacy and what came after, Dean slumped down in his seat. At last, the judge dismissed her, saying she should remain available in case they needed to call her again.

The police officer testified next referring to photos of the Anchi office in disarray, the loan forms used to get an appointment with Miss Polasky, the red scarf in a bag, and the gun they had found at the scene. The paparazzo told his version. At last, Prince Dobbs was called into the courtroom, pausing to take Stacy's hand where she sat by Dean and say, "God bless you," as he passed. Prince walked like a man completely healed, but with most of his swagger drained away. He wore his hair in small, light brown fuzzy dreads all over his head that created an almost halo effect. With his honey-colored face clean-shaven and still bearing the light scars of Stacy's nails, he'd dressed in a conservative suit and tie, no tats showing, when he took the stand.

The defense made sure to display to the jurors pictures of the bearded Prince wearing his knit cap taken as he sat on the sidelines of a Sinners game. Yes, he'd been dressed entirely in black. "But that's not my color no more, man." He had to testify to his height and weight and condition at the time. "Recovering from a previous injury. I'm a little lighter now from all the PT, but I'll be rock hard and ready to run by September."

"So you sustained no serious injury due to my client's actions."

"I wouldn't say that, oh no. I died and saw Jesus. I forgive your client for my suffering like the Lord said to do." Prince thumped his chest a few times with a sizeable fist.

"Still grandstanding," Stacy whispered to Dean.

"He was an arrogant asshole, now he's a jerk for Jesus, but I can stand the new version a whole lot better," Dean said.

Then, Kent's lawyer asked why Prince had come to Stacy's house that evening.

"To make amends, man, to make amends."

"For what?"

"For thinking she wanted to have sex wit' me when she didn't. She stomped my foot good and, uh, while leaving I fell down her stairs." Prince's eyes rolled in Dean's direction and cut away again. He'd saved his own dignity and spared his quarterback. "Dr. Funk, the team shrink, said I got to apologize. My apology was not honest. That's why I got shot, Jesus said."

Stacy was recalled to explain her relationship with Prince. "We've known each other from childhood. Our families are friends. I called off a date with him, and he took it badly, wanted to have sex. I didn't. I did defend myself and yes, Mr. Dobbs fell down my stairs. I reported his actions to the team."

"Have you always been a sexual tease, Miss Polasky, even in high school when you reneged on a promise to go to the prom with my client?"

Out of orders sounded. The gavel banged. The question brought the red to Stacy's cheeks. She blinked hard a few times. Dean knew the signs, but they would not make her cry. He'd tried to make her weep often enough as an obnoxious teen to realize that. Now, she'd shielded him from the whole Prince mess simply by leaving him out of it. She didn't have to answer the question, but damage had been done to her character. The lawyer asked about her relationship with Dean Billodeaux at the time. "We were seeing each other."

"After you dated Mr. Dobbs but before you tried to seduce my client."

Another out of order, but she answered anyway. "I did not date Mr. Dobbs, nor did I try to seduce your client." Stacy had regained her cool.

The defense attorney attempted to bring in the recent revelation that during a break in their relationship Dean had fathered a child with another woman—or had they been engaged in a *ménage a trois*? The judge ruled that irrelevant to the case.

The trial continued for several days with medical experts on Prince's condition, both mental and physical, and chance for full recovery. A parade of character witnesses testified that Kent Gonsoulin was a pillar of the community, a member of the Chamber of Commerce, a regular attendee at Ste. Jeanne d'Arc, and a good family man. He'd sold many a trailer to black people and had nothing against them, Kent said when called to the stand. As for Stacy, he'd misread her signals since she'd haggled over the fees and services to keep him in her office—which had a bedroom upstairs. Being such a beautiful woman, he simply couldn't turn her down. No, no, he'd never considered cheating on his wife before, but this opportunity was just too tempting. He sent Stacy an oleaginous smile that must have creeped out the two young women on the jury.

The prosecution countered with some of the same for Stacy, bringing in a few of her clients, not very good for business, but they all spoke of her professionalism and when working at the hospital, her compassion. They found two women in Chapelle who'd had sex with Kent, one a pro, the other a woman who'd gotten a big discount on her mobile home. Both said he could be a little rough but paid up later.

Lots of back and forth went on about Louisiana's stand-your-ground and concealed carry laws, until at last the jurors filed out to deliberate. Nine white men, two young Caucasian women, and one elderly black person, who believed in Jesus and forgiveness, returned a verdict of not guilty. Stacy did cry in Dean's arms on her purple sofa in the privacy of her apartment now staked out again by the press. "He went unpunished, and my reputation has been smeared all over the newspapers. I wish I were in Germany."

"You would have had to come home for the trial anyhow. It's over. Don't do this. Kent has lost his reputation and his black clientele. That wife of his might go for a divorce, Catholic or not. Think of poufy wedding dresses and tiaras and cake with raspberry filling," he said. "Aren't we supposed to pick out our china and silver patterns at Schifferman's this week?"

"Like you really want to do that." She blotted her eyes on a corner of the red scarf Mati dragged onto her lap when he came to lick her face.

"No, but I will—for you. Trust Leslie. He has good taste."

Stacy gave him a watery smile. "You were there for me every day, Dean. Thank you."

"Don't thank me either. I'm going to ask you to stand by me come the Fourth of July. That's when Ilsa says the baby is coming. She disagrees with the doctor by a good two weeks, and she has a pretty strong will."

The birthday of the nation and possibly of his child, Stacy would be there, she promised, and not in Germany.

Chapter Thirty-Six

Whether she practiced German precision or simply wanted to ruin Dean's holiday, Ilsa called him at five a.m. on the Fourth saying she thought she'd gone into labor. He must come at once to take her to the hospital, the same one his mother had used to give birth. She knew he'd planned to go to the ranch for the usual blowout picnic with his extended family and took it as an affront that her obstetrician had forbidden her to travel outside the city. Ilsa implied Dean put the man up to restricting her to New Orleans where she wouldn't be seen by his kin. He had to wonder if she'd somehow induced labor on her own.

"My family knows you're pregnant and due any moment. Believe me, answering their questions would wear you out. Besides, you still look very beautiful." Dean did not lie about either fact. Though clearly with child, she'd maintained a belly most people who knew about these things would put at six months. The doctor kept telling him not to worry.

"What if you are three hours away when the baby comes?" Ilsa inquired. "Am I to take a taxi or call an ambulance?"

"Whichever you want. Listen, Nurse Shammy says first births rarely go quickly. I'd have plenty of time to come back and be with you."

"She is an old, childless woman and was a nun.

What does she know?"

"A lot. She saw my mother through two difficult pregnancies and cared for those babies afterwards. She'll be waiting at your house to do the same for you and Beck."

The name had been another area of contention. She wanted Beckmann Billodeaux. Dean considered that too long and finally offered his dad's suggestion of Beck Mann Billodeaux. Ilsa rather liked that. "He will be the little Mann, *nein*?"

Mawmaw Nadine grumbled about the lack of a saint's name, but it wasn't her call. He'd wait a while to tell his grandmother the child would be raised Lutheran.

Ilsa demanded he attend Lamaze classes with her though she didn't intend to have a natural birth. Dean believed she still hoped to supplant Stacy and feeling the baby move in her belly, holding her between his legs at the classes and rubbing the small of her back would be steps in that direction. At least, he'd learned to diaper and swaddle a baby doll, not that he'd be practicing on the real thing very often with interviews already ongoing for a permanent nursemaid. When Ilsa suggested, "Come, Dean, move in with me. We do not need the big, fancy wedding," he'd set her straight again. He'd be a good father, but not her husband or lover.

The five a.m. call also woke Stacy lying beside him in his big bed with the leather headboard. His sheets smelled of lavender again, and he enjoyed it. "Right, I'll be over to pick you up shortly." To Stacy, he said, "Ilsa says it's time to go. She's in labor. You ride with Tom to the picnic. I'll call with updates."

"Hmmm, did you sit in a coffee shop waiting for

updates when the trial went on and on? No, I'll be at the hospital. Tom can drop me there before he heads out."

"If Ilsa sees you, she'll probably give birth to that kid in one massive spasm of anger."

"Then it will be faster." She shot him an enigmatic smile. "I'll stay out of sight. I know plenty of people at the hospital. Just check in with me now and then."

"It's going to be a long day."

Dean's prediction came true. Though Ilsa was in labor, she'd only progressed two centimeters. The doctor, whose clothes under his open white lab coat said he'd planned to go saltwater fishing, assured them the birth was in no way imminent and suggested they walk the halls until Ilsa reached five centimeters. He left instructions for the epidural to be administered at that time. She achieved five centimeters at noon, then lay like a log in her bed watching Fourth of July celebrations around the nation on the television. Dean fed her ice chips on demand. Hours passed.

He met Stacy in the main lobby whenever he took a break. She went outside and relayed any news to the partygoers at the ranch. They had lunch and dinner together taking their meals from the cafeteria to a staff lounge where they would not be observed together.

"She's not in any pain, but she's still bitching about everything possible. She's hot, she's cold, go get her more ice chips."

"I guess I'd be irritable, too, if I'd had an enema and nothing but ice chips since dawn."

"Just lost my appetite for this burger, but I know you. You might do the princess act very well, but you would suck it up and walk it off—if you could walk, which she can't any more."

Stacy brushed away his troublesome curl. "It won't be much longer."

At eight-thirty p.m. the doctor proclaimed them ready to go. In the meantime, he'd caught three good-sized redfish he told Dean as they followed the gurney to the delivery room. Even with Dean holding up Ilsa's shoulders and much grunting and pushing on her part, his son did not enter the world until nine p.m. "Narrow pelvis. Good thing the child is small, or we'd have a C-section to perform. Nice work, Mama. Apgar score of nine.

"Only a nine?" Dean questioned.

"What, he is not good enough for a ten? Let me see," Ilsa demanded.

"The birth weight is a little low, six pounds, two ounces, but he's lively. Nothing to worry about. Here you go, Dad. Take him to the nursery while we clean up Mama."

Dean secured his son, swaddled and capped, in a football carry and walked the long hallway to deliver him safely to a nurse ready for the hand off. All the way, the baby squinted up at him with pale eyes as if impressing his father on his mind. Dean wondered if his own dad had felt as helpless as he did shouldering this great responsibility for the first time when he'd snatched his son from a lawyer and driven away. If he had, Joe Billodeaux would never have let on. Dean smiled down on the infant. "Welcome to the world, Beck. I'll do the best I can."

He found Stacy and brought her to the viewing window. "He's puny and bald and has blue eyes. There's never been a bald Billodeaux. You think they could have mixed up the DNA test?"

Stacy squeezed his arm. "No, the way he's moving those arms and legs, he's yours. Besides, Mawmaw said your cousin Randi was bald for months. They had to tape bows to her head. Now she has lots of black curls. I think the eyes will change to brown. If not, he takes after Ilsa, and she is very beautiful."

"You should have seen him a little while ago all covered in gunk and blood. Not so pretty then."

"Oh, Dean, I wish he were ours, bald or not.'

"Me, too. I'm still up for starting a family right away.'

"No, we have problems to solve and people to call right now."

They walked outside. Fireworks crackled over the river and exploded in a hazy nimbus of light in the warm and humid air. Closer by, families popped strings of Chinese firecrackers and maybe some of those bangs belonged to handguns as well. Dean called his family with the news that Beck had come into the world. Tom got on the line and said they were shooting off a big display called Shotgun Wedding in his honor.

"Nothing shotgun about the wedding, bro. Do they have one called Shotgun Daddy? By the time Stacy and I have our own, I should be really good at this fatherhood thing."

"You've got plenty of backups. We're all here for you." Tom passed the phone along to so many people the battery ran down.

"I'd better go say goodnight to Ilsa and thank her for my son."

"That would be the Dean Billodeaux way to handle it. I'm proud of you. Go, I'll wait out here and enjoy the fireworks."

Dean returned shortly saying Ilsa wanted to rest. They drove back to the condo in silence with revelry exploding all around them. Both their worlds had changed tonight.

Chapter Thirty-Seven

Dean learned weddings were considerably more work for a man than being present at childbirth. Choosing the groomsmen, no sweat, he figured. He had five brothers, Tom to serve as best man and the others to do duty as ushers, except for Teddy and T-Rex. Ted would stand at the altar using his sticks. T-Rex rebelled against wearing short pants and being a ring bearer. He got his own tuxedo just like the rest of the men. He'd walk Mati, trained to carry a white straw basket in his mouth holding the rings Velcroed onto a pink silk pillow, down the aisle on a leash. The rest of his duties included making sure Mati used the fireplug beforehand and tugging him back from any attempts to raise his leg in the church, a serious responsibility. T-Rex filled the pocket of his tiny tux with dog treats to assure cooperation.

In return for these tasks, Dean learned he was expected to give his brothers a gift. Easy, the latest gaming system for all but Tom who already owned one. His best man, best friend, and brother received the deed to the condo. Stacy had convinced her groom they should live near, but not too near, Ilsa in the Garden District so he could easily visit Beck during his scant free time during the season. The idea still made him uneasy, but for the good of the child, he'd do it.

No white horse and carriage to transport them to

the reception at the Roosevelt Hotel. Because of the ever-voracious press, they'd have two white stretch limos with heavily tinted windows take them there and Mariah's bouncers running crowd control. Big-hearted Mariah attended all dolled up and sat in the front row on the bride's side accompanied by her oxygen tank because Stacy had no parents to sit there. With the Sinners team and staff, both past and present, and the huge Billodeaux clan plus some of Stacy's best clients attending, the huge cathedral didn't have an empty seat. Great to see Rex Worthy and his wife, Tricia, looking good after a double mastectomy and reconstruction. The Rev, his wife and family, Dr. Connor Bullock, Little Joe and tall Riley with her NBA fiancé filled a row in a big way. Prince Dobbs was there only because Mama Nell said everyone on the team had to be invited just like back in kindergarten. Don Juan gave Dean a wink and a broad, white smile. Angel, who had sold him out to the press after the drunken incident at Paco's, received no invitation.

Now, the music sounded and all Dean had to do was stand in front of everyone waiting for his bride, frozen in the pocket ready for the big play. Stacy had taken the term "white wedding" literally. His sisters marched down the aisle clad in that color though he knew Xochi had campaigned for something brighter. Each wore a chaplet of pale pink roses in their dark hair and carried the same in their arms, first tall Lorena, then Jude and Annie, then finally Xochi. Edie scattered dried rose petals from a basket onto the white runner and T-Rex, a full head taller, kept Mati on a short leash administering light tugs each time they approached one of the arrangements of pink and white flowers on the ends of the aisles. Lots of oohs and ahs before the organist segued into the traditional wedding march and his bride appeared on Joe Billodeaux's arm.

Dean's hands went sweaty, and his mouth turned dry as they never did during a game. Stacy appeared to be a fairy tale princess right out of the storybooks. She wore her golden hair down because he'd asked that of her and covered in a veil, cathedral length, secured by a small tiara of white and pink diamonds given to her by the aunt and uncle who raised her. Her dress, definitely poufy, had a strapless bodice embroidered with pink roses and a wide silk overskirt drawn up over a petticoat of tulle secured in the center with a pink gem. A couple of months ago, Dean Billodeaux wouldn't have had the words tulle or overskirt or cathedral length veil in his vocabulary, but his mom and sisters talked of nothing else before the wedding. His bride looked magnificent.

Baby Beck began to scream, and eyes turned his way. Mawmaw Nadine reached back into the second row, groom's side, and fairly ripped the child from Ilsa's arms. Dean could tell his grandmother's lips whispered "Dodo", the old Cajun word urging an infant to sleep. Beck settled on her wide, comforting bosom and quieted. Dean had only one worried moment to wonder if Ilsa had pinched the child to upstage Stacy,

No matter now, his bride approached the altar and was given away by her uncle. Their vows from the Book of Common Prayer took such a short time. Mati at a discreet gesture from the bride sat up on his haunches and offered them the rings in the slightly gnawed basket—his of titanium, hers a circlet of pink and yellow diamonds set in eighteen-carat gold. The communion following lasted longer as any baptized Christian who wished to partake came to the rail. Cuddling Beck, Mawmaw Nadine staunchly remained in her seat, as did all his Catholic relatives. Mariah with a what-the-hell shrug climbed the steps in her stiletto heels, her gold sequins and portable oxygen tank shining, and accepted the host and a pretty good slug of wine.

The wedding party exited the cathedral through a long tunnel of white canvas straight into the waiting limos. A police escort got them swiftly through traffic to the Roosevelt, once the Fairmont Hotel where his honorary Aunt Stevie and Connor Riley had held their reception. Closed after Hurricane Katrina and restored, the floors of place gleamed again with mosaic tiles, and the gold and white Waldorf-Astoria Ballroom awaited the guests with a cocktail reception and a sit down dinner of Surf and Turf accompanied by champagne. Tall glass columns held arrangements of white roses with pale pink edges and a cascade of ivy and stephanotis down the sides. Brian Lightfoot, the Sinners' punter, had handled all the flowers and done his usual tasteful and outstanding job.

With drinks, dinner, toasts, the cutting of a wedding cake of ornate opulence, and all the other wedding rigmarole out of the way, the dancing began. Stacy waltzed first with her Uncle Joe and then her groom, both men light on their feet and quick with the turns. Aunt Stevie got misty-eyed recalling her reception when Dean paused to talk to her as other men cut in for a dance with the bride. "Your birth mother planned the whole event, a daisy extravaganza since I just didn't care about the details. She was excellent at her job, Dean. Remember that much about her, the good part."

Daddy Joe joined them. "That's the night I seduced your mother for the first time by pretending to be too drunk to drive home alone. The tabloids thought I'd taken up with a teenager she was so small. Good memories. I hope you and Stacy will be as happy as me and Tink."

"TMI, Dad, but yeah, that pretending to be drunk works for women, too, evidently." Dean watched Ilsa hand the baby off to his mom, who immediately slung a table napkin over the shoulder of her pale blue silk suit to cuddle him, and rush to where Prince Dobbs held court within a ring of young women. Ilsa had insisted on attending and bringing the child though none had been invited except Edie and T-Rex, and she'd worn white as if it were her day, too.

Prince shed his tuxedo jacket and discarded a set of gold nugget cufflinks to roll up his sleeves to the shoulders. He beckoned to Stacy just finishing a dance. No, he would not do his biceps performance at their reception. Dean, backed up by his dad, headed for the group in time to hear Stacy say, "Please, not at my wedding!"

"No, no, you got me all wrong. I tell you that Cyril is a genius. He turned my penis palm into a Celtic cross. Get a look at my other arm. The skull is now the head of Jesus Christ who has his dreadlocks crowned with thorns. These show I am a changed man." Still, Prince flexed his fully regained muscles beneath Ilsa's eager fingertips.

"So strong. I would have liked to see that penis palm," she remarked.

"Oh, I can arrange to let you see the real thing, honey—I mean after you recover from having Dean's baby, and we pray together about it."

Aunt Stevie guided her beautiful and blonde teen model daughter Josee away from the exhibition of tattooed flesh and drafted a pleased, bespectacled, and age-appropriate Trinity Billodeaux to lead her in a dance even though he stood a head shorter than his partner. Dean backed off and reclaimed Stacy. He whirled her out onto the dance floor again. "Sounds like praying together is a new euphemism for sex in Prince's vocabulary. He did work hard to recover, I'll give him that."

"What worries me is the way Ilsa is stroking Prince's arm and his still substantial ego, the man could end up as Beck's stepfather. Xo says his aura is a bright orange now and most of the black is gone, so maybe he has changed."

"I wonder what my psychic sister has to say about us."

"That we are enveloped in the violet haze of love."

"She's got that right."

****

At midnight the bride and groom departed though the party went on for several more hours. A white limousine shot off into the night heading for the airport as a decoy. In the morning, the newlyweds would depart, not for Germany as they'd said, but to a secluded Caribbean isle to hone their salsa dancing and play in the waves for a week. Crammed in between training camp and the start of preseason games, they would make the most of it.

The newly married couple slipped upstairs to a

bridal suite to spend the night. In no hurry because they knew how well their bodies fit together, what each of them enjoyed best, they cuddled together in bed, Stacy's golden head lying close to Dean's heart.

Raised in a household that revolved around football, she knew there would be special occasions missed in the future and perhaps even births without Dean by her side. She accepted that. She'd have the love and comfort of the Billodeaux family to see her through. Because of Dean's one slip, Ilsa would always be part of their lives and Beck, too, the child not a burden like his mother. Anastasia Marya Polasky planned to manage that like true royalty.

"Was your wedding day all you wanted?" Dean asked.

"What I dreamed of all my life."

"Not bad for a big lout, huh?"

"I hereby raise you to the rank of handsome prince—which you have been all along." Stacy moved from his embrace, straddled his narrow waist, touched her fingertips to both sides of his shoulders as if she held a sword, and kissed his forehead with its wayward curl. "Arise, Prince Dean."

"Glad you finally admitted that—and I am already arisen."

Stacy did not answer except to say, "I think I'd like to be on top tonight."

"Oh, no! The wedding was yours. The honeymoon is mine."

They tussled in the sheets for position, and so the marriage of the princess and the lout began.

A word about the author...

Once a librarian, now a writer of romance, Lynn Shurr grew up in Pennsylvania Dutch country. She attended a state college and earned a very impractical degree in English Literature. Her first job after graduating really was working in a burger joint. Moving from one humble job to another, she finally buckled down and got an M.A. in Librarianship.

Lynn found her first reference job in the heart of Cajun Country. For her, the old saying, "Once you've tasted bayou water, you will always stay here," came true. She raised three children not far from the Bayou Teche and lives there still with her astronomer husband.

When not writing, Lynn likes to paint, cheer for the New Orleans Saints and LSU Tigers, and take long road trips practically anywhere. Her love of the Bayou Country, its history and customs, often shows in the background for her books.

Contact Lynn at www.lynnshurr.com
visit her blog at www.lynnshurr.blogspot.com
or write her at lynn.shurr@yahoo.com

~*~

Other Lynn Shurr titles
available from The Wild Rose Press, Inc.:
GOALS FOR A SINNER
WISH FOR A SINNER
KICKS FOR A SINNER
PARADISE FOR A SINNER
LOVE LETTER FOR A SINNER
THE CONVENT ROSE
A WILD RED ROSE
ALWAYS YELLOW ROSES
A TRASHY AFFAIR
MARDI GRAS MADNESS
COURIR DE MARDI GRAS